Reader
by Ja

"These people aren't perfect. There are no pretty ribbons and bows. There is no fairytale romance. What there is is slow and real, hurting, misunderstanding, over reacting, groveling, holding, kissing, loving, and hoping."
—Prism Book Alliance

"Definitely recommend this one, especially for those crazy gamers out there. You know who you are."
—The Blog of Sid Love

"One of the things I admire most about Jamie Fessenden's writing is his ability to vary his style to complement his story… Excellent job, Jamie. Thank you very much for sharing Danny and Jake's story with me."
—Rainbow Book Reviews

"I think what it comes down to is that this author's writing style just works for me. He is funny and it jives with my tastes in every way."
—My Fiction Nook

"I loved this book. Absolutely loved it. Jamie Fessenden is such an amazing writer no matter what type of story he tackles, and this one hit me right in the gut."
—Mrs. Condit & Friends Read Books

"Fessenden has a great handle on combining solicitude and humor in his prose, which is not an easy task."
—Smoocher's Voice

"This is a great book. It is, in turns, funny, heartbreaking and heartwarming."
—The Novel Approach

By JAMIE FESSENDEN

Billy's Bones
By That Sin Fell the Angels
The Christmas Wager
Dogs of Cyberwar
The Healing Power of Eggnog
The Meaning of Vengeance
Murder on the Mountain
Murderous Requiem
Saturn in Retrograde
Screwups
Stitch (with Sue Brown, Kim Fielding, and Eli Easton)
We're Both Straight, Right?

Published by DREAMSPINNER PRESS
http://www.dreamspinnerpress.com

MURDER
ON THE
Mountain

JAMIE FESSENDEN

Dreamspinner Press

Published by
DREAMSPINNER PRESS

5032 Capital Circle SW, Suite 2, PMB# 279, Tallahassee, FL 32305-7886 USA
http://www.dreamspinnerpress.com/

Murder on the Mountain
© 2014 Jamie Fessenden.

Cover Art
© 2014 Reese Dante.
www.reesedante.com
Cover content is for illustrative purposes only and any person depicted on the cover is a model.

ISBN: 978-1-63216-202-1
Digital ISBN: 978-1-63216-203-8
Library of Congress Control Number: 2014943202
First Edition August 2014

Printed in the United States of America
(∞)
This paper meets the requirements of
ANSI/NISO Z39.48-1992 (Permanence of Paper).

Acknowledgments

I OWE a big thanks to my friend Austin for going up to the summit of Mount Washington and interviewing the rangers stationed there for me—in the middle of February, no less! I would also like to thank the rangers there who took the time to answer my questions. Any inaccuracies in the novel concerning the way a murder investigation is handled on the summit should not be attributed to them.

1

JESSE KNEW he had no one to blame but himself. True, Steve had made volunteering to work in the Mount Washington Observatory sound romantic, which had been a lie. There was nothing romantic about cleaning up after seven people, washing dishes, and cleaning toilets. Steve was there with him, but their romance had died months ago. Yes, the view was spectacular, but now that the two of them had settled into just being friends, the view wasn't enough to make up for the tedium of the job.

Still, Steve hadn't forced him to volunteer, and Jesse had read the job description: one week on top of Mount Washington, bunking with three full-time staffers and two interns. The observatory studied weather patterns and climate on the mountain famed for having the worst weather in the world. And to free up the staff for their jobs, volunteers came in to do the cooking and cleaning in week-long shifts, from Wednesday to Wednesday. Jesse's shift was almost over, and he couldn't wait to pack his things and book it back down the mountain tomorrow. He just wasn't a mountain man. He knew that now. There was a stark beauty to the landscape, especially on days when it was possible to look out over the entire Presidential Range. But above all, it was windy and fucking cold. What Jesse had been longing to do more than anything this entire week was curl up in front of one of the propane heaters with a good mystery novel.

In the meantime, he still had catfish with lemon butter to scrape off the industrial cooking pans used in the observatory kitchen. Steve had cooked it, so Jesse had the honor of cleaning it. He couldn't really complain about that part—it had been delicious. Steve was a great cook.

Jesse didn't really mind getting cleanup duty. But he was still glad to finish up and escape for a while.

He passed through the common area, where one of the observers—Leo—was napping on one of the three brown couches. Bandit, the black-and-white angora that resided in the observatory, glanced up from her nap between Leo's feet before deciding Jesse wasn't exciting enough to wake up for. Jesse was half-tempted to take a nap on one of the other couches, but he really needed some fresh air, even if it required bundling up. It was October, and the monitors in the station indicated a moderate fall day at the base of the mountain. But the temperature on the observation deck was a good fifteen degrees lower. Nobody with any sense would wander around outside without a ski jacket.

He spent some time on the observation deck of the Sherman Adams building, the large crescent-shaped structure that housed not only the observatory but also the ranger station and the museum, though the view wasn't very impressive since everything was shrouded in fog. There was a husband and wife trying to look out over the Presidential Range with binoculars and bitching about the fact that they couldn't see anything. The only other person there was a young man, probably just a few years older than Jesse. He wasn't half-bad to look at—kind of thin and pale, with cool blue eyes. Jesse casually wandered over his way to see if he could strike up a conversation.

The guy wasn't wasting his time trying to see out through the mist. His focus was on the Cog Railway station below the observation deck, about a hundred feet away. Though what he was looking at, Jesse had no idea. Maybe just waiting for the next train.

"Hey," Jesse said as he walked up beside him. They were close to the edge, which could be dangerous in high winds, but it was pretty calm at the moment.

The guy glanced up at him and said distractedly, "Hey."

"Are you waiting to take the train down?"

The young man looked at Jesse as if he was annoyed, and then looked away again. "No, I'm camping."

He was lying. Jesse knew what kind of gear was suited to camping on the mountain. He'd done it himself a couple of times with Steve, back when they were dating. And this guy just wasn't dressed for it. His jacket was a good-quality ski parka and the hat pulled down over his hair was a warm knit bobble cap, but he hadn't brought a scarf or gloves. And where was his backpack? Even if he'd left most of his gear back at a campsite somewhere, he seemed poorly dressed for the weather. He might have been an idiot, of course. They weren't unheard of. State park volunteer rescuers had to risk their lives often enough to save hikers who were trapped by sudden blizzards or suffering from hypothermia when the temperatures dropped. But Jesse suspected this guy had come up on the train earlier in the day. He was just brushing Jesse off.

So screw him.

Jesse said, "Cool," and wandered away, leaving him to watch the train platform. The Cog was due in soon. Jesse thought it might be worth going down to see who got off. If he was lucky, there might be a cute guy or two who could spare him more than one-word sentences before he had to get back inside and start preparing dinner with Steve.

He went down the steps from the observation deck and arrived at the platform just as the Cog was pulling in. The train was kind of an oddity. Due to the steep incline it traversed on its climb up the mountainside, the engine and water tank had to be tilted toward the front so it would be level while running. This meant it was aimed at the ground when the tracks were level.

In a few minutes, he heard the rattling of metal wheels approaching, and it wasn't long afterward he saw the slow-moving train coming out of the mist, belching steam. It didn't move much faster than a man walking, if the man were walking on level ground, but the fact that it was coming straight up the mountain made the climb a bit less than an hour. That was a lot faster than a hiker could climb the mountain, especially in the winter. Of course, tickets were a little steep. Jesse had never ridden the train himself.

He glanced up to see if the guy he'd spoken with was still watching from the deck, but he couldn't find him. Maybe he was on his way down.

There weren't many people on the train this trip—just eleven. Six weren't particularly interesting to him. There were a couple of little kids, around nine or ten years old, attached to an elderly couple. He assumed they were the kids' grandparents. And there was a married couple in their thirties. Male and female, despite the fact that New Hampshire had adopted same-sex marriage a few years ago. Jesse could see their wedding rings but guessed they might be newlyweds from the way they were hanging all over each other.

Four of the passengers looked about Jesse's age—one girl and three guys. And they were sticking by each other as they got off the train, so he guessed they were a group of college friends taking a tour. They had another girl with them, perhaps about sixteen or seventeen. She had the same long blonde hair and delicate features as the older girl, so Jesse assumed they were sisters. One of the guys was decent-looking, if a bit scruffy, but it was the other two—obviously brothers—who caught Jesse's eye. They were redheads and so starkly handsome they could have been models.

"Stop leering," a voice said behind him, and Jesse turned to see Steve smirking at him. Fortunately, they were far enough from the platform that the passengers couldn't overhear them.

"I can look."

Steve didn't have to ask which ones he was looking at. "Think they're twins?"

"No." Jesse directed his gaze back to the brothers again, trying not to be too obvious about it. True, they looked almost enough alike to be twins. "You see the one with the green scarf? He's the older brother. Maybe by a year or two."

"They look the same age to me."

Jesse shook his head. "He keeps slapping his brother on the back, and he's ordering everyone around." The guy was pointing in different directions, asking questions, and waiting for the others to nod their understanding.

"So he's bossy," Steve said, unconvinced. "Some twins are like that—one always takes charge."

"I suppose," Jesse said. "But I don't think so."

Steve laughed. "Whatever you say, Jessica," he said, falling back on the nickname Jesse hated—Jessica, because he wanted to write mystery novels and was always observing people like the main character, Jessica Fletcher, in *Murder, She Wrote*. "I'm going back inside. Don't forget you have chocolate chip cookies to bake."

"I won't." Jesse let him go, his attention still focused on the tourists.

The younger brother seemed oddly complacent, as if he didn't care about anything going on around him. He was not only taking orders from his brother, but from the older girl as well. She wasn't making him march up and down the platform or anything, but she made him hold her purse when she got the bizarre notion to refresh her lipstick.

Girlfriend. Definitely. Unless they were married. But she had a ring on her finger. He didn't. More likely, they were engaged.

"Will you get rid of that fucking thing?" the guy's older brother asked, loud enough to be heard where Jesse and Steve were hanging out. "You look like a fag."

The girl gave him a scathing look, but his brother just held the purse out as if it didn't matter to him what happened to it.

The girl took it back with an irritated snatch of her hand. "Don't be so macho."

Whatever else she said was too low for Jesse to overhear, but just before the group of friends moved away toward the observation platform, the younger brother glanced around and his gaze fell on Jesse. It was just for a moment, but as their eyes met, Jesse saw something that disturbed him, something… off. The guy smiled slightly, but even from that far away, Jesse could see there was no joy in that smile. It wasn't just that he seemed sad. It was the look of someone who'd given up caring about anything. And his eyes….

They seemed completely lifeless.

DINNER WAS going to be tortilla pie, another dish Steve cooked particularly well. Jesse had baked his cookies for desert, and they were cooling on the counter. Now he was helping to dice up tomatoes and lettuce for the main dish.

"They were cute," Steve said, referring back to the brothers they'd seen on the platform a couple of hours ago, "but if you ask me, the friend was much cuter." Steve always went for the scruffy types, which was part of the reason he and Jesse were no longer together. Jesse was a bit straight-laced—he kept his black hair pretty short and never let his beard get beyond five o'clock shadow, even when every other guy at the observatory had given in to a full beard.

"Do you think he's gay?" Jesse asked. He didn't really care, but speculation about the sexual orientation of cute guys was always a source of entertainment.

Steve shrugged as he put his shoulder into stirring the pot of thick refried beans. "Didn't really get a chance to talk to him. He didn't *look* gay…." Meaning he didn't look like the type to go clubbing—perfectly coiffed and dressed in clothes that cost a fortune. Steve hated guys like that.

Before Jesse could think of a response, Reggie burst into the kitchen. He was still dressed for outside and he was panting a bit, as if he'd been running. "Hey! Are either of you guys free?"

Jesse and Steve stared at him blankly for a second before Steve asked, "Why?"

"We have a missing person," Reggie said, wiping his mouth with the back of a thick insulated glove. "A guy who came up on the Cog. His friends are freaking out. The sun's going down soon, so anyone who can join in the search would be appreciated. Carol and Leo are already out there with Rory."

Steve glanced at Jesse. "I have cornbread in the oven…."

"You deal with that, then," Reggie said. "Jesse, come out if you can. Make sure you have one of the walkie-talkies."

He took off, and Jesse followed, stopping to bundle up near the door. He was already wearing long underwear and a sweater over his long-sleeved shirt. That was typical everyday wear for the staff. He slipped on the same boots and ski jacket, but he opted for a balaclava underneath his ski cap to keep his face warm, and thick mittens instead of gloves.

Outside, the fog had grown heavier and more dangerous for an inexperienced tourist wandering around the peak. The observatory and surrounding buildings were in the middle of an expanse of barren rock—not a solid slab, but a moonlike landscape of massive boulders and rubble that could be treacherous to navigate even in the best visibility. In conditions like this, it would be easy for someone to fall and hurt himself or even stumble into a crevasse or off a cliff. As the sun began to set, the temperature dropped dramatically. Wandering around lost could prove fatal for someone not adequately dressed.

Jesse caught up with Reggie, who told him, "His name is Stuart. He came up here with his older brother and three friends a couple hours ago, and he's been missing for about an hour. No real hiking experience, and he's not properly dressed for anything but a day hike. Gray-and-yellow jacket with a yellow knit ski cap. Ted's been having a hell of a time with his friends." Ted was one of the park rangers currently stationed on the peak. "They're totally freaking out, not that I blame them. But the last train is heading down in a half hour. They need to be on it, whether we've found their friend or not."

Jesse was shocked to discover the guy he'd been observing on the platform earlier was the one missing. It felt almost as if he knew him, even though they hadn't spoken. Jesse could see the older brother and the others arguing with Ted on the platform. He could understand them not wanting to leave, under the circumstances, but there were no facilities for them to spend the night—the entire Sherman Adams building was closed to the public after hours. And the last thing the rangers needed was to have *another* tourist get lost or injured wandering around the mountain at night, especially ones who weren't dressed properly for the weather. The safest thing was to leave the search and rescue to the rangers and the observatory staff while Stuart's friends and family returned to the hotel and waited for word.

Of course, that was easier said than done. Jesse couldn't imagine what it would be like to leave a family member behind, trusting strangers to find him. At any rate, he remembered what Stuart had been wearing, so he knew what to look for. There was no point hanging back at the station.

"Now don't go thinking you're some hotshot because you've been up here with us for a week," Reggie warned as they stood looking out across the gray landscape to the north of the observatory. "You're still inexperienced, and I don't want to have to send a search party out looking for *you*. Got it?"

"Yes."

"You should be able to see the light from the tower, even in the fog, so you keep that in sight. Watch where you're climbing and don't try anything macho."

Jesse bit back a wiseass reply and settled for nodding. "I know."

Reggie snorted skeptically but left him to it.

Jesse made his way across the rocks as the sky darkened, half the time having to use his hands as much as his feet. Despite the week at the observatory and having hiked up here a couple of times with Steve, Reggie was right, and Jesse knew it—he didn't know the area that well. So he circled around, keeping the tower in his field of vision. He shouted Stuart's name and heard others shouting it in the distance, but there was no answer.

As the last hint of sunlight faded from the gray sky, his walkie-talkie crackled. He answered it, speaking through the insulated fabric of the balaclava, and Reggie told him, "The train waited as long as it could. Stuart's friends and family have gone down to the hotel to wait. Nobody's reported anything."

"Roger. Still searching."

"Come in if you get too cold, and for fuck's sake, don't get lost."

"Got it."

It was maybe a half hour later, when the temperature had dropped to the point where Jesse was seriously considering going in to warm up a bit, that he found something. A large boulder at the top of a ridge with something dark on it. He was using his LED flashlight now, and as he approached, he saw the dark spot glistened in the blue-white LED light.

It was blood. An irregular spot about three inches in diameter, and it was frozen solid.

Jesse looked past the rock and saw Stuart lying at the bottom of a steep incline, as if he'd rolled down. He was lying face up and not moving.

"Stuart!" Jesse shouted. There was no response. He scrambled down as quickly as he could without slipping, only thinking to grab his walkie-talkie when he was at the bottom, kneeling beside the young man. "Reggie! I found him!"

"How is he?"

Stuart didn't look good. In fact, he didn't even look alive. His hat was missing and the right side of his head was caved in and covered in blood, frozen and coagulated in his short strawberry blond hair. Jesse wasn't sure, but he thought he might be able to see some of the guy's brain exposed, though it was hard to tell in all that mess. Stuart's eyes were narrow slits and his skin was pale and bluish. He didn't appear to be breathing. Jesse took off one of his mittens to feel Stuart's neck, searching for a pulse. The wind bit into his skin like needles. He didn't feel a heartbeat and the skin was ice cold. Jesse suppressed a shiver at the realization he was probably touching a corpse.

"I think he's dead."

"Jesus! Where are you?"

Jesse put his mitten back on and looked around. *Fuck.* The tower was out of sight. "Hold on!" He waved his light in the air over his head, ignoring Reggie's tirade about getting himself turned around. It made a column of light in the heavy mist, slicing through the sky like a spotlight, though it wasn't particularly bright. "Can you see my light?"

"Yes!"

Thank God.

"Stay put and keep the light on," Reggie ordered him. "We're coming to get you."

Jesse wedged the flashlight against a rock so it pointed straight up into the sky and left it there. Then he turned his attention back to Stuart, using the small LED light on his car keys to illuminate him. He was dead. At least, Jesse was reasonably sure of that. But he wasn't an EMT, so he could be wrong. He didn't know how to treat a head wound, but the one thing he was sure of was nobody could survive for more than a few minutes without his heart beating. It was probably too late, but he had to try. So he dredged up the CPR training he'd had a few years ago and went to work.

"HE'S DEAD, all right," Ted said, bending over the body in the light of their flashlights. He and Rory, the other park ranger, had come out to join Jesse, along with Reggie and Carol, the third full-time observer. He'd taken over Jesse's clumsy attempts at CPR, but Stuart still hadn't responded. "I'm making the call," Ted said. "I don't have a watch. Who's got the time?"

Jesse pulled a glove off and yanked his cell phone out of his pants pocket. "Six thirteen."

"We can't just leave him here," Rory said. "Let's get him inside."

Ted stood up and shook his head. "Leave him where he is. He's dead, and bringing him inside isn't going to change that."

"I don't see any point in letting him freeze solid."

Ted ignored him, using his flashlight to scan the path Stuart must have tumbled down.

"There's a rock up there," Jesse volunteered, aiming his own flashlight at the top of the ridge. "It's got a big spot of blood on it. That's probably where he hit his head."

Ted grunted and climbed up the hill to take a look at it. The others stayed down at the bottom with the body.

"It seems odd that he wasn't wearing a hat," Carol observed.

Jesse had been wondering about that too. "He was wearing one this afternoon, when he got off the train."

Ted must have overheard them, because he called out, "The hat's up here!" when he reached the top. "I can see it wedged between a couple of rocks, about… ten feet away from where he hit his head."

Jesse frowned and looked down at Stuart, whose dead eyes stared blankly back at him. Was it possible he'd taken his hat off before striking his head? Maybe he'd slipped and the hat had flown out of his hand just before his head hit the rock. It was possible, though it seemed unlikely.

Then Ted called down, "I can see a little blood on it."

That clinched it.

"He was murdered," Jesse said.

2

KYLE WAS sitting in his boxer briefs on the couch with a bag of microwave buttered popcorn and a beer, about halfway through *The Time Traveler's Wife*, when he got the call. He growled and got up to fish his cellphone from the jeans he'd tossed on the floor. When he saw the number on Caller ID, he snarled, "You've gotta be fucking kidding me!" and put the movie on pause.

"What is it, Roberts?" Wesley Roberts had been Kyle's partner since he made detective three years ago.

Wesley laughed. "Cranky. Did I catch you on a hot date?"

"Just watching a movie. By myself."

"What are you watching?"

"*The Hangover*," Kyle lied. "Is this why you called me? To talk movies?"

"You wish. Some kid got himself killed on the mountain tonight. The rangers think it might not be an accident, so they decided to call in the Major Crime Unit. Guess who got picked to look into it?"

Kyle set his beer down and ran a hand through his slightly-longer-than-regulation brown hair. "Jesus. They expect us to drive up the mountain at this hour?" It was past seven o'clock, and the summit wasn't a fun place to be after dark at this time of year.

"It's too foggy for that. They're gonna take us up on the Cog."

Well, so much for sobbing like a girl over Rachel McAdams and Eric Bana. God, what the guys in the department would think if they found out what Kyle did for fun.

"Fine," he told Wesley. "I'll be there in a half hour."

NORMALLY THE Cog was shut down in the afternoons, but in this weather, it was far safer to take the train to the summit than attempt to navigate the winding Auto Road, bordered in places by sheer cliffs. Fortunately the engineers were willing to make the trip for something this serious.

The railway station was shrouded in fog by the time Kyle and Wesley arrived from Concord, which meant visibility on the summit would be next to nil. It was almost nine now, and it would be nearly ten by the time they got to the top. God knew how long things would take up there, with the temperature below freezing. This was going to be a long, long night.

Accompanying Kyle and his partner were two EMTs from Androscoggin Valley Hospital, and Larry Turner, a park ranger. One of the EMTs looked familiar to Kyle, and he eventually remembered her from an attempted suicide case in Berlin—Claire, he thought her name was. The guy with her was new.

The trip up the mountain could be beautiful and breathtaking during the day, but in the darkness and fog, it was simply cold and boring. Kyle and Wesley sat side by side in one of the school bus-style padded seats, while Turner sat in the seat ahead of them. He turned around to face them with one arm draped over the back of the seat and spent the first part of the trip filling them in about the tourist who'd died on the summit.

"He was twenty-one, still in college, liberal arts major, staying at the Mount Washington Hotel for the week with his fiancée and some family. The poor guy was supposed to get married this Saturday."

Jesus. Kyle hated that kind of irony. "Why don't you think it was an accident?"

"Me?" Larry shrugged. "I haven't seen the body. But Ted says the way he hit his head before he fell looks suspicious. You two will have to figure out what's what."

"Terrific," Wesley muttered. The train car was heated, but it was still chilly. He looked decidedly unhappy, even bundled up in a heavy winter coat, hat, scarf, and gloves. Not that Kyle blamed him. If he'd liked wandering around the mountain in the cold, he would have become a park ranger instead of a police detective.

"Ted asked the kid's family and friends to go back down the mountain and wait for us to notify them."

"*Has* anyone notified them?" Kyle asked.

"No," Larry answered. Then he grinned. "We'll let you take care of that."

"Gee, thanks."

"Don't mention it."

"Did anyone make a list of who was at the summit when the decedent died?"

"Of course," Larry said, reaching into his jacket to produce a folded piece of paper. "Ted faxed this to me. There were ten passengers that arrived with him on the Cog, and seven people went down when the train descended. The next train was the last of the day, and it carried four passengers. Those four plus Stuart's four friends went down on the last descent. There were probably four or five people already at the summit. That's hard to determine 'cause hikers come and go as they please."

Kyle took the paper and glanced over it. Unfortunately, there weren't a lot of names, beyond the four who'd arrived with the victim. Ted had taken their names, as well as those of the other four passengers who'd gone down with the last train. Some of the others might be gathered from the Cog ticketing office tomorrow.

"Thanks," he said.

By the time they passed Halfway House, the ranger had run out of things to tell them, so Kyle brought out his Kindle and read by the LED reading light built into the case. He'd loaded up an old Agatha Christie short story, since his partner was sitting right beside him, and there was no way in hell he was going to risk Wesley getting a glimpse of what he'd been reading earlier today—a raunchy romance about a "straight" widower falling for another man.

Having sex with a man had been a fantasy of Kyle's for a long time, even when he'd been married. Not that he'd ever considered cheating on

Julie. She'd known about his fantasies, and fortunately, she'd thought they were sexy. They hadn't been the type of couple who could even contemplate a threesome. But it had been fun to pretend, now and then.

Now that she was gone, his sexual desires toward men had become more intense. He wasn't quite ready to date yet, though Julie had passed away five years ago, but he'd begun to think about it more often. And when he did, he thought about both men and women.

He wasn't ashamed of being bisexual, but it wasn't something he felt comfortable confiding in the people he worked with. And he certainly didn't want Wesley to see the smutty romances he enjoyed. It wasn't that he felt they made him less manly or anything like that, but the ribbing he'd have to endure would be unending and a huge pain in the ass.

As the train passed the monument to Lizzie Bourne, a hiker who'd died near the summit in 1855, more sensed than really seen in the darkness and heavy fog—Kyle had made this trip several times by now—he snapped off his Kindle and slipped it back into a pocket inside his jacket. Then he zipped up again.

The train pulled into the station, and Kyle and his companions stepped out into the bitter cold gray fog. The wind wasn't all that bad tonight, but the temperature was much colder than it had been in Concord, and he knew any exposed skin would be in danger of getting frostbitten.

"Jesus!" Wesley complained, pulling his scarf up to cover most of his face. "It's fucking cold!"

Kyle snorted. "Very observant. No wonder you're a detective."

"How about you fuck yourself?"

"It'd be a better time than this."

Kyle moved toward the station, where Ted and Rory were coming out into the cold to greet them. Three other people were following them, and he assumed they were observatory staff. Everybody was bundled up so much he couldn't really identify them, though one appeared to be female.

"Hey, Kyle," Ted said. He extended a gloved hand and Kyle shook it, and then greetings and introductions went around the tiny circle. The three from the observatory turned out to be two Kyle had met before— Carol and Reggie—and a volunteer. The volunteer really had no business being there. A crime scene was no place for a gawking college student.

But when Ted introduced the kid as Jesse, the young man stepped forward and pulled his balaclava down to show his face, and Kyle came close to forgetting any objections he had.

The kid was gorgeous. Not handsome in a rugged, masculine sense, but beautiful. He had large, soft brown eyes and full, sensual lips that seemed somehow familiar, though Kyle was certain they'd never met. Then the kid looked up and him and parted his lips slightly, and it struck him—Ingrid Bergman. Something about Jesse looking up at him in the fog with those big, beautiful brown eyes reminded Kyle of Ingrid Bergman in *Casablanca*, saying good-bye to Bogart on the runway.

Christ, I must really be lonely, Kyle thought.

"Jesse, this is Detective Dubois," Ted said as Kyle extended his gloved hand.

Jesse seemed to find something about Kyle's face fascinating, to judge from the way he was staring. "Detective."

Here's lookin' at you, kid popped into Kyle's mind, but he just said, "Jesse."

As Ted introduced Jesse to the others, Rory took Kyle aside for a moment and asked, "Do you want us to send him inside?"

"The kid?"

"Yeah. He's got some kind of hard-on for murder investigations—he wants to be a mystery novelist—so we've been letting him hang out. He's the one who discovered the body, but I've already verified that he was inside the observatory working with one of the other volunteers from the moment Stuart Warren got off the train right up until search parties were sent out." Normally, the person who discovered a body might be a suspect—murderers often pretended to find their victims in order to divert suspicion. But Jesse had a pretty solid alibi. "We can send him inside if you want," Ted finished.

Kyle looked back at the young man. Once again, his eyes met Jesse's, and he felt a sharp tug deep in his chest. *God, he's beautiful....* "Well... do you think he'll get in our way?"

Ted shrugged. "I think he'll keep out of your hair if you tell him to. He's a good kid."

Normally, a civilian had to fill out a form, and get approval from headquarters, if he wanted to tag along on an investigation, but the kid had already been at the scene. If he stayed far enough back from the scene, Kyle could have him fill the form out tomorrow. That would still be breaking the rules, but as long as the kid didn't get hurt, it probably wouldn't get Kyle into too much trouble.

Hopefully.

"Okay." Kyle nodded at Jesse, and the young man hurried over to him. "Ted says you discovered the body?"

"Yes, sir."

"And you're researching police procedures for a mystery novel?"

"I've written some short mysteries," Jesse admitted. "But I've been wanting to do a full-length novel."

Kyle nodded, only mildly interested. Half the people in the United States claimed to be working on a novel. But who was he to stomp on someone's dream? "If you promise to keep back—stay out of our way and don't touch anything—you can tag along and see how it's done."

"That would be awesome!" Jesse said. "I won't bother you. I promise."

Kyle smiled at him and was rewarded with a beautiful smile in return. Behind Jesse, Wesley gave Kyle a look that clearly said "What the fuck?" but Kyle just shrugged and turned his attention back to the job. If they didn't want to spend their entire night freezing their asses off on the summit, he'd have to take charge. He told Ted, "Okay, let's go."

Somebody had marked the spot with a super-bright LED lantern, wedged between the rocks to keep it from blowing away. It provided a beacon of blue-white light for them to follow. The two EMTs had the roughest time clambering over the rocks, carrying a stainless steel Stokes litter and other equipment, especially since the litter kept catching the wind and trying to sail away from them. The rangers surrounded the newcomers and did their best to illuminate the way with their flashlights.

The lantern was situated at the top of an incline, and Ted made certain everyone halted before they reached the edge. In the darkness, it looked like the slight drop-off was a cliff on the edge of nowhere. The fog shrouded everything beyond and merged with the low cloud cover to create the disturbing illusion they were standing at the edge of the world.

Beyond this point, there be monsters, Kyle thought.

The rangers aimed their flashlight beams down over the edge and motioned for Kyle and Wesley to come nearer. When Kyle approached their position, he looked down to see the body of a young man lying at the bottom of the steep slope, perhaps thirty feet away. He was face-up, his limbs splayed out like a starfish—an impression enhanced by the bright yellow-and-red patterns of his ski jacket—except that a large stone was propping up his right arm. His gloved hand looked like it was grasping at the air, though the movement it made was probably caused by the wind. The young man was clearly dead, eyes and mouth slightly open and rimmed with frost. Ted had made the call hours ago, before Wesley had called Kyle.

Ted went first, moving down the slope to put himself in a position where he could catch the others if they slipped. Kyle descended after him, followed by Wesley. He told the EMTs to wait at the top for now. They weren't going to be much use to the young man lying at the bottom of the slope. Mostly it would be their job to transport the body down the mountain and take him to the morgue.

When he reached the bottom, Kyle knelt and examined the body. "I doubt he lived long after the fall," he told Ted. "Poor kid."

"What makes you think this is more than just a tourist tripping and falling?" Wesley asked.

"We'll have to go back up to the top so I can show you."

They made their way back to the top of the incline, where Jesse was standing beside the others, craning his neck to watch without getting in anyone's way. For a moment, the idea popped into Kyle's head that it would have been cool to bring the kid down with them and let him get a close-up view.

Yeah, he thought, *and then I'd be eviscerated back at the station for letting a civilian fuck up the crime scene.* Why did he even care? Jesse was certainly attractive, but they'd only exchanged about four words. Still, Kyle kept having to check himself whenever his gaze wandered over in Jesse's direction.

"Look at this," Ted said, using his flashlight to illuminate a large boulder at the top of the slope. There was a large splotch of frozen blood on the top of it.

Kyle bent to examine it closely and said grimly, "So he hit his head and *then* fell."

"Looks like."

"Why couldn't he have tripped?" Wesley asked again.

"Because of this," Ted said. He gestured to Rory, who approached and passed a plastic baggie to Kyle. It contained a knitted hat in the same bright yellow and red of the decedent's ski jacket. When Kyle turned it over in his mittened hands, he could see there was a small amount of blood on the inside of the hat, near the brim.

"We found that wedged between the rocks over here," Ted continued, shining his flashlight on a small crevasse between two knee-high boulders, about ten feet from the rock with blood on it. "I was concerned the wind might pick it up and carry it off, so I bagged it."

Kyle nodded. The bag was a standard evidence collection bag, since the rangers often investigated crimes on the mountain and elsewhere in the state park. Ted had carefully labeled it with his name and the time the evidence had been collected, and Rory had added his own name and the time he'd taken custody of it under that. Kyle understood why Ted hadn't wanted to leave the hat where it was. Protecting it from the wind would have been extremely difficult, since just about anything they put over it would have been likely to blow away too.

"Did you take any pictures of it in its original position?" Kyle asked hopefully.

"Jesse did." Ted looked a little embarrassed. "I didn't have a camera—Rory dropped it a couple weeks back, and we haven't replaced it—so I asked him to snap some shots."

Frankly, that rendered the pictures nearly worthless, and Ted had to have known that. They might help Kyle and Wesley a bit, but they couldn't be used as evidence—not if they hadn't been taken by a trained crime scene examiner.

Jesse stepped forward and showed Kyle a picture he'd snapped on his cellphone of the hat lying on the ground between the rocks. He flipped through a few others that had wider shots, so the location of the hat could be identified more clearly. Kyle grunted in acknowledgment and said, "Thanks, kid." He wasn't happy about Jesse insinuating himself into the investigation again, though he supposed it hadn't been intentional. "Can you forward those to me, please?"

"Sure."

Kyle gave him the e-mail address he used at the station, then felt guilty as he watched the young man remove his mitten, then start to type the address into his phone with bare fingers. "Don't…. Why don't you wait until you're indoors, so you don't freeze your fingers off?"

"Okay." Jesse put his mitten back on.

Kyle turned back to Ted, aware that Jesse was still standing beside them, listening in. He decided to ignore that for now. He'd told the kid he could observe, after all. "Okay. The decedent was wearing the hat when his head struck the rock. Somehow the hat came off and blew away."

To his dismay, Ted said, "Jesse has a pretty good theory about that."

Kyle frowned, though it was probably mostly hidden behind his hat and scarf. For a moment, he thought about declaring playtime over and sending the kid inside. Then he relented. It was unlikely some punk fresh out of high school—or maybe college—would be able to add much to a real investigation. He probably got most of his knowledge of crime scenes from television. But he could take a minute to hear the kid out.

"Okay," he said, turning back to Jesse, "What have you got?"

It was like he'd uncapped a bottle of shaken soda. Jesse's words practically gushed out of him. "There's too much blood on the rock," he said. "If he was wearing the hat when his head struck, most of the blood would have been contained within the ski cap. The only explanation that would explain how all the blood got onto the rock would be if the hat came off and his head struck the rock a *second* time."

Kyle raised an eyebrow at him, preparing to dismiss him as a wiseass who watched too much *CSI*. "You think he tripped twice?"

"Let me show you," Jesse said. He motioned to Rory, who sighed good-naturedly but went to stand in front of the kid, facing him. Kyle suspected they'd rehearsed this earlier.

"So he and the killer had to have been facing each other," Jesse said. "The wound is on the right side of Stuart's head, which means he was facing away from the incline when he was killed. There was no place for the killer to stand except right in front of him."

"Assuming there *was* a killer."

"There was," Jesse replied confidently. He reached up and placed a hand against Rory's temple. "But he—or she, possibly—didn't have a weapon handy. Maybe it hadn't been planned. So the killer reaches up and grabs Stuart's head like this—" He curled his fingers into the yarn of Rory's knit cap. "—then slams it down against the rock."

He went through the motion slowly, with the ranger humoring him and allowing his head to be shoved downward. At about the level of the rock Kyle had seen, Jesse yanked Rory's head back and the ranger's cap came off his head. "He pulls back and the hat comes off. But he just tosses that away—" Jesse let Rory snatch the hat out of his hand. "—so he can finish the victim off. He probably doesn't even see where the hat lands."

Jesse grabbed Rory's hair this time and shoved the ranger's head down one more time. "This time, Stuart's head is already bleeding and bare, so it leaves a big spot of blood on the stone. Then the killer lets go and the victim rolls down the hill."

Kyle wanted to dismiss the idea as some crackpot amateur theory cooked up by an overactive imagination. Except it wasn't all that improbable. He mulled it over for a minute while Rory put his hat back on. If the kid's theory was correct, there would be more signs of it—hair ripped out on the side of the head opposite the wound, for instance—that might show up in the autopsy report. At least it would be worth checking out.

Kyle shrugged and said, "Okay, Jesse Fletcher. I'll look into it."

He'd meant it as good-natured ribbing, but even with his face mostly obscured by the balaclava, the way Jesse's eyes darkened made it very clear he didn't appreciate the joke.

"Thanks," he said. But he no longer sounded at all pleased. Kyle felt a twinge of guilt for shooting the kid down, even if it had been unintentional. But he wasn't there to pat Jesse on the back and tell him how clever he was. He was there to find out who'd killed that poor kid lying frozen at the bottom of the hill.

Kyle nodded and went to talk with the EMTs.

KYLE AND the rest of his team kept at it until after midnight, examining the scene and taking statements from everyone who'd been present when the body was discovered. After giving his statement, Jesse had been ordered back inside by Reggie to finish doing the dishes. Kyle was sorry to see him go—even more so when the kid refused to look at him as he left.

Fuck me. I don't have time for this shit.

When they finally called it quits and made sure the area was sealed off as well as could be expected with yellow tape held down by rocks, he and Wesley and the two EMTs took the body down the mountain on the train. Larry stayed up at the ranger station with Ted and Rory.

The trip down was a bit shorter—about forty-five minutes, thanks to gravity giving the train a boost. At the bottom, an ambulance was waiting to take the body to Concord for an autopsy at the state medical examiner's office. Kyle took Wesley to where his Subaru wagon was parked in the station parking lot.

Unfortunately, their night wasn't over yet. Nobody had informed the victim's friends and family of his death, so it was their job now. It was late, but Kyle had no doubt they were still awake, worried sick about Stuart. Leaving it until morning would be cruel and telling them over the phone would be almost as bad. The least he could do was deliver the terrible news in person. So he drove to the Mount Washington Hotel in Bretton Woods, where they were all staying.

The Mount Washington Hotel was a Victorian landmark about six miles from the Cog Railway, and Kyle had to pass it to get to the highway anyway. It was gorgeous, palatial, and extremely expensive. Kyle had lived in this area his entire life, and he'd never even thought about spending a night there. Even off-season, rooms could go for about $300 a night. At some times of the year, it was twice that. The hotel was a true resort, boasting a number of activities from golf to skiing to tennis to horseback riding. It had indoor and outdoor pools, hot tubs, and a spa.

In short, it was swanky. Wesley whistled as they pulled up in front of the hotel portico and a valet came down the front steps to greet them. "These kids must come from money, if they're having the wedding at this place."

"Maybe," Kyle answered noncommittally.

They climbed out of the Outback, and he handed the keys to the valet. The porter held the door open for them as they entered the grand lobby. It was a cavernous space that had changed little in over a hundred years, with a high ceiling and rows of white square columns. Oriental carpets marked off spaces for comfortable upholstered couches and chairs, and an enormous stone fireplace, with a moose head mounted above it, contained a blazing fire.

Kyle led his partner past the lounge area until they came to the front desk near a broad staircase. He showed the concierge his badge. "We need to speak with Todd Warren. I understand he's staying here." Todd had left his contact information with Ted before he and his friends left the mountain. He seemed to be the only one directly related to Stuart.

"I'll see if he's in."

The concierge called up to the room and spoke to someone there. Then he asked Kyle, "Would you like him to come down, officer?"

Telling a man in the hotel lobby that his brother was dead seemed pretty crass. "No. What's his room number? We'll go to him."

THEY FOUND the room on the fourth floor, and Kyle knocked. The kid who answered the door wasn't Stuart's brother—that was obvious. He was a good head shorter than Stuart, and his unkempt hair was dark brown. He had something that might have been trying—and failing—to become a beard on his chin, and he looked up at Kyle with wide, frightened green eyes. Whether they were frightened of Kyle, or frightened of what Kyle was likely about to tell him concerning Stuart, wasn't immediately apparent. Kyle guessed this had to be Joel, a friend of the family who was listed in Ted's report.

"I'm Detective Dubois, from the state police," Kyle told him. He gestured to Wesley. "This is my partner, Detective Roberts."

The young man muttered something too softly for Kyle to make out, but he stepped back and opened the door. Kyle and Wesley entered and came face-to-face with Todd Warren.

Unlike his roommate, Todd was tall and strikingly handsome—even more so than his younger brother had been, though the resemblance to Stuart was unsettling. They could have been twins, despite the two-year age difference, and Kyle had the impression for a moment that the dead man had gotten up off the stretcher and said, "Just kidding!"

Todd was standing over his bed, shirtless, as if caught in the process of dressing, and in fact, the moment Kyle entered, Todd lifted a navy blue T-shirt in his hands and stretched it over his head. He was wearing faded jeans and his feet were bare, causing Kyle to reassess his conviction that the Warrens had money. Perhaps the bride's family was paying for this week, but neither Todd nor Joel was wearing anything that couldn't be picked up at Walmart. Like Todd, Joel was wearing worn jeans, and his brown sweater was unraveling a bit at the end of one sleeve.

"Have you heard anything?" Todd asked immediately, once his head emerged from the neck of the shirt. There was nothing tentative or frightened about him. He looked Kyle directly in the eye, daring him to deliver bad news about his brother.

"I'm afraid so," Kyle replied, meeting his gaze. "We found Stuart. But... I'm sorry. Your brother is dead."

Joel reacted first. He seemed to collapse in on himself, wrapping his arms around his body as if for protection or comfort. "I knew it."

Todd startled Kyle by growling deep in his chest, grabbing the glass tumbler off his nightstand, and hurling it against the far wall with an inarticulate cry. His face was contorted in pure unmasked rage. "*Motherfucker!*"

Wesley stepped back as if preparing for an attack, but Kyle forced himself to remain still. He couldn't blame Todd for this display of emotion, under the circumstances, though he wondered if he'd have to intervene to prevent the destruction of more hotel property. And Todd's temper might be something to file away for later.

Kyle waited patiently for the two young men to collect themselves, prepared to provide more detail, if they asked, or to simply leave them to their grief. If Stuart had been murdered, he would have to question everyone who'd been on the mountain with him, but that could wait until tomorrow.

"This whole thing was a huge fucking mistake," Todd fumed, pacing back and forth by his bed like a caged lion. "We should never have come here!"

Joel was staring blankly into space, obviously in shock. "How did... how did he die?"

Kyle didn't want to reveal telling details about the crime scene until he'd had the chance to question everyone, but he had to provide something. "It looks like he fell and hit his head."

"He shouldn't have wandered off on his own," Todd muttered.

"Fuck you!" Joel snapped. "Do you think he deserved to die because he wanted to take a walk by himself?"

Todd balled his hands into fists and took a few steps in Joel's direction, snarling, "He was my goddamn brother! And this bullshit wedding just got him killed! Don't tell me how I feel about it!"

Joel looked so helpless and small in comparison to Todd that Kyle felt compelled to step between them and place a restraining hand against Todd's chest. "Okay," he said soothingly. "Okay. It's nobody's fault. Sometimes—"

"This whole trip was Corrie's fault," Todd snapped. But he eased up, relaxing his fists. He glanced at Joel, who was glowering back at him, and then looked back at Kyle. "Can I go?"

"Where do you want to go, Todd?" Kyle asked, still concerned about the anger practically radiating off the young man's body.

"Just out. I need to be alone for a while." He added, "I'm not gonna break anything else."

Kyle nodded. He couldn't really do much to stop him. Sure, the guy had smashed a glass, but… well, Kyle was inclined to give him a break on that, under the circumstances. The hotel could take it up with him. The possibility Todd might have an ulterior motive occurred to him, but without anything more concrete to go on, Kyle decided to let him go. Maybe it was just what it seemed—he needed to cool off. "Just stay cool, okay?"

He watched Todd grab his heavy ski jacket and a pair of sneakers and stride out of the room, brushing past Wesley in the doorway. When his footsteps had receded down the carpeted hallway, Kyle turned to Joel and asked, "You think you're gonna be okay?"

"Why? Because my best friend in the world just died, or because I'm sharing a room with his psycho brother?"

"Both."

Joel sighed and unfolded his arms so he could run his hands through his tangled mop of hair. "Don't worry. He's a dick, but I doubt he'd really hurt anyone. He just… he's always been overprotective of Stuart."

"Did Stuart have a separate room?" Kyle asked.

"No, he was here with us." He made a sour face. "With Todd, anyway. He'd never be allowed to share a bed with *me*."

That seemed an odd thing to say. Kyle's bewilderment must have shown in his face, because Joel grimaced and pointed to himself. "Fag."

"Oh." Kyle still wondered at the way he'd phrased the statement. "He'd never be allowed to share a bed with me." Not "He'd never share a bed with me." Perhaps Stuart had been okay with Joel being gay—Joel claimed they were best friends, after all—but not Todd.

"I take it Stuart was supposed to marry this girl—" He consulted the list of names Larry had given him on the Cog. "Corrie Lassiter?"

"On Saturday," Joel replied. He sat down on his bed, still looking lost and confused. "This was supposed to be a vacation—sort of a wedding present to Corrie and Stuart from her parents."

"That's really tragic."

Joel laughed bitterly. "Yeah."

There was a long, uncomfortable silence. Then Kyle cleared his throat and said, "Can you tell us what room Corrie is staying in? We should go speak to her."

THAT CORRIE'S family was wealthy, Kyle had no doubt. The room the young men shared was nice, but a fairly standard hotel room with two queen-sized beds. The Lassiters occupied a luxury suite with three bedrooms and a living room with a fireplace, widescreen TV, wet bar, and another half bath in addition to the full-size bathroom off the master bedroom. The Lassiters themselves were quite well turned out. Kyle didn't know much about clothes, but he could tell Mr. and Mrs. Lassiter hadn't grabbed theirs off a rack at Sears. The three kids—apparently there was a brother Ted hadn't met on top of the mountain—looked a bit less tailored, but there wasn't a stray thread or worn patch to be found.

They were gathered in the living room area when the youngest girl let him in. She was a cute little thing with long blonde hair and wide blue eyes, perhaps about fifteen. According to Ted's report, this would be Lisa.

"Corrie...," Lisa said, her voice hesitant and fearful.

The young woman who stood up from her chair was extremely beautiful. Like her little sister, she had long blonde hair, a flawless complexion, and large blue eyes. But the ten-year age difference made an enormous difference. Her spotless white sweater and beige slacks clung to a delicate figure that curved nicely in the right places, and Kyle could see why any young man—well, any *straight* young man, anyway—would feel lucky to be marrying her.

She knew why he and his partner were there. He could see it in her eyes. But perhaps she didn't want him to say the words, which was why she remained silent for so long until he finally spoke.

"Are you Corrie?"

"Yes."

"I'm sorry. I have some bad news about your fiancé, Stuart Warren." Kyle watched Corrie's mother move silently to her side and put an arm protectively around her waist. "I'm afraid… he was found dead."

Corrie had clearly been on the verge of crying when Kyle walked in. Now the tears came as her face contorted into a mask of pain. Mrs. Lassiter folded her daughter into her arms and Mr. Lassiter strode across the room to place a comforting hand on her shoulder. Lisa ran to throw her arms around all three of them.

Only the young man stood apart, his eyes downcast. He was older than Corrie and the two young men Kyle had seen earlier—perhaps in his late twenties. His hair was a shade darker than that of his sisters, but he had the same large blue eyes and delicate, attractive features. He was tall and thin.

Why wasn't he included in the sightseeing trip? Kyle wondered. Perhaps he was too old to hang out with his sister's friends.

They seemed to have forgotten the two police detectives, and Kyle contemplated leaving. But a moment later, Mr. Lassiter patted his daughter gently on the back and broke away to come speak with him.

"I don't think Corrie will be much good right now, if you were hoping to talk to her," he said quietly. He was a distinguished gentleman, handsome and well groomed, his face appearing young, though his hair was gray. His wife, too, appeared a bit older than Kyle might have expected, as if they'd waited until middle age to have children.

"I understand," Kyle replied.

Mr. Lassiter lowered his voice and leaned in closer. "May I ask… how…?"

"There will be an autopsy, but for now, we believe he may have fallen and struck his head."

"Oh my God!" Lassiter gasped, still keeping his voice under restraint. "The poor boy. Have you spoken with his brother, Todd?"

"Yes."

"He must be devastated."

Kyle nodded noncommittally. "Mr. Lassiter, how long will your party be staying at the hotel?"

"We're booked in until Sunday," he replied. He shook his head wearily. "The wedding was to be Saturday afternoon."

"We would prefer it if you could stay in the area for the time being."

Lassiter looked taken aback, as if Kyle were accusing him of murdering Stuart. But he merely said, "We'll stay until our scheduled checkout time. I hope that will be adequate."

"What about Todd and Joel?"

"Their room is paid for up through Sunday," he said with a dismissive wave of his hand, "just as ours is."

"On your tab?"

Lassiter frowned, as if offended by talk of money. "Of course."

"Good night, then," Kyle said with a nod. "Please accept my condolences. You'll be hearing from us soon."

Lassiter opened the door, and Kyle had the distinct impression the man wanted to slam it behind them. But he didn't.

As he and Wesley made their way down to the lobby and then waited for the valet to bring the Outback around, Kyle wondered just how someone like Stuart Warren—a young man who, judging by Todd and Joel, had been just barely scraping by—came to be engaged to someone like Corrie Lassiter. Her family appeared to approve the marriage, arranging for the Warrens and Joel to have a very expensive week at one of the ritziest resort hotels in New England before the wedding, and then presumably covering the costs of the wedding on top of that, but Kyle was having a hard time reconciling the impressions he'd gotten of Todd Warren and Mr. Lassiter. If Stuart and Corrie were anything like their relatives, they seemed an odd match.

At any rate, the next step was clear. "I'd like to go back up the mountain tomorrow, when it's light out," he told Wesley. "Assuming the weather is good."

Wesley made a grumbling noise deep in his chest. "You don't think we suffered enough tonight?"

"We could barely see anything in the dark, especially with the fog so thick. There could be a footprint, some loose threads snagged on something… who knows? I'd just feel better if I took another look."

"There's a shitload of paperwork to fill out," Wesley said, "and if we're lucky, Vera will have the autopsy done by tomorrow afternoon." Vera was the state medical examiner in Concord.

"I'll tell you what," Kyle said. "You fill out the paperwork, and I'll go up the mountain by myself. I'll be back in time to go with you to Concord."

"You just don't want to deal with the paperwork."

"Damn straight."

Wesley snorted. "Fine. But it's past two in the morning, and we still haven't checked into a hotel. I'm sleeping in tomorrow."

"You do that."

Unfortunately, Kyle knew part of him was looking forward to going back for a completely unprofessional reason, and he'd just as soon not have Wesley along for that. He wanted to see that damned kid again. Not that he had any delusions of asking Jesse out or anything like that. For one thing, he was probably straight. Even if he wasn't, he was almost certainly interested in dating someone closer to his age than Kyle was. And after that failed attempt at teasing him, he might not want anything to do with Kyle, anyway.

But Kyle had watched his friends make fools of themselves just to be around an attractive woman for a few minutes. Why should he be any different?

FORTUNATELY, THERE was a hotel—an *affordable* hotel that they could expect headquarters to reimburse them for—directly across the road from the Mount Washington. It was called the Lodge and was a step up from a lot of the roadside motels Kyle had stayed in over the years. It advertised a pool and a spa, which he wouldn't be using, and about fifty rooms on two levels, connected by long balconies.

They ran into a slight problem when they checked in. Not that it was really bad. More… awkward. The clerk looked at the two detectives and asked simply, "Would you like one or two beds?"

Why she would assume they might be a couple, when they were both in uniform, Kyle couldn't imagine. Maybe she was just trying to cover her bases. But he really wished she hadn't.

Wesley snorted and clapped his hand on Kyle's shoulder. "What do you think, honey bear?"

"Two beds, please," Kyle said, shrugging Wesley's hand off.

"Aw, sugar lips, don't be that way…."

The clerk looked from one man to the other uncertainly until Kyle said, "Ignore him. We're not a couple. Two beds will be perfect."

As they walked up the stairs outside to get to their room, Wesley kept up the ribbing by calling Kyle "bunny" and "cuddle buns." Kyle did his best to ignore him—it was just horsing around—but he couldn't help but wonder if Wesley would think it was so funny if he knew Kyle really did like men. Not that Kyle was lusting after his partner. Wesley was okay-looking but not hot by any stretch. He had a pleasant face, but his hair was already creeping north at twenty-nine and he'd likely be bald in ten years. He was also getting a bit paunchy. But more to the point, Kyle just didn't feel any attraction to the guy at all. Probably for the best, since they had to work together.

The two men undressed quickly once they were inside, stripping down to their boxer briefs. They took turns using the bathroom and then crawled into bed, too exhausted to do anything else. It was getting close to 3:00 a.m.

Still, after they'd turned off the lights and Kyle muttered "g'night," Wesley giggled and replied, "Good night, pookie."

"Knock it off," Kyle said with a sigh, "or I'll crawl into bed with you and give you a big kiss on the mouth."

That made Wesley laugh and make kissing noises at him, but then he finally shut up and went to sleep.

WHAT A jerk.

Okay, Jesse hadn't really expected the police detective to shout, "My God, that's it! You've solved the case!" But it wasn't a bad theory. It explained the evidence. So why be a jerk about it? Was the guy that insecure about his job?

He'd been nice at first. And gorgeous—at least from what Jesse had seen of the guy's face peeking out from between his hat and scarf. He had a strong nose and dark razor stubble on his cheeks, but his mouth was unusually sensual for such a strong face, curved and delicate. His eyes, too, were a soft hazel, but they seemed to evaluate everything from beneath his sharply defined brow. He looked like a man full of contradictions, a fascinating mystery Jesse would love to unravel.

If only he hadn't been such a dick. And calling Jesse by the nickname he'd endured for the past few years in college didn't do anything to make him more endearing. No doubt he'd stumbled on it accidentally—it didn't take a genius IQ to make the connection—but he probably thought he was clever as shit.

It had been exciting to tag along after the policeman and his team, but after the big discoveries had been revealed, it was just nitpicky work— marking off the scene with tape tied down wherever it could be, scanning the ground for other evidence that could be bagged, photographing the scene, and mapping everything out. It was interesting, but in this cold, with Jesse pissed off at the detective in charge, it was only stubbornness that kept him from going inside.

Eventually, to his relief, Steve called him on his walkie-talkie and told him to get his ass back to the observatory to help with cleanup. There was a pile of dishes sitting in the sink with his name on it. So Jesse left the professionals to their work and went in out of the cold.

Lying in his room later that night, with Steve snoring gently in the bunk underneath him, Jesse was still fuming about the detective's attitude. He hated being dismissed like that. His theory had made perfect sense. If only there was some way he could learn what the medical examiner would find when she examined the body. He'd be willing to bet there would be some hair torn out of the guy's scalp. And he'd also bet there would be hair—some torn out by the roots—still inside the ski cap.

THE NEXT morning was Wednesday and the end of Jesse and Steve's shift. One of the coaches would be arriving soon to bring the two volunteers for the next weeklong shift and take Jesse and Steve down the mountain. But before that they still had to cook breakfast and clean up afterward.

Steve had whipped up some scone batter the night before and set up trays that could be taken out of the refrigerator and popped into the oven. In the meantime, he started frying up some omelets while Jesse set the table. His job was easy, for now, but he'd be doing those greasy dishes later as penance.

While they worked, Reggie hung out in the kitchen, chatting with them. "I felt bad for those guys last night," he said. "They didn't get out of here until close to one in the morning."

"Is that it, then?" Jesse asked him.

Reggie shrugged. "More or less. But the area is still roped off, in case they want to search it again or something."

"Is the body gone?"

"Of course. They took it down with them."

"What happens next?"

Reggie laughed and picked up one of the glasses Jesse had just set to go get himself some juice from the refrigerator. "What happens next is you serve breakfast and clean up. Then we'll wave a tearful good-bye as they take you away. If you want to bug the police about shit after that, be my guest. Just don't bring me into it."

Jesse wasn't sure if he wanted to talk to the detective again or not. Well, if he was honest, he had to admit he did. But what he'd say to someone who obviously thought he was a complete loser, he couldn't imagine. The guy was unlikely to give him any real information.

He was still brooding over this a couple hours later as he sat in the sun outside, his ass being chilled by the boulder it was parked on and his bags at his feet. He was half-hoping the police would come back before the coach got there—maybe to do a more thorough search of the area—so he'd have a chance to ask them some more questions. But they might be dealing with paperwork or autopsies instead that morning. That was the problem—Jesse didn't know what the correct procedures were, and he was frustrated to be missing such a great opportunity to find out more.

Steve startled him out of his thoughts by tossing his rucksack on the ground beside Jesse's.

"Still moping because they took your body away?"

"Don't be an ass," Jesse grumbled as Steve pushed him over to make room for himself on the rock. "I don't *want* the poor guy to be dead."

"But now that he *is* dead, you want to solve the crime."

"Well… kind of." Mostly, he wanted to write mysteries. But he had to admit it would be really cool to *solve* one.

Steve shook his head. "Well, maybe you'll get lucky and someone will keel over with a butcher's knife sticking out of his back when you get back to Dover."

Jesse frowned at him, but he didn't dignify that with a response. He heard the sound of a vehicle coming up the road and automatically reached for his bags, thinking it was the coach. But when he straightened up, he saw a Subaru Outback coming up the road instead. He turned away, losing interest, but as the wagon pulled into the broad parking area near the depot and came to a stop, Steve nudged him. Jesse turned back and felt an odd little flutter in his chest. The person stepping out of it was wearing a state police uniform.

It was Detective Dubois.

"Here's your chance," Steve said with a wry smile. "Go tell him it was Miss Scarlet in the library with the revolver."

"Fuck you."

Steve laughed. Then he leaned forward and kissed Jesse on the cheek. "You're cute. Too bad we turned out to have nothing in common."

"We have shared memories of scrubbing dishes and cleaning the toilet."

"That we do."

As tempting as it was to follow the police detective inside the observatory, Jesse couldn't think of a good excuse to do so. If he was too obvious about chasing after the guy, he'd lose what little dignity he still had left. So he gritted his teeth and stayed put. Maybe he could find a way to drift inside and nonchalantly wander over to the ranger station in a few minutes.

Steve eventually abandoned him to go inside and use the restroom. Jesse picked up his paperback again but really couldn't get into it, so he tucked it into his backpack.

Then he heard footsteps approaching and turned to find Rory and Dubois walking toward him. Jesse was so startled he jumped immediately to his feet, as if he'd been caught napping on the job. Of course, his job had more or less ended an hour ago.

"Hey, Jesse," Rory said when they drew near. "Detective Dubois is here to take a look at the scene again."

The detective smiled, his teeth so white and perfect he looked like a model in a toothpaste commercial. He wasn't wearing a hat or a scarf this morning, and Jesse could see he had a strong, angular jaw. The dark five o'clock shadow from last night was gone, though there was already a hint of it creeping back, as if he had a difficult time keeping it at bay. His chestnut hair seemed a bit long for a policeman, and the morning breeze tousled it.

"Jesse," the detective said, extending his hand.

Jesse shook it, marveling at how strong his grip was. "What's up?"

"Well, first I wanted to thank you for e-mailing me those pictures you took last night."

"No problem."

"Also," Dubois went on, "I, uh... I was feelin' a little bad about brushing you off last night. I didn't mean to insult you."

Jesse shrugged, trying to appear as if he hadn't given it another thought. "No big deal."

The detective glanced out across the parking lot in the general direction of the crime scene. "If you want, you're welcome to tag along again. Not that it's likely I'll find anything new, but I wanted to get a better look in the daylight."

"That would be great!" Jesse said. It came out a bit more enthusiastic than he would have liked, and Dubois turned those soft hazel eyes back on him and smiled again.

"Same rules apply," he said. "Don't touch anything, and don't walk inside the marked-off area. I don't want you contaminating the scene any more than you and the others did when you found the body." Jesse must have looked irritated at that, because the detective quickly added, "Not that you did anything wrong. You had to find him and do what you could to rescue him. Then the rest of us tromped all over it in the dark last night. But now we've got to keep things from getting any worse. Understand?"

"Of course."

"All right, then," Dubois said with a nod. "I have some forms I need you to fill out this time, to cover both last night and today. Is there anyone here who can watch your stuff for you?"

"I'll put it in the station office."

WITHOUT JESSE'S flashlight to provide a beacon, it was a challenge to find the exact spot, even with it marked off by crime scene tape. In some places, the landscape near the summit looked like an unbroken field of flint gray boulders with little to differentiate one boulder from another. It made Jesse think of the moon—or Mars, except that it wasn't orange. No trees grew up this high, and very few plants, other than lichen on the rocks and small patches of grass, diapensia, and dwarf cinquefoil between them.

But Rory knew the mountain well, and Jesse had wandered around outside the observatory enough to know his way around. He remembered the position of the observatory not long before he'd reported in and how far away it had looked. Dubois was patient and didn't complain when they had to backtrack.

They'd only been out there a few minutes when Rory's walkie-talkie buzzed for his attention. He answered it, and Jesse overheard Carol ask, "You going be much longer? Jesse's ride is waiting to take him down."

"We're still searching for the right spot."

Dubois looked at Jesse. "Where are you supposed to be going?"

"Just down to the bottom of the Auto Road," Jesse answered. "My car's parked there."

"Do you have a schedule to keep?"

Jesse shook his head. "Not really."

"If you want to wait until I'm done up here, I can take you down in a couple of hours."

"Sure."

Rory relayed the message to Carol and arranged for someone to pack Jesse's bags into Dubois's wagon. Then they went back to the search.

Jesse decided to see just how much the detective was willing to discuss about the case. "Did they already perform an autopsy?"

Rory frowned at him, but apparently the question wasn't out of line because Dubois responded, "Not yet. He was sent to Concord for the autopsy—they're all done there, at the Office of the Chief Medical Examiner. And before you ask," he added, "even if I could tell you what they found, I have no idea. I haven't gotten the report yet."

A moment later, they spotted the yellow tape fluttering in the wind, still anchored to the ground by small rocks. Jesse and Rory stayed outside it while Dubois carefully picked his way through the space, photographing everything again in the different lighting conditions and crouching frequently to examine things that might have been missed.

In the morning sun, the blood on the rock at the top of the slope was a dark brownish-red splotch. It had been frozen last night, but Jesse knew it would have coagulated quickly after thawing this morning—within minutes—and then after an hour or so, the yellowish serum would have separated out from the clots. From where Jesse stood, he thought he could see small dark lines where this had run down the rock face. Dubois peered at the stain closely and took several shots of it with his digital camera. Then he straightened up and snapped several pics of the rock in the context of the landscape from different angles.

Jesse scanned the area around them, commenting to Rory, "Stuart and his killer would have had to come out here together."

Rory gave him a shrug, as if to say "How should I know?" but Dubois overheard him and said, "Yes." He gave Jesse a half smile, a bit like the smile Humphrey Bogart used to wear in the old detective films, and said, "Now tell me why."

"Because there are no landmarks," Jesse replied, raising his voice. "Not if they didn't know the mountain. Stuart couldn't have arranged to meet someone all the way out here. And if he was wandering around lost in the fog, what are the odds the one person who would find him—without getting lost himself—would be the person who wanted to kill him?"

"It could have been someone he just bumped into," Rory suggested.

"Some random Joe who just felt like killing a helpless tourist?" Dubois asked, eyebrows raised. "That seems unlikely. Maybe if he was desperate for cash, but the victim wasn't robbed. We found his wallet and cash in his pocket."

Jesse nodded. "So either he met someone near the observatory, or it was one of the people he came with. Then they walked out here together, maybe even before the fog set in. They wanted to get away from people."

Rory looked as if he was trying to puzzle that out, but Dubois gave Jesse a wide grin. "You're gonna make a good mystery writer, kid."

I already am *a good mystery writer*, Jesse thought. But he didn't correct the detective. Dubois had clearly meant it as praise.

The detective glanced down the slope, perhaps debating the best way to climb down, and then turned back to say, "So Stuart probably knew his killer. The right side of his head was smashed in. Which means, as you pointed out, if he was standing here"—he pointed to a relatively flat spot between the rock with the blood stain and some other smaller rocks—"and it wasn't just a case of him slipping and falling, Stuart had to have been facing toward the observatory, away from the slope he fell down after he hit his head. Someone *could* have stood behind him, but there isn't much room. So most likely, Stuart was facing his killer when the guy—or woman—grabbed him."

"So maybe they were arguing," Jesse said. "Or maybe Stuart thought they were just having a friendly conversation…."

"Until it was too late," Dubois finished.

4

KYLE HAD married in college but lost his wife to lymphoma just three years later. For the past five years, he'd felt as if dating would somehow betray Julie and everything she went through—everything *they* went through together. Truthfully, it hadn't been hard to avoid it. He hadn't seen anyone who even piqued his curiosity in all that time. He worked long hours and filled his free time with sappy romantic movies he knew Julie would have liked, computer games she probably *wouldn't* have approved of, and maybe a bit too much masturbation.

That's why his first sight of Jesse Morales had broadsided him. Christ, the kid was gorgeous! Smooth olive skin, black hair, and big brown eyes a guy could get lost in. Kyle assumed, with a last name like Morales, Jesse had to be Latino or Puerto Rican or something. At any rate, he was the most beautiful man Kyle had ever laid eyes on.

Kyle had been attracted to men a few times in his life, before he met Julie and lost interest in anyone but her. Bisexuality hadn't been "cool" back then—everyone had assumed you were just in denial about being gay—so he'd more or less kept it to himself. Except for Julie. She'd thought it was sexy that they both found men attractive and had liked to compare notes about actors in the movies they watched together.

But to be this strongly attracted to a man—that was new. Kyle wasn't sure how to handle it. Particularly since Jesse was so young. Not so young as to be off-limits, really, but... well, he didn't look much over twenty. That was a pretty big gap. Kyle had just hit thirty this summer. At any rate, Jesse was probably straight, and he was definitely leaving soon.

So Kyle needed to put all this out of his mind and focus on the task at hand. It was one thing to let the kid tag along a bit and get a feel for what an investigation was like. It was entirely another to think about flirting with him.

They climbed down the slope for a closer look at where the body had been found, Jesse and Rory still staying outside the yellow tape. In the daylight, Kyle saw several spots they'd missed the night before, where streaks of blood marked the path the body had taken as it rolled. He photographed each one and pulled out a notebook and pencil to sketch where each was in relation to the scene. It was painstakingly slow, but Jesse and Rory waited patiently and didn't try to talk to him while he was working.

When they were finally examining the small pool of blood where Stuart's head had lain, dark and coagulated now, Jesse commented, "That doesn't seem like much blood, considering how bad the head wound looked."

"Was he breathing when you found him?" Kyle asked.

"No. I tried CPR, but... I think he was already dead. I couldn't find a pulse."

"If he was already dead, he wouldn't have bled much, even from a large wound. The heart isn't beating and forcing blood out of the body."

Jesse nodded and looked a little pale as he stared at the spot.

Kyle glanced around one last time, then tucked away his notepad. "That's about as good as I can manage out here," he said finally. He turned to Jesse. "Are you set to leave?"

"Pretty much."

"Then let's hit the restrooms and head out."

JESSE SAT in the passenger seat of the Outback, watching the landscape scrolling by outside the window—the breathtaking view of the other mountains in the Presidential Range, the often-terrifying sheer drops that bordered the Auto Road in places. Kyle kept glancing at his passenger's delicate profile and found himself hating the idea of saying good-bye to Jesse at the bottom. He knew it was stupid. The kid had a life to get back to.

"Are you in college?" he asked.

"I just graduated from UNH. English major."

Kyle grunted noncommittally. *What the fuck do you do with an English major?* "Do you need to major in English to be a writer?"

Jesse laughed and shook his head. "No, I don't think so. I just love reading and writing, and I couldn't get enough of it. I'd like to write full-time someday—be able to live off it, I mean."

"The next Stephen King?"

"I wish! Or maybe the next Harlan Coben."

"The way you observed so many details at the scene and how focused you were.... You've got a knack for investigation. Or writing about it, at any rate."

He was pleased to see Jesse color and look away shyly. It was very cute.

"How did you end up at the observatory?" Kyle asked, hoping he wasn't starting to sound creepy. He wasn't trying to grill him—just keep the conversation going.

"That was Steve's fault," Jesse replied with a wry smile. "He's volunteered there before and loves it. We dated for a couple months last year, and he convinced me to go hiking a few times. It was fun, so I let him talk me into volunteering."

That answered one thing—Jesse was into men. It was ridiculous how happy that knowledge made Kyle. He wanted to ask if he was seeing someone now, since it sounded like he and Steve were no longer an item, but that would definitely be stalkerish. Better not.

He stayed silent so long, trying to think of something innocuous to say, that Jesse finally spoke up. "So, how long have you been a detective?"

"Three years." Then, because he always felt that he had to explain why it seemed like such a short time, he added, "I was on the force for five years before that. I came in right after college."

"Eight years? How old are you?" Jesse asked, as if he'd expected Kyle to be younger than that. He looked flustered right after he asked it and quickly said, "Sorry. That's none of my business."

Might as well throw it out there. "I just hit thirty last July. Now you have to tell me *your* age." *Subtle.*

"Twenty-three. I took a year off after high school."

Seven years. Not as bad as Kyle had thought. But was it still too big an age gap? Maybe. Certainly he'd get some ribbing from his friends over it, in addition to the whole "But he's a *dude!*" thing. And Jesse might think he was too old. Any way he looked at it, Kyle just couldn't see it happening.

"Totally legal," Jesse added with a slight laugh.

"For drinking?"

Jesse glanced away, a coy smile on his lips, and said, "That and other things."

Jesus. Was he flirting?

Calm down, Kyle. Take a deep breath. He probably just meant sex with other *guys. You're just hearing what you want to hear.*

Then Jesse said something that cooled him off a bit. "Is your wife on the force too?"

Kyle took a long time to answer while he tried to figure out why the hell Jesse would ask about his wife. Then he realized—the ring. He'd noticed Kyle's wedding ring.

Dammit.

"I'm widowed," Kyle replied slowly, keeping his eyes focused on the road. "Julie was an artist. Oil paintings, mostly. She was just getting started with that—getting some paintings into some local galleries—when she got cancer. She passed away almost five years ago."

"I'm sorry."

Kyle took a breath and rubbed his thumb against the simple gold band he'd been wearing for so long it felt like part of his skin. "It just… never felt right to take it off."

Jesse was quiet for a long time, so Kyle shot him a quick glance. He was smiling sadly and looking away out the window. Kyle wanted to kick himself for being a downer, but really, what else was he supposed to have said? Jesse would assume he was straight now, and off-limits, and there was no way to correct that impression without Kyle making a complete idiot of himself. But maybe that was for the best.

When they got to the bottom of the mountain, where the Auto Road came out on Route 16 near Gorham, Kyle had another moment of panic at the thought of Jesse taking off and disappearing forever. He'd said when Kyle took his statement that he lived in Dover, almost three hours south. It was completely irrational, since he knew there was nothing he could do to prevent it, but Kyle couldn't help it—he needed to delay the inevitable a little longer. "How do you feel about stopping for lunch? I'll buy."

"You don't have to do that."

Is that a brush-off? Kyle was so out of the loop, he couldn't tell. Maybe Jesse was just being polite. Kyle grinned at him, trying to hide his nervousness. It felt like he was asking Jesse out on a date. "I'd like to. It's the least I can do for all the help you gave me this morning."

Lame. He probably thinks I'm a total weirdo.

But Jesse smiled and said, "Okay, sure."

IF DETECTIVE Dubois was completely straight, Jesse's gaydar had to be on the fritz. Not that the man was really doing anything overt, but Jesse kept getting the impression he was… interested. And God knew *Jesse* was interested.

Dubois had been married, and Jesse sensed genuine sadness when Dubois spoke about his late wife. A man who still wore his wedding ring five years later was still missing his wife and perhaps not really interested in dating—not seriously, at any rate. But he kept giving Jesse looks out of the corner of his eye. Jesse had seen looks like that often enough. They usually came just before a guy asked him out or at least propositioned him. He wasn't usually interested in one-night stands, but with a guy this hot… well, he'd be willing to consider it.

They ate at the Glen View Café, across the highway at the base of the Auto Road. It was a restaurant attached to a store selling hiking supplies and underneath a hotel. The décor was rustic, with a large fireplace at one end of the room and wide plate glass windows along the side facing the mountain. The food was decent—mostly homemade. Steve had taken Jesse there for breakfast last year, before they hiked up the Auto Road. The cafe also had tourist packages that included boxed lunches for hikers to take with them.

After they'd both ordered simple cheeseburgers and a big plate of chili cheese fries to share, Jesse asked, "So what happens next?"

Dubois looked startled. "What do you mean? I guess I take you to your car."

"No, I mean with the investigation."

"Oh." Was it his imagination, or did Dubois look disappointed? "I'm afraid I can't really tell you anything too specific."

"I understand. I wouldn't want you to tell me anything confidential...."

"Yeah, you would," Dubois said with a grin.

Guilty as charged. "Well, okay," Jesse admitted, "I would love to hear all the details. But you can at least tell me about the procedures you go through, can't you? Like I told you, I want to write detective novels."

Dubois sat back and thought about it a moment. "Like I said, the body was sent to the Office of the Chief Medical Examiner in Concord for an autopsy. My partner and I will probably drive down there this afternoon to get the report. Wesley—Detective Roberts—filed an initial report this morning, but we'll have to update it with the information we get from the coroner. Then we'll probably head back to the hotel to interview the family and friends of the victim in detail. We broke the news about Stuart to them last night, but we haven't taken statements yet. And that's... pretty much all I can tell you."

"Statistically," Jesse said thoughtfully, "it most likely had to be one of the three people who arrived on the train with him."

"What about the other train passengers?" Kyle asked. Then he grimaced, as if he hadn't meant to say that, but he continued, "Or the people already at summit?"

Jesse shook his head. "If they didn't know him, they wouldn't have been likely to kill him. Most murders are committed by someone who already knew the victim. So it's most likely to be one of the three who came with Stuart."

"Four," Dubois corrected.

"I'm not counting the teenage girl. Do you think we should?"

"What's this about 'we'?" Dubois asked, frowning. "I'm buying you lunch, not inviting you to be my partner in the investigation."

Jesse felt his face flushing. "Sorry."

"It's okay."

The waitress brought their chili fries out and told them the burgers would be out soon before running off to wait on some new arrivals to the café. Dubois picked a fry off the plate and popped it into his mouth.

Something occurred to Jesse that he hadn't thought of before, simply because it seemed so ridiculous. But it wouldn't necessarily seem ridiculous to the detective. "Wait a minute. I'm a suspect, aren't I?"

"Why do you say that?"

"I discovered the body. You have no way of knowing I didn't kill him and then just *pretend* to discover the body."

Dubois quirked an eyebrow at him. "Except that both Reggie and Steve say you were inside preparing dinner right up until the time he was reported missing."

"Reggie didn't actually see me until about that time," Jesse said. "And Steve could be providing an alibi because of our past history together. Besides, I could have found Stuart wandering around out there, lost in the mist, and *then* killed him."

"Though that's statistically unlikely, if you'd never met him before," Dubois said with a wry smile. "You said so yourself."

"Maybe I'm a psychopath."

"Jesus, kid! What are you trying to do? Get yourself arrested?" Dubois sighed and reached for another chili fry. "I don't consider you a suspect. If I did, I wouldn't be having lunch with you, and I sure as hell wouldn't be telling you anything about my private life. If it gets you all hot and bothered, I'll concede that you're a person of interest."

Why do you want me all hot and bothered? Jesse wondered. But he didn't ask the question out loud. He decided to change the subject. "Do you read mystery novels?"

Dubois gave out a sharp laugh. "My *work* is a mystery novel. Why would I want to read about it when I'm trying to relax?"

"Fair enough," Jesse replied, though he was a little disappointed. He'd been hoping for common ground. "What *do* you like to read?"

The detective hesitated so long in answering that Jesse began to wonder if he'd said something wrong again. Finally Dubois sighed, frowned, and said, "Nothing."

"Nothing?"

"Let's change the subject, okay?"

Jesse blinked at him for a moment. How the hell could discussing favorite books be a sensitive subject? "What? Are you into yaoi or something?"

"Yaoi?" Dubois asked, his face screwed up like he'd just seen something disgusting. "What the fuck is yaoi?"

"Never mind. It was just a joke."

"What is it?"

"It's, um… Japanese comics. But they're… gay… and pornographic…."

For a second, he thought Dubois might tell him to go fuck himself. He didn't look at all happy about what Jesse might be implying.

"I'm sorry," Jesse said hurriedly. "It was just a joke."

"Do I look gay to you?"

"No!"

Dubois shook his head, but if he'd been angry, it appeared to be fading. "Look, Jesse…."

"I'm sorry! I didn't mean to imply anything!"

"Will you shut up a minute?"

Jesse shut up.

Dubois's expression softened and he leaned across the table. In a hushed voice, he said, "Look, I'm only telling you this because you told me… about you and Steve. So, obviously you're gay or bi—"

"I'm gay."

"Okay," Dubois said. "Well… this is just between you and me, okay?"

"Sure."

"I'm not… completely straight."

Jesse had figured that out, of course, but he didn't say that. "You're bi?"

"Yeah." Dubois looked uncomfortable, and he glanced around again before continuing. "Julie—my wife—she knew about it, even before we were married. But nobody else. I never… acted on it."

"I understand." Jesse couldn't resist smiling at him. "It's really cool that you told me."

"Yeah. I guess. I probably shouldn't have."

"I'm not going to spread it around."

"Thanks. I appreciate that." Incredibly, Dubois's hand was shaking when he picked up his water to take a drink. Jesse realized this had been a really big deal to him. He'd just come out—to someone who was pretty much a stranger. It was obviously something that made him really uncomfortable.

"So is that why we're having lunch?" Jesse asked.

"What? So I could come out to you? Fuck, no."

Jesse laughed. "That isn't what I meant. I mean, did you ask me to lunch because…." He found himself too embarrassed to complete the sentence.

But Dubois understood where he was going. "Because I think you're cute?" The detective looked at him sharply, and for a moment he seemed irritated. But then his brow unfurrowed and he smiled. It was an adorable, shy smile. "Well, maybe."

"I think you're cute too," Jesse said. Then he amended that to "Or rather, 'hot.'"

Dubois looked intently into his eyes for a long time. Then he sighed and shook his head. "This is fucked up. My brain must have shut down or something."

They were interrupted by the waitress returning with their burgers, and all conversation stopped for the few moments it took her to set their plates in front of them and ask if they needed anything else.

After she'd left, Jesse said, "You know… I don't have to drive back to Dover tonight." Dubois didn't look entirely pleased to hear that, so Jesse quickly amended, "Not that I'm going to drop into the station or anything. But I could stay in a hotel for a couple days. We could go out." He hoped it didn't sound like he was trying to get laid. He wouldn't *mind* getting laid, of course. But he didn't want to sound as if that was his top priority.

Dubois frowned. "I don't know if that's a good idea, kid."

I'm not a kid, Jesse thought. But he didn't feel like arguing semantics at the moment. "Sure it is," he insisted. "We can go someplace out of the area. Just for dinner."

A little making out and heavy petting would be nice too, but he didn't say that out loud.

Dubois sighed and took out his cell phone. "What's your number?"

Jesse gave him his cell number and watched the detective punch it into his phone. A moment later, Jesse's cell buzzed. He took it out of his pocket and started to save the number under "Dubois." Then he changed his mind and asked, "Can I get your first name?"

The detective smirked at him. "It's Kyle." While Jesse typed that in and saved it, Dubois continued, "But look, I don't know if I want to do this or not. I mean, I've never…. I'll call you tonight, okay? Even if I decide I don't want to get together, I'll let you know. I won't be a jerk about it."

Jesse didn't know what the best response would be to encourage him to accept the date, so he just said, "Sure, Kyle."

BEFORE GOING up the mountain a week earlier, Jesse had parked his car at the Stage Office, which was just at the other side of the parking lot in front of the Glen View Café. He could have walked there, but Kyle insisted on driving him the short distance to his car. The detective promised to call him later and then drove away. Jesse had sort of hoped for a quick good-bye kiss, but he couldn't say he was surprised when that failed to happen. Kyle seemed uncomfortable with the idea of dating a man, regardless of his obvious interest, and still uncertain he wanted to date *anyone* yet. Jesse was fairly inexperienced at relationships, but he felt he understood. He thought it was romantic that Kyle still missed Julie. In a twisted way, it made him more appealing, even if he ended up rejecting Jesse because of it.

But Kyle wasn't the only reason Jesse wanted to stay in the area a couple more days. He sat in his car and counted the money in his wallet. Just over two hundred dollars. That was a lot by Jesse's standards. He'd saved up for this trip, figuring he might need it for gas or food or possibly for a cheap hotel. But it wasn't enough for what he wanted to do now.

He put his wallet away and turned the key in the ignition. After sitting a week, the battered old Geo Prizm was reluctant to start, but it caught eventually. He let it idle for a couple of minutes and then pulled out onto Route 16. The bulk of the mountain was between him and his destination, so he had to drive north and curve westward around it before turning south again.

The Mount Washington Hotel was way out of his league. He could tell as he pulled onto its palatial grounds in Bretton Woods that the measly wad of twenties he had in his pocket wouldn't even pay for a single night there. He drove up a long winding drive, passing a vast expanse of golf course on his right, and pulled up in front of the hotel. The valet who took his keys looked at his car as if it might fall apart the moment he climbed into it.

First order of business: find out if there was a room available and how much it would cost. Jesse entered the cavernous foyer and had to search around before he noticed the front desk far off to his left.

Fortunately, the concierge was trained to be cheerful and friendly to everybody and managed not to look at all surprised by Jesse's rough appearance when she said, "Welcome to the Mount Washington Hotel! How may I help you?"

"I'm looking for a room for the next few nights," he replied.

She typed something into the computer. "We have a few available. Would you like a single?"

"Yes."

"We don't have any singles with single beds," the woman said apologetically. "We do have one with a queen-size."

"How much is that?"

She told him and it took all his self-control to keep the horror out of his expression. He said, "Let me check something. I'll be right back."

He found an area of the foyer away from people—not difficult, since it was the size of about two tennis courts—and dialed his father on his cell.

"You're not serious, Jesse!"

"Consider it an early Christmas present," Jesse told him.

"I've got news for you, son. I love you, but I've never spent that kind of money on you for Christmas—not once in your entire life."

"I need to stay in the area a couple more days, Dad. There's some stuff going on. It's important."

His father didn't ask "What stuff?" Jesse had spent one summer driving across the country in his Geo and another summer learning the ropes on a lobster boat in Maine. When he was in high school, he'd nearly burned down the garage trying to work his way through a book of chemistry experiments. As long as he wasn't exploring the fine art of serial killing, Mr. Morales pretty much let him follow his muse.

But there were limits. "So find a cheap motor inn somewhere."

Jesse knew that wouldn't allow him to do what he'd been hoping to do—sidle to up Stuart's brother and friends and see if he could get them chatting. He didn't want to do anything to interfere in the investigation, but maybe he could gain some insight into which of them had been holding a secret grudge against the guy. If he could get them drinking at the bar or something like that, maybe he'd learn something Kyle could use.

But it wasn't worth putting his father in debt. "I guess I could," Jesse admitted. "One of the reasons I want to stay is so I can see this really cute guy again. I suppose it doesn't really matter which hotel I'm in for that."

"Does this 'really cute guy' know you exist?"

"Yes. We might be going out to dinner tonight."

"Who is he?"

So Jesse ended up telling his father about Kyle—leaving out Kyle's name and profession. That pretty much made him a thirty-year-old widow Jesse met on the mountain. Jesse half-expected that the seven-year gap, or the fact that Kyle was still grieving for his wife, would get him a lecture, but his father wasn't really the type of parent to do that. He knew Jesse was a romantic and there was no cure for it.

"All right," his father said, when Jesse had finished describing Kyle, "I logged in and checked my bank account while you were mooning over this guy you think you're going to marry." Jesse hadn't actually said *that*, but he let his father finish. "It's looking pretty good, and I hate to get complacent about my financial stability, so I might as well let you wipe me out."

Jesse couldn't help but laugh at that. His father had a fairly decent income, or he wouldn't have asked for the money in the first place. "Be serious, Dad. I don't want it if it's really going to set you back."

"Just give me the hotel phone number," his father said. "I'll give you two nights, and you can charge your meals to your room. Any massages, drinks, or prostitutes will have to come out of your pocket. Understand?"

Jesse swore he'd love his father for all eternity and never put him in a home and forget about him. Then he walked across the lobby and simply handed his cell to the concierge. Within a few minutes, he had a room at one of the nicest resorts in the state.

6

AFTER DROPPING Jesse off at the Stage Office parking lot and fretting all the way back to the Lodge about whether he'd made a mistake giving the kid his phone number, Kyle called his partner to see if he'd heard back from the OCME in Concord.

"Not yet," Wesley told him, "but the last time I called, they said Vera was in the examination room."

The clock on Kyle's dashboard read 1:20. They still had plenty of time. "You want to drive down and catch her when she gets out?" Concord was just an hour and a half away.

"Sure. Pick me up at the room."

VERA WAS still busy when they arrived in Concord, so they took up seats outside the examining room. Kyle and Wesley had talked about the case on the drive down, so there wasn't much else to say at the moment. Wesley played *Angry Birds* on his iPhone, and Kyle snuck a peek at the sappy romance novel he was reading on his Kindle, sitting far enough away from Wesley that the other man wouldn't be able to look over his shoulder. Thankfully, he was already well past the cover with its seminaked man on it. Julie had known about this guilty pleasure of his and had sometimes read the same novels so they could talk about them. They'd watched movies together and, if he commented on a guy having a nice ass, she'd just weigh in with her own opinion. She'd never made him feel weird about it. But she'd been the only one he'd ever told about his bisexuality. He'd trusted her absolutely.

Could he trust a twenty-three-year-old kid obsessed with murder mysteries… and maybe with a hard-on for detectives? Probably not.

"Kyle? Wesley?"

They glanced up to see Vera standing in the doorway. Instinctively, Kyle shut the Kindle off and pocketed it. Then he stood up. "Hey, Vera. You got anything for us?"

She gave him a tolerant smirk. "Am I allowed to have a cup of coffee first?"

"Sure," Kyle replied with a grin. "I'll buy."

The hospital cafeteria was nearly empty at the moment, so Kyle bought a cinnamon roll for Vera and coffee for both of them—Wesley could fend for himself. Then he led the medical examiner to a table in the corner. How the woman could eat anything after conducting an autopsy was beyond him—he'd been present for a few and always had trouble keeping the contents of his stomach down, never mind eating more. But Vera had been doing this a long time. She was made of much sterner stuff.

"You'll get my report later today," she assured him after taking a healthy swig of her coffee, "but there weren't many surprises." She paused a moment for Wesley to come over and sit down with his coffee. "The injury to his brain killed him before he lost much blood. There was also an injury to his neck, like we often see in car accidents, where the head has been jerked around a bit. There were also some odd lacerations in the scalp on the left side, and some hair was torn out."

"Like someone grabbed his hair?"

"Possibly. There were also multiple abrasions and contusions on the body and limbs."

"From falling down the hill?" Wesley asked.

Vera shrugged. "How they got there, it isn't really my job to determine. There was debris in the head wound—dirt, mostly, and some fragments of lichen."

That, Kyle was certain, would have come from the rock his head had struck. But the forensics lab would have to match Vera's findings to the samples they'd taken at the scene.

Vera took a bite of her cinnamon roll, chewed, and swallowed, and then added, "I found something else interesting, when we bagged up his clothes."

"What?"

"Twenty thousand dollars."

THE MONEY had been concealed in an envelope, and the reason nobody had come across it when they searched Stuart's pockets for his identification was that it had been tucked inside his underwear. Vera had sealed it inside an evidence collection bag because it was soaked with urine. Stuart had voided his bladder when he died.

So obviously he'd been hiding it. More than that, he hadn't felt it would be safe enough in his pocket.

The big question was, where did someone like Stuart, who was unlikely to have ever possessed twenty thousand dollars, get that kind of money? And why would he take it to the top of Mt. Washington instead of leaving it in his hotel room? Was he planning on giving it to someone? Or had someone given it to *him*? What for? Drugs?

Maybe that's why he wandered off, Kyle thought as he drove to the station from the hospital. *Maybe he was planning on meeting someone, and they exchanged the envelope.*

But then what? Did the exchange go wrong somehow, and the other person killed Stuart? If that were true, then wouldn't it mean the killer couldn't be any of the four who accompanied Stuart on the railway? After all, if Todd had wanted to exchange something with his brother, he could have done that in their room. The same went for Joel. And certainly Stuart could have arranged a meeting with his fiancée without waiting to get to the summit.

So who was he meeting? Or did he really just carry twenty thousand dollars around in his crotch all the time?

As soon as Vera signed over Stuart's clothes and personal effects to them and gave them the autopsy report, Kyle and Wesley would be stopping by the station to drop off Jesse's Ride-Along paperwork, then heading back to the Mount Washington hotel. It was time to collect statements from Stuart's friends and family.

But what really bothered Kyle was the strong temptation to discuss the case with a certain twenty-three-year-old he really shouldn't be talking to at all.

ROOM 320 was at the end of a long corridor, and it was pretty small considering how much Jesse's father had paid for it. But it was beautiful. The original woodwork was still present from the early 1900s, and the furniture might have been original as well. The carpeting looked right for the time period, though Jesse suspected it had been replaced at some point. It seemed unlikely the original carpet would be in this perfect condition over a century later.

His first impulse was to strip naked and rub his body all over the sheets in the softest-looking bed he'd ever seen. He didn't do that, though he filed it under things he might want to do later. For now, he dropped off his bags and changed into his best clothes. Not that they were much better than his worst clothes, but at least they were clean. Then he headed downstairs.

Let's see, he thought. *If I were a murderer, would I prefer to hang out in the foyer or the bar?*

He checked the foyer first but wasn't surprised when he didn't see any of Stuart's companions there. What the hell was there to do in a foyer, anyway? Read? Sit in front of the enormous stone fireplace and get into a staring contest with the moose head above it? Of course, they might not be motivated to drink in the afternoon either. But if they were hanging out in their rooms, Jesse would have no way of bumping into them. He might like the idea of playing detective, but that didn't mean he'd be willing to pull a TV detective show maneuver like dressing up as housekeeping or room service to get access to someone's room.

If they were the kind of people who preferred to go horseback riding or get massages in the afternoon, Jesse was likewise doomed. He'd never be able to afford to do those things. He could check the swimming pool—the outdoor pool was closed, but there was an indoor one—but first he'd check the bars.

The hotel had four of them. The bar in Stickney's Restaurant on the basement level was nearly empty, and he didn't see anyone he was looking for hanging out there. The Cave, across from that, which claimed to have been a speakeasy in the prohibition era, appeared to be closed for renovations. The Princess Room on the main floor was a bit ritzy, but he poked his head in anyway. Completely empty. The Rosewood Bar was also on the main floor, and it offered a beautiful view of the mountains through its plate glass windows, but it was small and a bit cramped. There were people in it, but again, nobody Jesse was looking for.

There was one more place he could think of to check before heading down to the pool. It was a large semicircular room off the foyer, with entrances on either side of the moose head fireplace, called the Conservatory. There was a fireplace in the center that shared a chimney with the foyer fireplace, and the tall windows along the outer wall looked out upon the golf course and the mountains beyond. It was here Jesse stumbled across the dark-haired guy he'd seen with Stuart on the train platform. He was seated in one of the wicker loveseats by himself, drinking what looked like orange juice and gazing out at the view.

As it turned out, Jesse didn't have to come up with some lame way to start a conversation. The guy glanced up at him when he drew near and appeared to recognize him. "Hey."

"Hey."

"You were on the summit yesterday, weren't you?" the guy asked.

"Yeah. I was working at the observatory."

"You want to sit down?"

Well, that was easy.

The guy introduced himself as Joel, and Jesse quickly discovered he wasn't drinking orange juice. When Jesse sat on the loveseat, facing Joel so their knees were almost touching, he could smell vodka on the guy's breath. It seemed he'd been sitting there for a while, sipping screwdrivers.

"Did you hear what happened last night?" Joel asked.

Jesse nodded. "I'm afraid so. I was one of the staff called out to search for him." He wasn't sure it would be a good idea to mention he was the one who'd found Stuart. At least, not yet.

"Stuart was my best friend," Joel said wistfully. "He was…." Words seemed to fail him, and he took another sip of his screwdriver. "I can't fucking believe it. This is such bullshit!"

Apparently, the wait staff from the Rosewood wandered through the foyer and the Conservatory during the day to see if anyone needed anything, because one approached them and offered Jesse a menu. He ordered a ginger ale. When the waiter had wandered off, Jesse asked Joel, "What were you guys doing yesterday? Sightseeing?"

Joel didn't exactly say yes. Instead, he sort of shrugged noncommittally. "We're here for something like a vacation before the wedding. Stuart was supposed to marry my friend Corrie this Saturday." He made a sharp, bitter sound that might have been a laugh.

"I'm sorry."

"So, if you work up on top of the mountain," Joel asked, "why are you here at the hotel?"

Jesse shrugged. "We have weeklong shifts at the observatory. My shift ended, so I came down. I'm checked in here for a couple days to relax."

"Pretty fucking expensive way to relax."

Jesse raised his eyebrows and nodded. "Oh yeah. My dad's paying for it as an early Christmas present."

"Cool. I wouldn't be here if Corrie's family wasn't footing the bill. They let Stuart bring me and his brother along to be his best men."

The conversation died for a moment as the waiter returned with Jesse's ginger ale. Joel had finished his screwdriver, so he ordered another one. Jesse had a million questions, but most of them wouldn't have been appropriate in this context. He was supposed to be just a stranger sitting down for a drink to be friendly. If he started asking too many questions about Stuart's brother or his fiancée, that would probably give Joel the creeps.

When they were alone again, Joel said, "The police told us he fell and hit his head."

"Yeah."

"Did you see it?"

Jesse didn't want to reveal anything that would compromise the investigation, but he felt the guy deserved *something*. He said, "Yeah, I saw him. There isn't much to say about it, really. It looked like he hit his head on a rock and then rolled down a slope. He was already dead when we found him, I think, but we tried CPR. It… didn't…." He shook his head unhappily.

Joel was staring at his hand where it rested on the tablecloth, and Jesse realized tears were leaking from his eyes.

"I'm sorry."

Joel made no attempt to wipe his tears away. He said softly, "Yeah…."

"Would you like me to leave you alone?"

Joel shook his head. "No. Well, unless you want to leave. I guess I'm not very good company."

"You're fine," Jesse reassured him. He was tempted to put a hand on his arm, but most guys didn't appreciate that sort of gesture from another man. "I can't blame you for being upset. He was your best friend."

"Yeah," Joel said, but it sounded strangely distant, as if he were just saying it without really believing it. His head lolled a bit when he turned to look at Jesse. The alcohol was having an effect on him. "You know what the really fucked-up part is? Nobody really wanted this wedding. Not Stuart, not Corrie, not her family, not Todd… sure as hell not me. We should never have come here."

Jesse couldn't blame him for feeling that way, under the circumstances. Still, it was weird that he thought Stuart and Corrie hadn't wanted to get married. If they hadn't, and their families had also been against it, why had they been planning on going through with it anyway?

Joel stood up, a little unsteady on his feet, and said, "I think I need to go lie down for a while." He braced himself on the wicker armrest of the loveseat and looked Jesse in the eye. "Do you want to get together later?"

Jesse got the distinct impression he was being hit on. It was kind of sloppy, and he wasn't certain Joel really knew what he was doing at the moment. But that look was pretty intense for a straight guy. At any rate, Jesse wanted to talk to him further, so why pass up the opportunity? "Sure."

Joel smiled. "I'm in room 405. Call me for dinner?"

"Okay."

Joel leaned over and clamped him on the forearm, which seemed like a weird gesture. The way he squeezed it, lingering just a moment longer than necessary, seemed to confirm Jesse's feeling that he was being hit on. Though it could be difficult to tell with guys when they were drunk. Joel straightened up and left, walking slowly but not too unsteadily.

He really wasn't Jesse's type—that, plus he might be a murderer. So Jesse wasn't particularly interested in hooking up with him. But he felt bad for the guy. Jesse sensed Joel's feelings for Stuart might have gone a little deeper than just friendship.

WHEN KYLE walked into the hotel foyer, the first thing that caught his attention was Joel Owens entering the elevator at the far end, across from the main desk. This elevator had a man operating it, which was probably good. Joel looked like he was staggering a bit.

The second thing Kyle noticed was Jesse Morales coming out of the Conservatory.

Christ!

He'd given half a moment's thought to catching up with Joel, but the sight of Jesse drove that from his mind. Kyle strode across the foyer, directly toward him. Jesse was looking in the direction Joel had gone, but he turned in time to see Kyle approach. From the way the blood drained from his face, Kyle figured he had to be up to something.

"Oh, hi!" Jesse said with forced cheerfulness.

"What are you doing here?"

"Didn't I say I was going to get a room in a hotel?"

Kyle folded his arms across his chest and glared at him. He lowered his voice to avoid being overheard by some people sitting near the fireplace. "I guess I severely underestimated your net worth."

Jesse gave him a sour look. "You caught me. Normally I'd spend my summer resort-hopping in the Caribbean, but this summer I thought washing dishes and cleaning toilets would be more fun."

"It's October."

"They had me chained up all summer in the observatory. I managed to break free just before you arrived."

"Lucky."

"Look," Jesse said, exasperated, "can we please take this up to my room, instead of fighting out here like we're married?"

Unexpectedly, Kyle found himself smirking. "You have a weird view of marriage." He took Jesse's elbow to steer him toward the elevator, but quickly dropped his hand when he realized how it might come across. Instead, he merely gestured toward the far end of the foyer. "Lead the way."

THE ROOM Jesse led them to was small, though it had a large, comfortable bed and was still a step above most hotels Kyle could reasonably afford. The clothes Jesse had worn down from the mountain were strewn across the bed, and Kyle had to force his thoughts away from the thought of Jesse stripping out of them just a short time ago.

He closed the door behind them and said, "Okay, spill."

"What?"

"You can't afford this place any more than I can," Kyle growled. "Oh, sure—you *might* be wealthy and slumming it on the mountain for a week, but I don't think so. Or maybe you saved up all summer so you could splurge and relax after spending a week doing dishes."

Jesse shrugged and sat down on the bed. "Sure. That sounds good."

"It sounds like bullshit." There was a chair in the room, but it would have put him in the position of looking up at Jesse, and he didn't like that. So he stepped closer to the bed and stood over him. "Here's what I think happened. You got all hot and bothered about someone committing a murder, just like in your detective books, and you decided there was no fucking way you were gonna miss out on that. So you got a hold of some cash somewhere—parents, probably—and booked yourself into the same hotel all the suspects were staying in, hoping to snoop around and solve the case. Am I right?"

"You keep saying I'm 'hot and bothered' about things," Jesse said. "What—do you think I'm some kind of sex fiend?"

I wish, Kyle thought. Then he mentally slapped himself. "Stop changing the subject."

"Okay, fine." Jesse looked up at him and that coy little smile crept across his face again. "I'm not doing anything illegal. I'm just hanging out in the hotel."

"You're interfering with a police investigation."

That wiped the smile off Jesse's face. He frowned and reached up to grab Kyle's wrist and pull him down toward the bed. "Will you please stop looming over me like you're interrogating me?"

Kyle was shocked at the touch. Who the fuck did he think he was? He was lucky Kyle hadn't instinctively whipped him around into a defensive handhold. People just didn't grab police officers like that! But after just a slight amount of resistance, he gave in and sat down.

"This feels weird," he muttered.

"Because we're both on the same level now?"

"That and we're on a bed!" Kyle snapped. "And don't you ever grab a cop like that again. You understand? It could get you killed!"

Jesse looked wounded at that. "I thought we were friends."

"We took a half-hour drive together and had lunch. That makes us acquaintances, by my book—not friends."

"Fine," Jesse said, scowling. He flopped down on his back, which put Kyle above him again. Although this new position didn't make Kyle feel any better, because now it looked like they were on a bed and about to get busy. "Are you seriously going to arrest me if I talk to them?"

"Yes!" He was lying. Technically, there was no law against a civilian talking to a murder suspect. If there were, reporters wouldn't be able to interview them—or their friends hang out with them, for that matter.

"You can legally do that?"

Kyle stayed silent, having reached the limit of how far he was willing to take the lie.

"What if I told you I've already got some new information that you probably wouldn't have learned in your official investigation," Jesse asked, "since it isn't the type of thing they would have admitted to in public?"

Kyle leaned over him and scowled, uncomfortably aware he was in a great position to steal a kiss. "What are you talking about?"

Jesse looked as if he might try to bargain for a moment, but apparently he realized Kyle wouldn't go for that. He sighed and said, "According to a somewhat tipsy Joel—who I think was hitting on me, by the way—nobody wanted this wedding to take place. Stuart, Corrie, Corrie's family, Stuart's brother, Joel—they were all against it."

"That's hard to believe, considering how much this must have cost the Lassiters."

"Which ones are the Lassiters?"

"Corrie and her family," Kyle responded, realizing too late that he'd just given the little bastard more to work with. He decided to change the subject. "Please tell me you weren't considering whoring yourself out for information?"

"You mean letting Joel fuck me?" Jesse lifted himself up on his left elbow until their faces were close together. "No. I'm not really attracted to him."

He was looking so intently into Kyle's eyes that Kyle had to look away. *Just who* are *you interested in?* he wondered. But he was afraid to learn the answer to that question, so instead he asked, "What if you *had* been interested in him?"

"Then wouldn't that have just been me hooking up with some guy I thought was hot?"

"And maybe a murderer," Kyle pointed out, quashing the feeling of jealousy that rose up in him. *You've just met him,* he told himself. *You don't have any claim on him.*

"That's true. Being a murder suspect is kind of a turn-off."

"I'm glad to know you're not the type who gets off on dangerous men."

"There you go again," Jesse said, the coy smile returning as he lowered himself back onto the bedspread. "Speculating about what turns me on."

He looked amazing like that, gazing up at Kyle through sleepy lids. This was the first time Kyle had seen him without a bulky sweater and ski jacket, and the black cotton shirt he was wearing clung to a thin but well-defined musculature—the body of a young man who might not be athletic but certainly exercised and took care of himself. The bottom of the shirt had ridden up when Jesse leaned back, exposing a small band of smooth, bare skin. Kyle felt a strong urge to run his fingers along that patch of stomach and slide his hands up under the shirt.

"I think I'm starting to get an idea what turns you on," he said hoarsely. "I mean, it's been a while, and I'm pretty rusty at this, but… you're flirting with me, right?"

Jesse laughed, and for a moment Kyle was afraid he'd call him an idiot and tell him he was flattering himself. But he didn't. "You want me to back off?"

"I already told you I used to be married. To a woman." Then, in case that didn't get the point across, he added, "Happily."

"It was very sweet. She was a lucky woman to find a man who loved her so much."

"Doesn't that make me off-limits?"

"You're bi. You already told me that."

Kyle nodded. "But I'm still… not really over it."

"I'm flirting with you," Jesse said, "because I've been getting the feeling you're attracted to me. All you have to do is say, 'Not interested.'"

Kyle looked deep into those beautiful brown eyes and tried to find the words to tell Jesse to back off. He didn't need some cocky punk tagging along after him. But there was no way in hell he could lie to Jesse about how strongly he was attracted to him. While he leaned over the young man, struggling, Jesse lifted his arms and wrapped them around Kyle's back. Then he gently pulled Kyle down on top of him until their lips met.

It had been a long time since Kyle last kissed anyone in passion. In the back of his mind, he'd always thought he'd hate it, that it would never feel right to kiss another person. But he'd been wrong. He didn't want to compare kissing Jesse to what it had been like to kiss Julie—that wasn't fair to either of them. But he found he didn't have to because they were so different. Kissing Jesse was like nothing he'd ever experienced before— rough in places, as he'd fantasized it would be like to kiss a man, but surprisingly soft and warm and yielding when it needed to be. Jesse's lips were amazing, and the taste of him was clean and delicate. Kyle couldn't stop himself from plunging his tongue into the depths of Jesse's mouth, yearning for more.

When he finally had to break the kiss and breathe, he realized he'd been grinding his erection into Jesse's hip through their pants, and the inside of his underwear was uncomfortably damp with precome. *Christ.* "I can't do this now. I'm on duty."

"Can you come back tonight?" Jesse asked breathlessly.

Kyle wasn't so sure that would be a good idea. They hadn't even known each other for twenty-four hours, for fuck's sake! Was this how fast people moved now? "I don't… I think I need to slow down a little."

He was terrified Jesse would decide he wasn't worth the effort. He seemed like someone who decided what he wanted and just went for it—not at all like Kyle. But Jesse smiled up at him and asked, "What about that date, then? You were going to think about that."

Kyle grunted and nodded. "Yeah. I guess we could go out to dinner someplace. I know a good—"

"Oh!" Jesse interrupted, his eyes widening in distress. "I can't do dinner."

"Why not?"

"Because I promised Joel I'd eat with him." Kyle's irritation must have shown on his face, because Jesse quickly added, "Come on! This is perfect and you know it. He's liable to tell me things you'd never get out of him."

"And if he suspects you're talking to the police, you could end up dead!"

"Then we can't let anyone here see us together," Jesse replied. "Wait for me outside—say nine o'clock—and I'll come out to meet you. We can go out for a drink, and I'll tell you all about it."

Kyle didn't like this plan. In fact, he hated it. But it was clear Jesse wasn't going to stay out of harm's way. "All right," he said. "But don't think I'm condoning this just because I'm not handcuffing you to your bed for the night."

Too late, he realized how that sounded. He felt his face redden as Jesse raised his eyebrows and smirked up at him.

9

Wow.

Kissing Kyle had been like…. Jesse was having a hard time figuring out how to describe it. Like sticking his finger in an electric socket. His whole body was pulsing with energy, yet somehow he just wanted to lie there and experience it, not get up for the next hour or two. His cock was so hard it hurt, straining to break free of his jeans. He wanted Kyle to rip his clothes off and make love to him, but apparently that would have to wait. It was frustrating, but he thought he understood. The guy wasn't a virgin, but he'd never done it with a man before. In a way, it must be kind of like starting over again. For once, Jesse was the one with all the experience.

Weird. Jesse didn't think of himself as *experienced*, exactly, though he'd certainly had sex with a few guys. And he wasn't shy about sex. Not at all. *I hope he doesn't think I'm a total slut.*

He actually whimpered when Kyle lifted his body off his and straightened up.

Kyle looked down at him and scowled, but his voice was gentle when he said, "God, you're beautiful." Then he sighed. "This is such a bad idea."

"I understand sleeping with men isn't the kind of thing that generally furthers a police officer's career, Kyle," Jesse said quickly, hoping to head off any second thoughts Kyle might be having. "You can trust me not to spread it around, even if things don't work out between us."

"Can I?" Kyle sat down on the bed beside him again. "Look, there *are* gay cops. *Out* gay cops. We've got one in my unit that I'm aware of. He seems to be doing all right. So I guess I'm being kind of cowardly. But up until this moment, my being bisexual—it's all been kind of theoretical. Julie knew about it and made me feel comfortable about myself. But I never told anyone but her."

"I'm totally cool with it," Jesse interjected. "I wouldn't feel threatened by you finding a woman attractive. Or even another guy, for that matter."

Kyle raised his eyebrows. "You're getting a little ahead of yourself, don't you think? You're talking like we're going to start dating when I'm still trying to wrap my head around maybe sleeping with you—*once*." He looked into Jesse's eyes and pressed his lips together tightly for a moment. Then he said, "Of course, we don't have to do that—have sex, I mean. Maybe you'd rather I make up my mind first about dating…."

Jesse found it kind of cute how uncertain this imposing and somewhat abrasive police detective could be when it came to this topic. "Look, Kyle," he said softly, "I'd like to get to know you and all that. I do kind of like the idea of us dating. But I don't really have a problem with having sex first, before we decide everything."

Kyle chuckled. He gave Jesse a warm smile and reached out a hand to ruffle his hair. "I'll pick you up at nine and take you out for a drink. We'll figure the rest out after that."

"Okay."

Kyle bent forward to give him a brief, tender kiss. "I gotta go. Stay out of trouble, okay?"

And then he left.

He was right, of course. They'd just met and it was a bit soon to think about a relationship. Jesse tended to leap feet first into them, and so far that hadn't worked out so well. Few of his boyfriends had stuck around more than a month. Once the physical attraction stopped being a novelty, it generally turned out he had little in common with the guys on campus. His fascination with crime fiction had seemed too morbid to some. Others had been put off by his total lack of interest in sports, or on the flip side, his lack of interest in clothes and celebrity gossip. Hiking with Steve had been fun and romantic, so that relationship had lasted the longest—about two months. And they'd managed to stay friends after it ended, which was a bonus.

But Kyle was different. In addition to the strong physical attraction—incredibly strong physical attraction, at least as far as Jesse was concerned—Jesse felt a stronger connection to Kyle than he'd ever felt with another man. There was that seven-year age gap, but that didn't seem insurmountable. Not if they were really compatible otherwise.

Of course, Jesse thought, *I could just be a psycho stalker. That would suck.*

Eventually, he realized he'd been lying on his bed thinking about this for far too long. He needed to get out and do something with his day. He didn't want to piss Kyle off, but he couldn't just stay in his room all the time. Besides, Kyle hadn't forbidden him to go out into the hotel.

Joel was expecting him to show up before dinner, but it had only been a short time since they'd parted at the bar. He was probably still sleeping. Before he'd run into Joel, Jesse had been considering checking out the indoor pool, so that seemed like a good plan now. After all, it was midafternoon. What kind of trouble could he get into there?

ABOUT TWENTY minutes later, clad in a thirty-dollar pair of swim trunks from the spa gift shop, Jesse was standing at the edge of the hotel swimming pool, looking at exactly the kind of trouble Kyle had wanted him to avoid—Stuart's brother. Jesse still didn't know the guy's name, but he recognized him instantly. He was by far the most handsome man at the pool, and stripped down to a Speedo, he was practically a work of art. He cut through the water as smooth and silent as a shark, though his turns were awkward. Jesse guessed he'd never been trained as a swimmer—he was just naturally fit and athletic. And if Kyle hadn't already caught his eye, Jesse could see himself falling for a guy like that—hard.

Stuart had looked an awful lot like his brother. Jesse hadn't seen him out of his clothes, but now he was even more convinced Joel had had the hots for Stuart.

He couldn't get away with standing at the edge of the pool staring at the guy for an hour, so Jesse dove in and did a few laps himself. He wasn't a great swimmer, but he enjoyed splashing around a bit. It was fun, but he couldn't stop himself from plotting ways to start a conversation with Stuart's brother before the guy got bored and left.

It turned out he didn't have to. He came up for air after crossing the pool again, gripping the tiled edge just as a voice asked, "You're Jesse, aren't you?"

Jesse wiped the water out of his eyes and looked up into a man's crotch. The owner of the crotch was squatting at the edge of the pool, his legs spread wide to display a rather nice package tightly wrapped in a red Speedo. Jesse recognized that Speedo and quickly raised his eyes to see Stuart's brother gazing back at him with striking blue eyes.

"How do you know my name?"

"Joel said he ran into one of the volunteers who worked on the summit," he replied. "A guy named Jesse. And I recognize you from the train platform."

Jesse hefted himself up out of the water and plopped his wet ass down on the tile. "Yeah," he gasped. "That's me."

The young man extended his hand. "My name's Todd. The guy who died was my brother."

"I'm sorry," Jesse said, shaking his hand. "That's really rough."

Todd nodded and looked away at the pool. A family with a bunch of kids had arrived, and it was getting kind of loud in there. "Joel said you saw him. You know, after he died."

"Yeah."

"I think I'll hit the showers. You all set?"

He was clearly inviting Jesse to follow. Did he want to talk, find out more of the gory details? Or was he afraid Jesse had seen something incriminating, so now he was planning on killing him? Jesse decided the latter was unlikely, since Todd would have to kill off every ranger and observatory staff member on the mountain if that was his plan. He couldn't be that stupid. The possibility that Todd wanted a quickie in the shower occurred to him, but he dismissed that as unlikely too. Todd wasn't leering at him like a man with sex on his mind.

"Yeah," Jesse replied. "I'm done here."

He followed Todd into the locker room, trying hard not to get fixated on that perfect ass in front of him. He wasn't sure if Todd would react well to being ogled. There was something about him—a set to his shoulders, perhaps, or the way he tended to ball his hands into fists—that made him seem… pissed off. Of course, his brother had died senselessly just twenty-four hours ago.

The locker area was surprisingly small for a resort like this. It was just one room about five feet square, with lockers along three of the walls. Nobody else was in there with them, which was good, since they were practically rubbing against each other as they stripped out of their swim gear.

In those close quarters, Todd said quietly, "I don't know why the idiot had to wander off like that. You wouldn't believe some of the shit I protected him from when we were kids—bullies at school, our drunken jackass of a father…. And then I turn my back on him for five minutes and he goes and gets himself killed!"

He slammed the locker shut and stood glaring at it, stark naked, clutching his towel in a tight fist.

Jesse tried not to let his eyes wander. The poor guy was miserable—he didn't need someone checking out his dick. "Were you just up there sightseeing?"

"Yeah. It was Corrie's stupid idea."

"Corrie?"

"The spoiled rich girl he was supposed to marry this weekend."

Jesse tried to sound casual, laughing slightly as he said, "I take it you don't like her much."

Todd snorted and got an ugly smirk on his face as he glanced around to make sure they were still alone. Then he came closer and lowered his voice to just above a whisper. "She only liked him 'cause he let her boss him around all the time. I mean, sure, she has money. So marrying her wasn't a completely stupid idea. But she didn't love him. Five minutes after the honeymoon, she'd probably be fucking the mailman."

Dude! Jesse thought. *Have you forgotten I'm a total stranger?*

Todd seemed to be one of those people without internal filters, which normally made Jesse a little uncomfortable. But he tried to push his discomfort aside. This might be useful to Kyle, so he might as well encourage Todd to tell him all about it. He laughed again and said in the same hushed tone, "Well, mailmen can be pretty hot."

"Yeah," Todd said with a sneer. "You wanna hear something? I mean, stop me if it makes you uncomfortable to talk about shit like this...."

Jesse wasn't exactly sure what shit he was going to talk about, but he replied, "Sure, go ahead."

"I fucked her."

Jesse's jaw must have dropped, because Todd laughed again. "Seriously," he added.

"You mean... while they were engaged?"

"Yeah." Todd held up a hand. "Now, don't get me wrong. I didn't sneak around behind my brother's back or anything like that. I just wanted to show him what she was really like. So one night, when the three of us were hanging out together, I told her about this time Stuart and I had a threesome with this chick I was dating. And you could tell she was gettin' all turned on. She kept asking us for details. So I said, 'Hey, let's do it.'"

Jesse was struggling not to let his expression convey what a pig he thought Todd was. He was obviously one of those jerks who liked to tell everyone about his conquests. And... Christ! He was getting hard as he talked about it.

Apparently taking Jesse's wide-eyed stare for rapt attention, Todd continued, "So *she* talks my brother into it! He didn't even want to. But when she wants something, she always gets her way. I have to admit, it was really fuckin' hot."

"Obviously," Jesse said, glancing down briefly at the rather large erection jutting out at him.

Todd grinned and covered his crotch with the towel he was holding. "Sorry, dude. Got a little carried away. Anyway, I thought he'd wake the fuck up after that. Who wants to marry a girl who fucked his brother right in front of him?" He shrugged and shook his head. "But he still wanted to go through with it. Idiot."

Jesse closed his locker, feeling self-conscious about his body for the first time in his life as he stood there naked in front of this gorgeous and blatantly well-endowed chauvinist pig. But he kept his towel away from his dick. He'd be damned if he'd hide it just because it didn't resemble a power tool. It was a perfectly respectable dick.

Todd didn't seem to give a fuck about Jesse's dick. He didn't even glance at it. He turned and led the way to the showers. He was still semierect as he hung his towel up outside the stall he chose and said, "So you're gay, right?"

Jesse froze for a second, baffled by the sudden change in direction. "Why? Do I act gay?"

"Joel thinks you are. You knew he was, right?"

"Oh. Well… yeah. I am. And I kind of figured."

"He says you're meeting him in our room before dinner."

"Yeah."

"Are you actually going to dinner?" Todd asked. "Or are you just gonna fuck?"

Jesus. Jesse looked at him suspiciously. "Why? You're not hoping for another threesome, are you?"

"With two dudes? No. I'm not into guys. Stuart and I never touched each other, you know. Though it was kind of cool to watch him with Corrie."

Jesse wasn't quite sure what the point to all of this was, and it was starting to make him feel a little queasy. Was Todd trying to prove he was open-minded about homosexuality? If so, it was just coming across as sleazy. "Look, Joel's a nice guy, but I don't have any plans to have sex with him. I thought we were just going to dinner."

Todd looked relieved. "Good. Then I'll join you. I don't want to get stuck eating with the fucking Lassiters again. As far as I'm concerned, Stuart wouldn't be…." He seemed to have a moment of clarity, where the reality of the situation once again overwhelmed the cocky attitude. His face went grim as he continued, "We can eat down the road at Fabyan's. That should dodge them. They always have to eat over at the fucking Bretton Arms."

He grimaced and stepped into his shower.

Jesse had forgotten to turn on the spray during this bizarre conversation, so he did that now. While he waited for it to warm up, he wondered if anything Todd had told him could constitute a motive for murder. If anything, it sounded like Todd would rather have killed Corrie than his brother. Or maybe Stuart would have wanted to kill *him* after the threesome. Could Stuart have attacked him but lost the fight? Todd certainly looked like he'd be a formidable opponent.

10

KYLE HAD gone to Todd Warren's room first, but no luck. He'd knocked, then knocked a second time, and almost turned away when he heard someone moving around inside. So he waited. When nothing happened, he knocked a third time—louder.

A sleepy voice said, "Jesus Christ! Hold on a sec...."

A minute later, Joel Owens opened the door. He'd obviously been sleeping. His hair was a mess and he had pillow creases etched into the side of his face. He was attempting to hide his body behind the door and doing a lousy job of it, so Kyle could see he was wearing nothing but a pair of gray boxer briefs.

"What is it?" he asked groggily. "I was taking a nap."

Sleeping it off, more precisely. Kyle could smell the alcohol radiating from his pores.

"I'm looking for Todd," Kyle said.

"I think he went swimming."

"All right." Kyle gave him an appraising look, then mentally kicked himself when he realized he was assessing whether or not the guy might appeal to Jesse. He forced himself to focus on his job. "Go ahead and nap. I'd like to talk to you later."

"Can you come back after dinner?"

"Sure."

KYLE WASN'T particularly interested in cornering Todd in the swimming pool, so he changed course and went to find Corrie instead. He found her in her family's suite, along with the entire Lassiter clan again, but he immediately ran into a problem.

"I'll call our family lawyer," Mr. Lassiter stated. "You'll have to wait for him to arrive, if you'd like to talk to any of us."

"Oh, Daddy," Corrie said, rolling her eyes. "You're making it sound as if we're trying to hide something."

"It's standard procedure, sweetheart, and simply for our protection. I'm sure the detective understands."

Kyle did understand, though he was still annoyed by it. "How long will it take for your lawyer to get here, Mr. Lassiter?"

"Not long at all," Lassiter replied. "I called him last night, and he drove down this morning. He's booked into this hotel."

"All right. I'll wait."

And so he stood there while the Lassiters went about their business in hushed tones, as if he might overhear something incriminating. He was as relieved as they were when there was finally a knock on the door. Lassiter let the lawyer in—a large man in a tailored suit and glasses, whom Lassiter introduced as Charles McDonnell.

But while Kyle was willing to let McDonnell sit in during the interviews—he had little choice in the matter—on one point he was adamant. "I'd like to speak to each of you separately, apart from Mr. McDonnell's presence, of course."

Lassiter didn't like the idea of Corrie going off to be interviewed without him, but the lawyer assured him it was a reasonable request. So a few moments later, Kyle was sequestered with Corrie and McConnell in Corrie's bedroom, with the girl sitting demurely on the end of the bed and McConnell parked in the only chair in the room.

Kyle forced himself to refrain from pacing back and forth as he spoke with Corrie. "I understand you and Stuart were engaged, Miss Lassiter?"

"Yes," she replied, "we were supposed to be married on Saturday." She seemed oddly cool and collected for a young woman who'd just lost her fiancé.

"Please accept my condolences."

"Thank you."

Kyle flipped back a couple of pages in his notebook. "I'm curious how you met. According to what I could learn about Stuart Warren, he was from a very poor neighborhood in Rochester."

"And I've never wanted for anything in my life," she said wearily. "Obviously, you haven't spoken to my family yet."

"What would they tell me?"

She laughed. "That I'm a brat."

"Let's not get carried away, Corrie," McDonnell warned gently.

She ignored him, waving a hand in the air dismissively. "I'm not that bad. But Daddy wanted me to go to Harvard. I insisted on a state college."

"UNH?" Kyle asked.

"Any state college. It didn't really matter. I just wanted to…." She seemed to be having trouble finding the right words, and Kyle was tempted to suggest "slum it." But after a moment, Corrie said, "…have fun. Spend a couple years enjoying myself without worrying about grades."

"You don't have a very high regard for state universities, I take it."

She gave him a coy smile that made her opinion on that subject perfectly clear. Yeah, she was a brat, all right. And Kyle could see dopey college boys lining up around the block for the chance to date her.

"So how did you meet Stuart, exactly?" he asked.

"Through Joel. They had some kind of algebra for the math-impaired class together. And they were both having trouble with quadratic equations. Joel knew I was good at math, so I started helping them study."

"How did you know Joel?"

"We met the year before, in oil painting. I thought he was cute." She shrugged and rolled her eyes. Clearly she'd discovered the pointlessness of chasing after him.

"Then you fell for Stuart."

"He was adorable," she said, showing the first hint of sadness since they'd begun talking. "And so sweet. We dated for about a year, and then I proposed to him."

"You proposed to him?"

The coy smile came back. "Why would I wait for *him* to think of it? He could barely tie his shoes without me or Todd doing it for him."

"You make him sound… mentally challenged."

"No," she said, "he was smart enough—except when it came to math. But he was used to Todd always telling him what to do, always taking care of him. Did you know their parents died when they were teenagers?"

"No." Kyle hadn't had time to look deeply into anyone's background yet. So far he'd just tracked down addresses.

"Todd raised Stuart from the time he was sixteen. It's just been the two of them, for the last several years. Todd's really overprotective of him. He was totally jealous of Stuart spending time with me—at least, at first."

"But everyone gets along fine now?"

"Sure. I love Todd."

"NO, I didn't approve of the wedding," Lassiter admitted. He and Kyle were in the main bedroom with McDonnell. "But I'd like to see *you* try to talk my daughter out of doing something she's set her mind to."

"I can see where that might be a challenge," Kyle conceded, trying not to look too amused.

"I didn't have anything against the kid. He was decent enough, polite. God knows he was good-looking. Their children would have been beautiful."

"So you decided to just suck it up and throw them a nice wedding."

Lassiter took a sip of the scotch he'd poured for himself on the way into the bedroom. "Oh, I admit I fought it for a while, tried to talk her out of it. I mean, seriously—she's twenty-one. She hasn't even graduated from that kindergarten she chose to get a degree from. Did she tell you what her degree is in?"

"She's getting a BA in liberal arts," Kyle read back from his notes.

"Liberal arts!" Lassiter spat out. "She has an IQ of 150. She was an honor student in high school. She could easily succeed in anything she applied herself to. So what does she do? She *paints.* Naked men."

It didn't sound like such a bad career choice to Kyle, though he'd want to throw some naked women into the mix. Maybe he'd consider going into that if he ever left police work.

"She's neither old enough nor experienced enough to know what she wants," Lassiter continued. "I wouldn't have been at all surprised if they divorced two years down the road."

Kyle tapped his pen against the page he was writing on. "This is... perhaps not the most delicate question. Did Stuart stand to profit much from marrying Corrie?"

Lassiter snorted. "Of course. She's had access to her trust fund since she was eighteen. It isn't a fortune, but I'd be willing to bet it seemed like one to Stuart and his brother. Do you know what Todd does for a living? He's a cashier in a supermarket. Both their parents are dead, so Stuart was attending college through guaranteed government loans, studying *philosophy.*" He clearly found the notion absurd.

Fortune hunting sounded like a good motive for murder—if the murder had occurred *after* the wedding, and Corrie had been the victim. Then Stuart might have stood to profit from it. On the other hand, Lassiter himself hadn't wanted Stuart to marry his daughter. He was trying to pretend he'd accepted the idea, but it clearly still galled him. Would he have been willing to resort to murder to prevent it?

Or perhaps he'd simply resorted to bribery. Stuart had to have gotten the twenty-thousand from somewhere. That kind of money was a lot to the Warrens, but it wouldn't hurt Lassiter's bank account much.

"Mr. Lassiter," Kyle said slowly, "we found some money on the victim. A fairly large amount. Would you know anything about that?"

Lassiter shrugged. "No. Why would I?"

"I don't think you should say anything further," McDonnell said with a note of warning in his voice.

"I have nothing *to* say. I know nothing about it."

Kyle couldn't tell if he was lying or not. But if Lassiter *had* paid Stuart off, why would he then murder him?

11

JUDGING BY how grumpy Joel was when Jesse showed up at his and Todd's room, Todd had informed him Jesse wasn't interested in a quickie before dinner. To be fair, if Jesse hadn't been thinking about Kyle all day, and Joel hadn't been a murder suspect, he might have considered it. Joel was cute and available. He could have done worse.

But it wasn't going to happen.

"I still have to shower," Joel muttered as he let Jesse in. He was in his underwear and didn't seem to care much that he had company over. "Have a seat."

Jesse sat down on the end of the bed as Joel shucked his underwear to reveal a compact ass with a light dusting of dark hair and headed into the bathroom. *Christ*, Jesse thought. He'd had no idea how many naked men he'd be seeing when he checked into this hotel. He wondered if it was a perk included in the price of the room. He'd have to check the receipt when he left.

Todd was in the room and already dressed, since he'd showered downstairs. He was stretched out on his bed, using the remote to scan through the program listings on the hotel television. Not surprisingly, he was mostly checking out the porn. "You sure you don't want to slip into the shower with him?" he teased Jesse. "We've got about twenty minutes before our reservation."

"Not that I'm judging, but… do you think about anything besides sex?"

Todd laughed and shrugged. "That, and what I'd like to do to the prick who killed my brother, if they ever catch him."

Was he supposed to know that Stuart's death was murder? Jesse wasn't sure what Kyle had told him yet. He decided to play dumb. "You don't think it was an accident?"

"The police don't think it was an accident," Todd said grimly. "Corrie was down here about a half hour ago. She said this detective was asking her and her family questions about it."

"He hasn't talked to you yet?"

"We saw him last night. But he didn't say much about it then. Corrie said he's still up there, talking to her brother."

"Should we wait here for him?" Jesse asked. Then he amended that to, "You and Joel, I mean."

"Fuck it. I'm hungry. He can track us down at the restaurant if he's so anxious to talk to us." Todd turned to look at him, his eyes narrowed suspiciously. "When I talked to you at the pool... did you know he'd been murdered? You didn't say anything."

Shit.

"When we found him, it looked like he'd fallen and hit his head," Jesse hedged.

That seemed to satisfy Todd. He turned back to the television. A minute later, Joel came out of the bathroom, his hair dripping and the towel wrapped demurely around his waist. But that didn't last long. He whipped it off and tossed it over the back of one of the chairs while he rummaged through his suitcase.

Jesse was surprised by some large pill bottles Joel had packed in there. He leaned in to get a closer look, but he wasn't subtle enough. Joel caught the look and explained, "I'm not a dealer. I have migraines, so my neurologist has me on honking huge doses of vitamin B and magnesium."

"Cool," Jesse said, laughing. "Just curious."

"No problem."

"Hey, dickweed," Todd called out to Joel, "you want me to find something bi so we can both get off to it later?"

Joel made a disgusted noise and looked up at him. "Tell you what—you find something that turns you on, and I'll just jerk off while I stare at you going at it."

Todd blew him a mocking kiss and Joel shook his head, looking to Jesse for commiseration.

THE HOTEL had a shuttle that transported guests to both the extremely expensive restaurant at the Bretton Arms Inn and a much more affordable diner-style restaurant called Fabyan's Station. It was to Fabyan's that Joel and Todd took Jesse. The restaurant was comfortable, with a fake potbellied stove near the entrance putting out heat and burning with a propane flame underneath fake sticks of wood. A small train track with a toy train on it skirted the entire room near the ceiling, and all the décor was bric-a-brac from trains and train depots. The restaurant was situated at the entrance to Base Station Road, which passed between it and the hotel, eventually ending at the Cog Railway station.

Eating with Joel and Todd was an odd experience. Jesse couldn't tell if they hated each other or just enjoyed sniping back and forth. Sometimes the conversation seemed easy enough as they talked about heading back to Rochester on the weekend—apparently, Todd and Stuart had come up to Bretton Wood in Joel's car. Other times, they snapped at each other over minor annoyances like what to get for an appetizer. If they really didn't like each other's company, they could easily have eaten at different tables or different times. But they hadn't.

One thing was clear, though—they both found tolerating each other's company infinitely preferable to eating with the Lassiters. Corrie was a friend of Joel's, so he wouldn't have minded her joining them—Todd seemed indifferent—but the thought of eating with Mr. and Mrs. Lassiter was completely repellant.

"They've been… nice," Joel said, making the word "nice" sound as if he were scraping the bottom of the barrel for something pleasant to say.

"They've been total fucking snobs," Todd corrected.

Joel shrugged, but he didn't disagree.

"So, forgive me if this is too personal," Jesse asked, "but what happens now? It seems like you were all connected through Stuart. Are you going to see each other at all, after you go back home?"

Joel and Todd looked at each other for a minute, and then Todd shrugged. "I don't know. You're okay, I guess."

"Maybe," Joel said, frowning as he looked back at the mashed potatoes on his plate. "Now that I know you won't beat the shit out of me."

"I keep telling you, I'm not homophobic."

"As long as I kept away from him."

That was met with stony silence. Todd took a bite of steak and chewed it, looking past Joel as if he found something on the brick wall behind him incredibly fascinating.

"Oh fuck," Joel muttered after the three of them had been eating in silence for a few minutes. He was looking toward the door, and both Jesse and Todd turned to see what had caught his attention.

It was Kyle and his partner. The detective was scanning the room, obviously searching for someone. When his eyes landed on their table, Jesse thought he saw him hesitate just a second. Then he said something to the detective beside him. The other man remained by the door while Kyle strode across the room until he was standing by the table.

"Todd," he said. "Joel. Jesse. You know these guys?"

Kill me now. It was a question Kyle would be likely to ask, if he'd just known Jesse from taking his statement at the crime scene, and now stumbled across him having dinner with a couple of the suspects. "Um… I ran into them at the hotel."

Kyle nodded and turned his smile upon Todd. "Corrie told me you were planning on coming here for dinner. I don't want to disturb you while you're eating, but I'd appreciate it if both you and Joel could meet me back in your room later. Say in a couple hours? I have some questions I'd like to ask you."

Todd's face had turned to stone. Jesse suspected he'd been one of those kids who'd been questioned quite a lot by the cops when he was growing up. Maybe nothing extreme—minor vandalism, trespassing, perhaps some shoplifting—but enough to make him antagonistic. But he nodded and said, "Sure. We'll be there."

THEY TOOK the shuttle back to the hotel when they were done eating, and it stopped at the Bretton Arms Inn to pick up anyone returning from there. Apparently the Lassiters had just finished eating as well, because they climbed on board. Jesse recognized Corrie and her younger sister—whatever her name was—and he assumed the older man and woman who followed them were their parents. Todd and Joel were sitting with him in the back, so Corrie simply smiled at them and mouthed the word "hi" as she took a seat up front with her parents. Mr. Lassiter nodded perfunctorily at them before sitting down, but his wife acted as if she hadn't noticed them.

The young man who climbed aboard the shuttle last sent a chill up Jesse's spine. He was blond and blue-eyed and bore a distinct resemblance to Corrie. Jesse ducked his head down, hoping to avoid eye contact. The guy sat down without appearing to notice him.

Jesse stayed silent for the ride back to the hotel, and he hung back while the others were disembarking. But the moment he was off the shuttle, he caught up with Joel and grabbed his arm. "Who was that guy with Corrie's family?"

"You know Corrie?" Joel said, looking confused.

"She was with you two—and Stuart—on the train platform," Jesse explained. "And I assume the younger girl was her sister?"

"Yes. Lisa."

"But who was the guy?"

Joel shrugged. "Isn't it obvious? He's her brother. His name's Ryan. Why?"

Jesse realized he didn't have a very good reason for being fascinated by Ryan, so he smiled faintly and said, "He's really good-looking."

Joel frowned. "Yeah, I'm totally fucking surrounded by good-looking guys this week." He seemed pretty pissed off about it, and Jesse realized he was probably feeling insulted that Jesse hadn't been interested in *him*. But there wasn't much Jesse could do to make him feel better without leading him on and making things worse for both of them.

Joel started walking again and Jesse followed, but his thoughts were whizzing around in his head. "Ryan didn't go with you guys to the summit yesterday?"

"No. He doesn't hang out with us."

It was true that Ryan hadn't gotten off the Cog with the others. But that just created more questions. Because he *had* been at the summit. Just a few minutes before the train had pulled in, he'd been acting rude to Jesse on the observation deck.

LATER THAT evening, Jesse waited with growing trepidation for Kyle to call him. The detective was bound to be pissed off that Jesse had been eating dinner with two of the suspects. That probably hadn't quite met Kyle's definition of staying out of trouble. Jesse could handle being lectured or yelled at a little, but would this make Kyle change his mind about what they'd planned to do tonight?

It seemed like hours went by, during which time Jesse couldn't concentrate on reading or watching television. So he just sat on his bed, fretting.

Around 9:00 p.m., the phone rang and he jumped to answer it.

"Jesse, this is Kyle." His voice sounded curt.

Shit. He's cancelling.

"Hi" was all Jesse could manage.

"I have to type up these notes. It may take a while."

Jesse couldn't say anything. He waited for the words "so I won't be able to make it," but Kyle didn't say them. Eventually, the silence stretched on long enough that Kyle asked, "Are you still there?"

"Yeah! Yeah, I'm still here."

"Did you hear what I said? It's gonna take me two or three hours, probably."

"Okay."

"Are you still gonna want to go out, if it's close to midnight?"

"Yes! Please."

Kyle laughed gently. "That's what I was hoping you'd say."

TYPING UP statements and reports had never been particularly fun. Kyle had always found that to be the most boring part of his job, the same as pretty much any cop. But knowing there was a gorgeous young guy waiting to have a drink with him across the street and possibly getting bored and falling asleep.... Well, that was fucking hell.

It took all Kyle's willpower not to rush through the reports and to make sure they were done right. He kept glancing at the clock on his computer, and he could swear each minute he saw go by caused him physical pain. But he'd dumped the reports on Wesley that morning. He couldn't do it again tonight. Still, it didn't help that Wesley insisted on watching some dumb crime drama on the hotel television while Kyle worked. The loud noise, screams, and music were incredibly distracting.

By the time it was all wrapped up, it was 11:56 p.m. He stepped outside the room for a minute, standing in the ice-cold night air while he called Jesse's room on his cell. He was relieved when Jesse picked up on the first ring. "Hey. You still awake?"

"Yes! Are you coming over?"

"I just finished up. I'll be there in a few minutes."

Unfortunately, he still had to deal with Wesley. His partner was still sitting on his bed in his underwear, watching TV, and it would hardly be possible for Kyle to slip out without him noticing.

As it was, Wesley gave him a suspicious look when he came back inside. "What the fuck was that all about?"

Kyle pocketed his cell to give himself a moment to think. Then he replied, "I'm going out for a bit."

"Going out?" Wesley asked in surprise. "Where the fuck are you going at this time of night? We're in the middle of nowhere."

"I have a friend who lives nearby. We're just gonna meet up at the bar at Fabyan's."

"Cool!" Wesley said, sliding his legs around, as if he were about to get up. "I'll go with you."

Kyle had been afraid of that. He held up a hand. "Sorry, partner. Not this time. I'll buy you a drink when we get back to Concord. But this is… private."

Wesley put his feet on the floor with a thump and leaned forward to brace himself with his elbows on his knees. "Are you telling me you've got a fucking *date*?"

"Not really a date. It's just a couple drinks. The bar'll be closing in, like, an hour."

"What's her name?"

"None of your business."

Wesley laughed and shook his head. "Jesus." He slid back onto the bed and turned to the TV. "Fine. But I'll get it out of you sooner or later."

That's what Kyle was afraid of.

KYLE PULLED the Outback up near the entrance to the Mount Washington, but still in the shadows. Jesse came running out almost immediately, suggesting he'd been waiting for Kyle to pull up.

"Hey!" he gasped as he jumped into the vehicle and slammed the door. "God, it's fucking cold!"

Kyle smiled, surprised at how happy he was to find their "date" still on, despite the late hour. He put the Outback in gear and headed for the hotel's long, winding drive. "I'm afraid we won't have much time before the bar closes."

"That's okay," Jesse replied. "I mostly just wanted to see you."

Kyle looked away, embarrassed but pleased. He didn't talk as he guided the wagon down the drive to Route 302. Then as he turned onto it, he pointed at the hotel across the road. "That's where my partner and I are staying, by the way. Room 104."

"Does your partner know you're out with me?"

Kyle shook his head. "He knows I'm going to Fabyan's. I just told him it was with a friend." *God, I'm pathetic*, he thought. Jesse was seven years younger, and he had his act together. He didn't hide his sexuality. True, he didn't have a career to worry about losing—not yet. But Kyle probably wouldn't lose his job if he told Wesley he was bisexual.

I'm just a fucking coward.

If Jesse thought less of him for being closeted, he didn't say it out loud. He merely nodded and looked out the window at the train tracks that ran parallel to the road and the forest of spruce trees on the other side of them.

They pulled into Fabyan's parking lot at about half past midnight, which didn't give them much time. Kyle led the way inside, and they found seats at one end of the bar. Kyle ordered himself a beer, and Jesse surprised him by ordering a ginger ale.

"You don't want a drink?" Kyle asked. "I mean alcohol?"

Jesse shrugged. "Not right now. I just wanted to hang out with you."

"You don't… *not* drink, do you?" Kyle asked, afraid he'd offended him.

But Jesse laughed. "Sure, I drink. When I'm in the mood for it. But it's pretty late."

Kyle grunted and nodded. He was tempted to apologize again, but before he could say anything, the bartender returned with his beer and Jesse's ginger ale. The beer was bottled, since Kyle only drank Corona. The bartender opened the bottle and asked, "Do you want a glass?"

"No, thanks."

The guy left them and Kyle reached for the beer, but Jesse snatched it away. "Besides," he said, "if I had my own beer, I couldn't do this."

He took a healthy swallow and then put the bottle to Kyle's lips. Kyle flinched. Then he relaxed and allowed the contact. The glass rim was warm from the heat of Jesse's lips, and rather than tilt the bottle to give Kyle a sip, he slowly slid it back and forth along Kyle's lower lip until there was no mistaking the sexual nature of the gesture. Kyle felt himself grow hard.

He quickly snatched the bottle out of Jesse's hand and took a swig of beer to disguise his discomfort. He put the bottle down and gave Jesse an embarrassed smirk. "You are evil."

"If you let me."

Kyle glanced up to see the bartender watching them curiously. The man casually turned away to talk with another customer. It made Kyle uncomfortable to know the guy had caught on to him so fast, but he decided to ignore it. He was already skulking around, keeping things hidden from his partner. It didn't really matter what some guy he'd likely never see again thought about him.

"Do you want anything to eat?"

Jesse opened his mouth to say something, and from the look in his eyes, it was clear it was going to be raunchy. But apparently he thought better of it, because he smiled instead and took a sip of his ginger ale. "I'm fine," he said, setting the glass down.

"Do you mind if I ask you something?"

"No."

"Why me?" Kyle asked. "Why are you flirting with someone my age? You're gorgeous. You can't have any trouble finding guys your own age."

Jesse frowned. "Oh, stop," he muttered. "We're only seven years apart. That doesn't seem like a huge gap to me. I'm happy that you think I'm attractive—"

"The word was 'gorgeous.'"

"I'm not gorgeous. But thanks. For what it's worth, I think I look okay. But that isn't my problem when it comes to dating."

"No?" Kyle asked, raising one eyebrow at him. "What *is* your problem, then?"

"They all think I'm a nut job for being interested in murder."

Kyle chuckled and took a sip of his Corona. "So why are you interested in murder?"

"It's not because I've got a hard-on for violence or dead bodies or anything," Jesse replied defensively. "It's the puzzle that gets me—trying to figure out how they did it and why."

"And who," Kyle added.

"Yeah. You get that, don't you?" The look in Jesse's eyes was almost pathetic, a plea for understanding.

Kyle did understand. "That's why I joined the force," he said. "That and I hate the idea of someone like Stuart lying in a grave somewhere while his killer goes out partying, fucking… kicking back in a goddamned resort hotel…."

Jesse smiled and held up his ginger ale. Kyle clinked his beer bottle against the glass, and they both drank.

It wasn't long before the bartender shooed everybody out, so they retreated to the Outback. Kyle was reluctant to take Jesse back so soon, so he drove down Bay Station Road toward the Cog Railway, then pulled off the road in a wide, grassy spot where there were no street lamps.

"Is this the part where you murder me and ditch my body?" Jesse asked with a nervous laugh.

Kyle grunted. "Get your mind off that kind of crap for a few minutes, will you? I pulled over so we could be alone."

"We could go to my room."

"It's too dangerous. If anybody sees us together, they might decide to come after you." He looked around at the darkness outside and then glanced over his shoulder. "You wanna get in the back?"

"Are we going to have sex?" Jesse's face was faintly illuminated by the dash lights, and the look he gave the back seat was dubious.

Kyle laughed. "No. If I wanted to go that far, I'd take you somewhere comfortable and hopefully romantic." He got out of the wagon, closed the door, and then opened the back door and climbed in. "But we can cuddle, can't we?"

Jesse didn't bother getting out of the vehicle. He slid his lean body up over the CD holder and between the two front seats, slipping naturally and easily into Kyle's open arms. The engine was still running and the heaters were still warming the interior of the wagon, but Kyle felt the heat of Jesse's body against his own and suspected they wouldn't need that for long.

"That's better," he murmured, leaning forward to find Jesse's mouth with his own.

Jesse kissed him back without hesitation. The sensation was no less intense for Kyle than it had been on Jesse's bed that afternoon. He heard a low growl of desire and realized it was coming from deep in his own throat as he pulled Jesse closer. Soon he was leaning back against the closed door, one foot bracing on the floor and the other on the car seat, his crotch welcoming Jesse's body. Jesse lay along the length of him while they kissed, grinding his erection against Kyle's through frustrating layers of blue jeans and underwear.

Kyle explored Jesse's mouth deeply with his tongue, breathing into him and accepting his breath in return. He wanted it to go on forever, but suddenly Jesse stiffened. Kyle didn't understand the significance of it until Jesse's entire body twitched a couple times. Then he chuckled.

"Fuck. You just came, didn't you?"

Jesse buried his face in between Kyle's jacket collar and the collar of his flannel shirt. "Sorry," he said, sounding embarrassed but amused. "I don't usually do that. But with all the kissing and grinding and…. Jesus, you're hot!"

"Thanks for the ego boost," Kyle said, stroking his back affectionately. He desperately wanted to get off too—it had been hot while they were kissing, and to have Jesse *ejaculate* right there in his arms…! But whipping it out right now would just make the moment feel sleazy. As it was, it was kind of sweet. So Kyle settled for nuzzling the top of Jesse's head and saying, "You are such a fucking turn-on."

Jesse laughed. "Right now, I just feel damp." He paused and then lifted his face to look Kyle in the eye. "Do you want me to…?"

"No," Kyle replied, leaning forward to kiss him on the nose. "I just wanna bask in the fantasy that I'm a hot stud who can make guys come just by kissing them."

"It's not a fantasy."

Kyle smiled and moved his lips down to kiss Jesse on the mouth.

A SHORT time later, Kyle drove back to the Mount Washington. Still reluctant to put an end to the night, he held back on the long driveway, stopping the wagon a short distance from the portico. Unfortunately, the sight of the hotel brought back his concerns about Jesse staying under the same roof as the Lassiters, Todd, and Joel.

"It's dangerous for you to be here," he said, wishing he could think of something romantic to end their date instead of this.

"I'll be all right."

"If whoever killed Stuart finds out you and I are… friends…." He couldn't think of the right word. They weren't boyfriends—not yet. Not even lovers. "…and they realize they've told you something incriminating…. They might try to kill you, Jesse. Someone who's already committed one murder isn't going to balk at committing another to cover up the first. They assume they're going to get life or the death penalty for the first one, so one more won't make any difference. They don't have anything to lose. You understand?"

"Yes, of course," Jesse replied.

Kyle frowned. "Really? Then why do you keep tempting fate by nuzzling up to these guys?"

"I've learned some things," Jesse said, as if that explained it. Then he recounted something Todd had told him about a threesome between him, Corrie, and Stuart. Kyle had to admit that was useful intel. Jesse also relayed his observations about the ambivalent relationship between Joel and Todd and his suspicion that Joel may have been interested in Stuart to a degree that made Todd uncomfortable.

"How uncomfortable?" Kyle asked, his eyes narrow suspiciously.

"He seemed fine with Joel being gay," Jesse observed, "and they don't appear to have an issue running around naked in front of each other. But Joel seemed to feel Todd was putting up roadblocks between him and Stuart."

Kyle nodded. "It sounded like Todd wouldn't allow Stuart to share a bed with Joel, that first night I spoke with them. So he was overprotective of his kid brother—he didn't like him fucking around with girls *or* boys. That's a little weird, but it's not much of a motive for murder."

"Not for killing *Stuart*, at any rate," Jesse agreed. "But there's something else—Corrie's older brother, Ryan Lassiter."

"What about him?"

"He was at the summit the day Stuart was killed."

Kyle frowned at him. "His family said he went to Concord on business."

"The business of *murder*, perhaps." Kyle cocked his head at him and quirked an eyebrow, but didn't say anything until Jesse said, "Sorry. Too many mystery novels."

"I figured."

"But I *saw* Ryan at the summit just before the train arrived with Stuart and the others. He was standing on the observation deck. I spoke to him."

That got Kyle's attention. "What did you talk about?"

"Nothing. I tried to flirt with him a bit, but he brushed me off."

Kyle sighed and gave him a little smirk. "Am I just going to have to get used to the idea that you flirt with everybody?"

"Well… maybe," Jesse confessed. "But flirting isn't the same as fucking. I know the difference. I won't be unfaithful to you."

"I'm not worried about it." Kyle leaned forward and kissed him gently.

WESLEY WAS sound asleep by the time Kyle got back to the hotel room. Thank God. Kyle didn't turn on the light. He locked the door and stripped down in the darkness, then crawled into bed. Warm thoughts of cradling a sated Jesse in his arms lulled him to sleep despite the lingering, pleasant sensation of arousal still stirring in his loins.

He woke to daylight and the sound of the shower running. His cock was at full mast, and he quickly grabbed one of his socks to wrap around it. He hurriedly beat off, exploding into the sock just as the shower turned off. Kyle quickly tugged his boxer briefs back into place and scrambled out of bed to get to his suitcase. He managed to flip it open and stuff the damp sock into a side pocket just as Wesley came out of the bathroom, naked but for a towel around his waist.

"Hey," his partner said as he walked to his own suitcase and retrieved a hairbrush. "You wanna call for room service or go out for breakfast?"

"Room service," Kyle said. "I have something to do on the laptop before we head back to the hotel."

Wesley called the order in while Kyle showered and brushed his teeth. Then they both hung out in their underwear for a while as they ate.

As he'd feared, Wesley was still curious about what had happened the night before. "So, how did the hot date go?"

Kyle decided to go for misdirection. "Didn't you notice us fucking on your bed?"

"Must be a heavy sleeper."

"Guess so." When Kyle didn't add anything else, Wesley frowned and went on, "Come on! What gives? You know I'd tell you all about it."

Kyle shrugged. "It wasn't that big a deal. Just a couple of friends having a drink together."

That isn't a total *lie, is it?*

Wesley let it drop, but it was obvious he was pissed about it. For a minute, Kyle debated just spitting it out. *I'm bi, and I'm seeing a guy now.* But the thought filled him with dread. What if Wesley didn't react well? They had to work together almost every day. Was it worth potentially fucking up a good partnership when he wasn't even sure the relationship with Jesse was going to go anywhere?

Kyle forced himself to put all of it out of his mind so he could focus on the next step in the investigation. He turned on the laptop he and Wesley shared for the case, connected to the hotel's Wi-Fi, and did a quick search online. He found what he was looking for on one of the unofficial Mount Washington "fan" sites and downloaded one of the images. A few minutes with Photoshop, and he had exactly what he needed.

"Did you bring your iPad?"

Wesley pulled himself away from the morning news to glare at him. "What the fuck do you want with my iPad?"

"I wanna wipe my ass on it."

"Fuck you."

Kyle sighed. "Stop being an asshole. I need to load a picture on it before we talk to one of the suspects."

A few minutes later—once Wesley stopped being pissy—he had everything set up. Wesley decided to use the bathroom before they left, which gave Kyle a minute to dial Jesse on his cell phone. "Does Ryan Lassiter know you're staying in the hotel?" he asked when Jesse answered.

"I don't think so. I just saw him from a distance yesterday—that was the first time I'd laid eyes on him here."

"And he didn't see you?"

"Not that I know of."

Kyle bit his lower lip. "I'm gonna tell him we have a witness who saw him at the summit. He may remember talking to you, and if he knows you're in the hotel...."

"I'll avoid him," Jesse replied, not sounding terribly concerned. God, he drove Kyle *crazy*! "If I think I'm in danger, I'll call you."

Hopeless!

"You'd damned well better," he muttered.

KYLE FOUND it perversely satisfying when Ryan himself opened the door to the suite. He looked at the two police detectives standing on the doorstep with wide eyes, and Kyle suspected the alarm he saw there wasn't wholly his imagination.

"Ryan," Kyle said, smiling, "you might want to call your lawyer. I have some questions for you."

The young man looked frightened as he backed away and allowed the detectives to enter. Not surprisingly, Mr. Lassiter had overheard and was already coming toward them.

"What's this all about?" he demanded.

"We have a witness who places Ryan at the summit just before Stuart was murdered."

"He... or she... is lying. As we've already told you, Ryan was in Concord, meeting with Tom Corby to discuss Tom's promotion to VP of sales. Tom will swear to that."

"I'm sure he will," Kyle said, unperturbed, "but before he does so in a court of law, he might want to take a look at this." He held out Wesley's iPad with the photo displayed on it and had the pleasure of watching Lassiter blanch. "The observation deck has a webcam that snaps a picture every ten minutes," Kyle continued.

The original image had shown both Jesse and Ryan Lassiter, but Kyle had cropped Jesse out. What was left showed a pretty clear image of Ryan walking away from the edge of the deck toward the camera. It wouldn't be admissible as evidence, altered like that, but the original might be. Maybe not—photos, especially digital photos, were generally viewed with skepticism by the courts—but Jesse's eyewitness testimony might be enough to corroborate it. In the meantime, Kyle could use the photo to make Lassiter sweat.

"Nobody says another word until Charlie gets here," Lassiter warned his family as he went over to the hotel phone and dialed McDonnell's room number. The girls weren't in the room, and perhaps not even in the suite, but Mrs. Lassiter was sitting by the gas fireplace with an eBook reader in her lap, watching the drama unfold.

Despite his father's warning, Ryan was already panicking. "I was just delivering something—"

"Ryan!" his father snapped at him. Then into the phone he said, "Charlie! We need you up here right away. This... policeman...." Kyle suspected he'd wanted to say something a bit more insulting. "...is making accusations about Ryan."

"Oh yeah," Kyle said, smiling coldly at Ryan, "there's also the matter of the envelope. You know what was in that envelope, don't you, Ryan?"

"Don't say a word!" his father shouted from across the room.

Ryan's face was pale and his eyes were wide as he no doubt pictured himself going to prison for a murder rap. But he opened his mouth and immediately clamped it shut again without saying anything.

The lawyer would be there soon and everyone would clam up then, but Kyle tossed one more thing out there. "I'm just wondering what it was for. Drugs, maybe...."

"No!" Ryan gasped.

"Be quiet, Ryan!" Lassiter snarled as he slammed the phone receiver down and strode across the room.

"We just wanted him to leave!"

"Ryan!"

"Oh, Marty!" Mrs. Lassiter exclaimed. "You didn't!"

Lassiter looked at his wife, exasperated. "We can discuss this later, Meghan."

McDonnell showed up before things could spiral further out of control, and he quickly reined it all back in, demanding time to discuss the situation with his clients before Kyle could continue questioning them. But Kyle was content to say good-bye for now. He knew he'd get nothing more out of any of them in McDonnell's presence, but he'd gotten what he came for.

"WHAT THE fuck was all that about?" Wesley asked in a hushed voice. They were approaching the rotunda that connected the hallways, where an older gentleman in a uniform sat in a chair, waiting to operate the elevator for guests. Kyle put a finger to his lips and forced Wesley to wait until they were downstairs and out of the hotel.

He pulled Wesley aside as they waited for the valet to bring around the Outback. "Lassiter used his son as a delivery boy. Ryan never went to Concord. He went up the mountain on the Cog—probably on one of the morning trains. He waited for Stuart to come up with Corrie and Todd so he could offer Stuart a bribe."

The light dawned in Wesley's eyes. "The envelope with twenty thousand dollars in it."

"Mr. Lassiter wanted Stuart to bail on the wedding plans and disappear from Corrie's life forever."

Wesley shook his head. "Why wouldn't he just slip the envelope to Stuart at the hotel?"

"I don't know yet. Maybe because Stuart was never out of Corrie's, Todd's, and Joel's sight. Even if he tried to sneak out of his hotel room in the middle of the night, he was sleeping in the same bed as his brother and likely to wake him. So he and Ryan agreed to meet for a few minutes on the summit."

Wesley didn't look convinced, and Kyle had to admit that part still didn't quite make sense. It was hard to imagine they couldn't have bumped up against one another in a hallway or something to pass the envelope. Unless… maybe the meeting at the summit had been Stuart's idea? Had he proposed it, and Ryan accepted the inconvenience to keep him happy? That would mean Stuart knew he was going to be paid off. And he planned on taking the money.

So much for true love.

Had he already decided Corrie wasn't for him after she agreed to the threesome with Todd? So when Lassiter—through Ryan—waved a big wad of cash at him, he just decided "fuck it" and took the deal?

Even if all this was largely correct, Kyle couldn't think of a reason Ryan would want to kill Stuart after he'd taken the money. And if he *had* killed him, wouldn't he have taken the envelope back? Todd and Joel hadn't approved of the wedding anyway, so it seemed unlikely they would have been upset with Stuart for taking the money. And again, if one of them had killed him, wouldn't they have taken the envelope? They might not have known where it was, of course, since it was safely tucked in Stuart's crotch. But if Stuart had planned on returning to Rochester with them, they would have had other less risky opportunities to take it from him.

There was only one person who seemed likely to be furious with Stuart for taking that money and might conceivably be angry enough to kill him right then and there, as well as not really caring about the contents of the envelope itself.

Corrie Lassiter.

14

JESSE WASN'T too embarrassed about coming while he and Kyle were making out last night. It had been kind of nice having an orgasm while cradled in the detective's arms. But he definitely wanted a rematch. Kyle hadn't come, and neither of them had even taken their clothes off. Just the thought of what Kyle might look like under his uniform was enough to make Jesse painfully hard again, so he lay in his ridiculously soft bed at the Mount Washington and slowly jerked off, remembering the feel of razor stubble against his cheek, the softness of Kyle's warm lips…. His orgasm was intense and very messy. He lay there naked and wet for a long time afterward with his eyes closed, thinking his life couldn't possibly get much better than this.

A knock on his door sent him scrambling for some tissues to mop up with and some clothing. "Just a minute! Hold on," he added, as he extricated his right leg from the same pant leg he'd just put his left leg in and tried to find the correct hole. Somehow he'd misplaced his underwear, so for now he'd have to make do without it.

There was no answering voice at the door, but when he opened it, his shirt clutched in his hand and his chest still bare, he found Joel standing on the other side. Joel stared unabashedly at his naked torso for a moment, but Jesse couldn't blame him for that. He would have done the same under the circumstances. Still, he slipped the shirt on before saying, "Hey. What's up?"

Joel didn't look good. He seemed weary, and he didn't look as if he'd bathed since the day before. Certainly, he didn't look like a man hoping to get lucky. "Hey. Um… Todd and I…. Look, I kind of need to talk to someone. You seemed like…."

He was fumbling, probably not sure this was such a good idea, but Jesse took pity on him. Despite the fact that he knew Kyle would be annoyed with him, he said, "Come on in."

Joel flopped himself down in the chair, ignoring the dirty underwear—*That's where they got to!*—draped over the back of it. "Todd's driving me crazy," he said, rubbing his eyes.

"I can see where that might happen."

Joel snorted. "Yeah. But it's more than that." He took a deep breath and settled his head back, closing his eyes. "He jerks off in front of me."

"So he wasn't kidding about watching a porno later," Jesse said with a smirk as he settled himself cross-legged on the bed.

"Nope. He watched it, and he let me watch him go at it."

"He's kind of a pig."

"Yeah," Joel agreed, "but the thing is, I'm no angel. Normally, a hot guy like that masturbating in front of me… I'd be *happy* to watch! But…." He leaned forward and looked Jesse in the eye. "Can I tell you something? Something really personal? I know we just barely met."

Jesse found himself feeling a little uncomfortable. Prying into the events surrounding the murder was one thing, but he was discovering that went hand in hand with learning people's intimate secrets, and that felt kind of… icky. Still, he replied, "Sure."

"You can't tell Todd. It could get really ugly if you did."

Jesse raised his eyebrows. "Do you have a crush on him, or something like that?"

"No." Joel sat back and rested the back of his head against Jesse's underwear again. "Stuart was my boyfriend. I don't mean I had a crush on him. I mean I was in love with him, and he was in love with me. And yes, we fucked. Not just a one-time 'Hey, Joel, I'd like to see what it's like' kind of thing. We'd been sleeping together for almost a year."

Jesse stared at him, having no idea what to say. Finally, just to break the silence, he got up and leaned over Joel to pluck his underwear out from between the guy's head and the chair. "Sorry. This has just been bugging me. I didn't realize they were on the chair until you sat down."

Joel glanced at the briefs in his hand and laughed. "I didn't even notice. It's cool."

"I'm sorry about Stuart," Jesse said, tossing the underwear on top of his duffel bag. "I mean, I was before, but now…."

"Yeah."

Jesse sat down on his bed again, not sure where go next.

"I know what you're thinking," Joel said.

"Really? Because I have no idea what I'm thinking."

Joel smiled, but it looked sad. "You think I must be a total scumbag, hitting on you the day after my boyfriend was murdered."

"I hadn't thought that, really," Jesse said, "but now that you mention it, it is kind of an unusual thing to do, under the circumstances."

"I guess it was." Joel let his head fall back against the chair again—sans underwear pillow. "I just wanted to blot it all out for a few hours, to be fucked into oblivion. It wasn't because I didn't love him. I don't know what I'm going to do without him."

It still seemed a little weird. But Jesse wasn't here to foist his views of fidelity off on the guy. He sighed and leaned forward, looking Joel directly in the eye. "You're cute, Joel. And if I was single, I'd probably say, 'Sure! Let's go for it!' But I have a boyfriend, and I can't cheat on him." He was overstating the depth of the relationship between himself and Kyle, quite possibly, but that wasn't Joel's concern.

Joel nodded. "It was a really bad idea. Almost as bad as the one I had last night."

"Which was?"

"I got so horny, watching Todd pumping away, I almost begged him to let me suck him off."

"Jesus," Jesse groaned. "Do you think he would have flipped out on you?"

Joel shrugged. "Not really. He's kind of a redneck, but he's not so bad, once you get to know him. He probably wouldn't have let me do it—although you never know with him. Either way, I'm sure he would have tormented me for the rest of my life over it."

"Tormented?"

"Oh, you know—he'd make crude jokes and wave his crotch at me every chance he got."

Jesse smiled. "Yeah, I can see him doing that." But that was another thing that didn't quite add up. "Why did you and Stuart feel like you had to keep your relationship secret from him? I mean, sure, he's a pig, but he doesn't seem all that homophobic to me."

Joel screwed his face up as if he were having trouble coming up with the right words. "It's not so much that he's homophobic as... jealous."

"Jealous? Of Stuart?"

Joel waved a hand in front of his face. "I don't mean like incest or anything. But he was really weird about Stuart having friends—*any* friends. He didn't like me being Stuart's friend, and when he found out I was gay, he started watching me all the time, making sure I didn't—" He lifted both hands and wiggled his fingers. "—grope Stuart with my faggy little hands."

Jesse couldn't help but snort at the image he'd painted. "But he didn't mind when Corrie started groping Stuart?"

"He didn't like that either. But Corrie didn't let that stop her. She has more balls than I do. In a... you know... figurative sense." Joel glanced over at the desk, where the cleaning staff had placed fresh glasses and a carafe of water the night before. But he scrunched his nose up as if the thought of water nauseated him. "Do you wanna go get some coffee?"

"Sure. I should probably shower first."

Joel gave him a mischievous smile. "Can I watch?"

"No," Jesse replied with a smirk as he stood from the bed and went to scrounge some clean clothes out of his bag. There weren't many left. "Like I said, I'm not available." Not to mention the attempt at flirting had been clumsy and unappealing.

Jesse wasn't sure how serious Joel had been, but he didn't look insulted by the refusal. He was still smiling, at least. "So who is this mysterious boyfriend?"

"I met him while I was working at the observatory," Jesse hedged.

Fortunately, that seemed to satisfy Joel's curiosity. He seemed bored already, picking up one of the empty glasses and filling it with water from the carafe. "They say most murder victims know their murderers."

Jesse found the reminder a little disturbing, considering he was currently alone with one of the murder suspects. Maybe he should put off that shower? He'd seen *Psycho* a few too many times. "I've heard that."

"Which means one of us had to do it—one of us here for the wedding."

"Well, statistically. It's always possible some random hiker killed Stuart."

"Yeah, but why?"

Jesse shrugged. "Why would anyone in the *wedding* party want to kill him?"

"I've been thinking about that a lot," Joel said. "I know *I* didn't do it. Todd's a little psycho, but he's been watching out for Stuart since their parents died. I can't believe he would ever hurt his brother. That leaves the Lassiters."

"Didn't you say Corrie was a friend of yours?"

"Yeah. I hung out with her in college. I introduced her to Stuart. I never would have done *that* if I'd known where all of this was going."

"But you put up with it, when she started sleeping with your boyfriend?" Jesse asked, puzzled.

Joel looked miserable when he responded. "Yeah. Stuart kept telling me he was just leading her on. I didn't like it, but... I couldn't get him to stop. He kept insisting I was the one he loved—this was just for fun. And then he started fucking her. And then suddenly he was *marrying* her...."

This was the first hint that Stuart hadn't been a complete angel. Perhaps he'd been more like his brother than Jesse had thought. But at the moment, he was less concerned with Joel's fucked up love life than figuring out why it came to such an abrupt and unpleasant end.

"Do you think Corrie's capable of murder?"

Joel had raised the glass to his lips. Now he snorted and had to put it down again.

"Should I take that as a 'no'?" Jesse asked, giving him a wry smile.

Joel cleared his throat a few times. "Jesus. I don't know. She can be a real spoiled bitch when she doesn't get her way. But I have a hard time imagining her killing anyone." He took another sip of water, looking thoughtful. "On the other hand, she's the only one with a motive."

That perked Jesse's ears up. "A motive?"

"Yeah," Joel said. "You remember how I said nobody wanted this wedding?"

"Yes."

"Todd thought the whole Lassiter family was a bunch of rich snobs and Stuart should stay the fuck away from them. Corrie liked Todd, despite the fact that he treated her like shit. If she had her choice, she would have picked Todd over Stuart—count on it."

Jesse remembered the threesome, which Todd said Corrie had wanted more than Stuart had. "You think she would have killed Stuart to be with Todd?"

"No," Joel said, shaking his head. "She could've just married Stuart and fucked around with Todd on the side."

"Charming."

Joel laughed. "Don't think she wouldn't have. Todd might actually have had a problem with it—he's a fuckload more loyal to his brother than to her—but the three of them might have worked something out."

"That still doesn't really give Corrie a motive to kill Stuart."

"*Unless*," Joel said dramatically, punctuating the word with a wave of his glass and causing the water to slosh a bit, "Stuart backed out, ran off, and left her at the altar. Then she'd lose him and Todd both."

"Do you think he was going to do that?"

Joel paused and looked at Jesse for a long time before he drained his glass and set it back on the desk. "You know, the more I talk to you, the more I realize… we're not very nice people. Me, Stuart, Todd, Corrie, the Lassiters… I can't imagine you being as much of an asshole as every single one of us is."

Jesse shook his head in bewilderment. "What the hell are you talking about?"

"Stuart told me Mr. Lassiter offered him some money to bail on the wedding. A *lot* of money. And I told him to take it. Just take the fucking money so we could get the hell out, go to New York or California or somewhere, where we could be ourselves and live together. Fuck Corrie and Todd and everyone else."

He was right. Jesse wouldn't have been able to do that. Then again, he'd never had a brother like Todd, who might have made him so afraid to come out of the closet that he ended up trapped in a marriage he didn't want. "Do you really think Corrie would have been so freaked out by Stuart jilting her that she would have wanted to kill him?"

"Maybe," Joel said. "Especially since she was terrified to tell her parents she was pregnant."

15

WHEN KYLE and Wesley returned to their hotel room, they found an e-mail waiting for them with a fax attachment. Several pages, in fact, sent over from McDonnell's office. Kyle expected to discover it was some kind of cease and desist, threatening him if he didn't back off from the Lassiters. What he found was a report from a private investigator the Lassiters had hired to look into the background of their future son-in-law.

Very interesting.

The Lassiters were attempting to redirect suspicion away from them, he knew, but if they felt there was something incriminating in the file, Kyle wasn't averse to taking a look at it.

The Warrens' adult lives hadn't been terribly interesting. Oh, sure—to the Lassiters, Stuart's shoplifting incident four years ago, Todd's car repossession, and his arrest for public urination in a parking lot probably made the boys seem like low-class degenerates. To Kyle, it made them seem like half the guys he grew up with.

Their childhood was more interesting and far more unpleasant. Their father had been a cop, which probably contributed to Todd's thinly veiled hostility toward Kyle. The guy hadn't been a very *good* cop. He'd had a serious drinking problem and was cited for using excessive force more than once during an arrest. Eventually he was suspended, and shortly after that, he was relieved of duty.

Apparently, the drinking got worse when he was off the force. The neighbors called the police on him more than once for knock-down, drag-out fights with his wife, and child services had the boys removed from the home for a year, when Todd was fifteen and his brother was thirteen. According to what the private investigator had turned up, there was some evidence the boys had been physically abused. But a year later, everything was more or less back to normal—Mr. Warren was supposedly going to Alcoholics Anonymous, and the boys were back living with their parents. But according to interviews with neighbors later, everyone knew Mr. Warren was off the wagon more than he was on it.

During this time, according to what the PI uncovered, Mrs. Warren had not only stopped sleeping with her husband, but she was openly going out to clubs at night and screwing around with other men. Friends and neighbors pretended not to notice… until one summer night.

Mrs. Warren had been out dancing in Portsmouth. Mr. Warren had stayed home, drinking. When his wife came home, Todd and Stuart's father shot her several times in the chest with a Smith & Wesson M&P45—a standard police-issue pistol, though he must have obtained this particular one on his own. She was killed instantly. Neighbors called 911, but not before one more shot was heard. Mr. Warren had committed suicide, shooting himself in the head with the same pistol.

By the time the police and ambulance had arrived, the teenage boys—sixteen and fourteen years old at the time—were outside the house. They'd climbed out an upstairs window onto the porch roof and jumped down. They never returned to the house, except for a couple hours under the supervision of a social worker a few days later. They were allowed to pack up some of their personal belongings. Eventually, they were sent to live with grandparents—on their mother's side—in nearby Dover, NH. But apparently they didn't like living there. As soon as Todd was eighteen, he moved out and found a job and an apartment back in Rochester. Stuart moved in with him, even though he was just sixteen and his grandparents had legal custody. Nobody cared to order him back with his grandparents, so he and Todd continued to live together until the present time.

Again, the Lassiters seemed to believe their tragic childhood made the Warrens psychologically unstable—they'd even gone so far as to underline the investigator's comments along these lines. Kyle wasn't so sure about that. It was a rough thing for teenage boys to go through, but people could be surprisingly resilient. Todd clearly had some anger issues, and perhaps his brother had as well. But did that make them murderers?

Still, Kyle was curious about this second—or rather, first—tragedy in Todd and Stuart's lives. He gave a call down to Concord. It was an old case, before his time, but someone might remember it. And maybe he could get the case notes sent up to him.

THE TWO detectives assigned to the case—Malone and Carson—were no longer with the Major Crime Unit in Concord. Nobody seemed to know where Carson was. He'd moved to California years ago and was presumably working for a PD out there. Malone, however, was still in Concord. He'd transferred to the Terrorism Intelligence Unit, but it wasn't hard to track him down. Kyle had to leave messages, but eventually the officer called him back. Kyle took the call through Skype so Wesley could listen in.

"Yeah, I remember that case," Malone said. "Jesus. Cases like that were why I had to get out of Major Crimes. Husbands and wives blowing each other's brains out really gets to you after a while."

"No shit," Kyle agreed.

"So why are you digging that one up after all this time?"

"Because their son, Stuart, was just murdered on the summit of Mount Washington," Kyle answered, and Wesley added, "His older brother is one of the potential suspects."

Malone sighed and muttered something obscene under his breath. "What do you want to know?"

They didn't learn much from Malone that they didn't know already, though he was able to fill in some detail. There were powder burns on Mr. Warren's right hand, indicating he had, in fact, pulled the trigger. That hand was also covered in spattered blood—his own. The trajectory of the bullets that killed his wife came from the vicinity of the living room couch about fifteen feet away, and they traveled upward, as if the gun had been fired while Mr. Warren was sitting down. She was shot four times in the torso, and two of the bullets pierced her heart. The shot that killed Mr. Warren was fired at point-blank range underneath Mr. Warren's chin, aimed upward into his cranium. He never got up from the couch and he was found sitting up, the gun still in his hand where it rested in his lap. The gun had a ten-round magazine, and it still contained five rounds.

"The kids were upstairs when it happened," Malone went on, "probably asleep until the gun went off."

"Probably?" Kyle asked.

"When we interviewed the older one—um… Todd—he insisted he was jerking off."

Wesley screwed up his face in disgust. "Why would he tell *you* that?"

"Have you talked to him? He likes to yank your chain. At least, he did when he was a sixteen-year-old punk. Anyway, I don't care if he was finger-painting with his own jizz. He and his little brother crawled out Stuart's bedroom window after they heard the shots. They had enough brains not to run down and see who was shooting who."

After Malone had given them everything he could think of, Kyle thanked him and disconnected the Skype call.

"Fuckin' A," Wesley muttered, getting up out of his chair to stretch. "Those kids had to be screwed up after something like that."

Kyle frowned. "That's certainly what the Lassiters think."

"They're right!"

"Yeah," Kyle said, "maybe Todd and Stuart ended up with some trust issues or phobias or something. Who wouldn't? But that doesn't make them psychopaths. Everything we've learned so far indicates Todd was protective of Stuart—and maybe this is why. But that doesn't convince me he'd ever kill him."

Wesley flopped down on his bed. "I guess not. So where does that leave us?"

"Taking a trip down to Dover," Kyle said.

"What for?"

"I'd like to talk to the grandmother." Their initial inquiry into Stuart's identity had turned up only two surviving relatives—Todd and their grandmother. The old woman hadn't been contacted since the boys had lost touch with her years ago, but supposedly she was in an assisted living community in Dover.

Wesley spread his hands wide. "Why? You haven't established any connection between what happened to Stuart's parents and what happened to Stuart. Or am I missing something?"

Kyle wasn't sure. Perhaps it was just that it seemed like such a bizarre coincidence—three murders in one family. But Wesley was right. He didn't have anything to tie the two incidents together. "Call it a hunch," he told his partner. He stood up and closed the laptop. "If I don't get anything useful this interview, I'll drop it. But we don't have many other leads at the moment."

Wesley sighed and shook his head. He picked up the TV remote and turned the television on. "Fine."

"You can stay here if you like," Kyle suggested. He was kind of hoping Wesley would take him up on that. The idea had just popped into his head that this might be a way to spend some more time with Jesse. Not taking him along on the investigation, of course, but there wouldn't be any harm in bringing him along for the ride, would there?

Wesley snorted and said, "No fuckin' way. If you're going, I'm going. I need to get out of this fucking hotel room."

Kyle prodded the inside of his cheek for a moment as he thought things through. Then he sighed and said, "Turn off the TV."

"Why?"

"Just do it, please."

Clearly reluctant, Wesley flipped it off, then tossed the remote on the bed beside him. He looked at Kyle with his eyebrows raised expectantly.

Kyle sat down on the edge of his own bed, bracing his elbows on his knees. "Look… I think it's time we had a talk."

"Is this about sex? 'Cause I basically figured that out in summer camp."

Kyle snorted. "Shut up. I'm trying to be serious for a minute. It's about *me*. And some shit I've been dealing with."

Wesley's brow furrowed, somehow making him look both concerned and baffled at the same time. Kyle couldn't blame him. He was kind of hitting the guy with this out of the blue. But it was either this or come up with another lame excuse for sneaking out tonight. Wesley was his friend, wasn't he? The closest he had to a friend right now, anyway. He at least deserved the chance to show that he was cool… or not.

"You know I was married to Julie for five years," Kyle went on.

"Sure."

"And I was really happy with Julie. I loved her and loved… you know… *being* with her…."

Wesley looked uncomfortable, and Kyle couldn't blame him. Could he have phrased it any more awkwardly? "Dude."

"Sorry," Kyle said, giving a halfhearted laugh. "I'm just trying to say I like women."

"This is news?"

"No. But… what I'm trying to get at is… I like men too."

Wesley was beginning to look irritated now. "You're gay?"

"No. Bisexual."

"Since when?"

Kyle shrugged. "Since always. Julie knew about it. But I've never told anyone else until this week."

Wesley didn't appear to pick up on the distinction between "this week" and "now," which was what Kyle would have said if Wesley had been the first person he'd come out to. Instead he screwed up his face in disgust and asked, "So you two were into threesomes with other dudes?"

Kyle groaned and stood up. "No! Julie and I were monogamous. I've never even had sex with a man." He started pacing in agitation.

"Then what difference does it make?"

"It makes a difference because I've met someone—a guy. And I've started… I guess 'dating' would be the right word."

He watched the light of comprehension come into Wesley's eyes. "That's who you were with at the bar last night."

"Yes," Kyle replied. "And I'm going to have dinner with him tonight. At least, I hope so."

"Fuck! You're gonna leave me alone again?"

"Sorry."

Wesley appeared to be mulling something over for a moment. "Wait a minute," he said finally. "How the hell did you meet this guy? Did you pick him up in a bar?" His expression clearly showed his distaste for that kind of hookup.

"Fuck you," Kyle snapped, coming to a stop at the head of Wesley's bed so he could glare down at him. "You really think I'm that sleazy?"

"We've been here three fucking days. How else did you meet him?"

"How do you know I don't know him from before we came up here?"

"From where?"

Kyle slumped down on his bed again. "Never mind. I did meet him this week," he admitted. "But I didn't pick him up in a bar. He was working on the mountain the night we got called up there."

Kyle could practically see the gears turning in Wesley's head as he tried to pinpoint who'd been on the summit that night. "It's not Ted, is it?"

Well, at least Ted was good-looking. Wesley could have picked worse.

"No," Kyle said. "His name's Jesse Morales."

"Jesus!" Wesley practically shouted. "The *high school* kid?"

"He's not in high school, for fuck's sake. He's twenty-three. He just graduated *college*."

That seemed to mollify him, but Wesley grumbled, "Still seems kind of young."

"Yeah," Kyle agreed. "But he doesn't seem to think the age gap is a big deal. I mean, will it be that big a deal ten years from now?"

"Dude, you're not gonna be with this kid for ten years." He raised a hand when Kyle glared at him. "All I'm saying is nobody starts dating and meets Prince Charming on the first try. If you want to fuck around with some cute young thing, fine. You deserve to have a little fun. But don't go thinking you've found true love fresh out of the gate. You've got more sense than that."

He had a point, Kyle knew. But he didn't want to think about that. Being with Jesse felt right. All he wanted was time to see where things went. "That's all fine," he told Wesley. "But what I need to know right now is if you're cool with this."

"With what? With you being bi? Or with you chasing tail during an investigation?"

Ouch. Kyle wasn't sure if "tail" was the right word for it, but he got the gist. And Wesley might be right. "Well… let's start with the first part."

Wesley shrugged, then grinned and tossed one of the extra pillows at him. Kyle snatched it out of the air to avoid getting hit in the face. "Dude," Wesley said. "It's cool. I don't care about that."

Well, that was something, at least. "But you want me to stop seeing him?"

"Like you'd fuckin' listen to me."

Kyle laughed and tossed the pillow back at him. "No. Not in the long term. But I can tell him to back off during the investigation, I guess."

Wesley gave him a sour look. "I suppose it's not much different from when I was dating Sharon, is it?" Wesley didn't have a great track record. Most of his girlfriends didn't stick around longer than a few weeks. But Sharon had lasted longer than most—almost a year. Wesley had even talked about marrying her before she got a great job offer in New York. "I mean, she and I went out to dinner and stuff, even when I was on a case. And it's not like this guy is under suspicion or anything."

"I was hoping you'd see it that way," Kyle said, "because I have a big favor to ask."

16

JESSE KNEW it wasn't a good idea to keep hanging out with the suspects, but after Todd had joined him and Joel for coffee, he'd mentioned that Corrie and her younger sister, Lisa, would be going to the pool with them later. Jesse's curiosity was aroused. He hadn't had a chance to speak with Corrie yet. This might be the only chance he'd get. It probably wouldn't accomplish anything, but still… after what Joel had told him, he was dying to find out more about her. So when Todd invited him to come along, he accepted.

He wasn't convinced Joel had given up trying to get into his pants. And of course, going swimming meant he had to change in the locker room, giving Joel a perfect opportunity to check him out naked—which he did. He tried to be subtle about it, but he was a lousy actor. Not that Jesse was overly worried about it. Checking out wasn't the same as making a pass, and despite the fact that the three of them were packed in pretty closely in the small locker room, Joel didn't make any attempt to touch him.

Corrie Lassiter was beautiful. Even a gay man could see that. In a cerulean blue one-piece swimsuit, she looked absolutely stunning. Jesse couldn't help checking to see if she looked pregnant, but if she was, he couldn't tell. Perhaps she was just a few weeks along, or maybe Joel had lied.

Todd, true to form, gave her a lecherous look up and down as she approached them at the pool with Lisa following behind, dressed in a pink one-piece. But she seemed to like the attention. She smiled at him coyly, returning the appreciative look.

The look she turned on Jesse, when Joel introduced him, wasn't anywhere near as sexually charged, but she smiled warmly and said, "The boys told me about you! It's so nice to meet you."

I've heard about you too, Jesse thought, but he didn't think he should mention that. "I'm so sorry for your loss," he said.

"Thank you."

"Hey!" the other girl interrupted. "I'm Lisa." From the grin and sidelong glance she was giving Jesse, it was apparent at least *one* of the Lassiters thought he was cute.

"Hi." *God save me.*

The fifteen-year-old hung out with him at the edge of the pool for a while, both of them sitting with their feet dangling in the water. While they watched the others swim, she rattled on about how much more fun it would be at the hotel if her and Corrie's parents weren't there and if she'd been able to bring her best friend with her. Only after she'd been going on like this for a few minutes did she think to add, "Oh! And yeah, if Stuart was still alive!"

"Of course."

"He was really nice," she said, as if trying to make up for her previous oversight.

"So I've heard."

"Well… more kind of… quiet. He didn't talk much. But Corrie really liked him."

That was nice, considering the fact that she'd planned on marrying him.

Something caught Lisa's attention and her expression clouded. "Jesus! There's fucking Ryan again."

Jesse glanced up to see the young man standing out in the basement hallway that led past Stickney's and several touristy shops, looking into the pool area through a large plate glass window. He panicked for a moment, trying to hide his face behind his hand. But Ryan wasn't looking his way. He seemed to be watching the swimmers—one in particular.

"He's so fucking creepy," Lisa said, her face screwed up in disgust.

"That's your brother, isn't it?"

"Ugh. Yes. Fortunately, he doesn't stare at *me* all the time."

No, Ryan wasn't staring at her. He seemed to be staring at Corrie. After a moment, he glanced away and wandered back down the hall. That *was* pretty fucking creepy. Was he lusting after his own sister? Jesse suppressed a shudder at the thought that he'd tried to flirt with the guy at the summit.

Corrie swam over to them and climbed out of the water, her lithe body flexing as she raised herself up, drawing the attention of more than one straight man there. When she stood and walked over to one of the deck chairs, Lisa followed her.

"Did you see him?" she asked in a low voice.

Corrie reached for her towel and nodded. "Yes."

She toweled off and sat down in the chair, declining to comment further. But Jesse saw his chance to talk to her, so he stood and walked over to her side as casually as he could manage, flopping down in the deck chair beside her. Corrie smiled at him while her sister went back to the edge of the pool, but she didn't seem interested in talking. She watched Todd take a few dives off the low diving board, while Lisa, her interest in Jesse forgotten, challenged Joel to race for a few laps.

Corrie watched Todd take another dive. Only when he'd disappeared underwater did she sigh and muse aloud, "Things were so perfect a few days ago."

Jesse nodded sympathetically, but he didn't really know what to say to that.

She continued, "We were having such a good time together—all four of us. And Lisa too. My parents were being pissy in private, but they're always that way."

"It was nice of them to host the wedding here," Jesse said. "It's the nicest hotel I've ever been in."

Corrie shrugged, as if she'd seen much nicer hotels. "Daddy insisted upon a certain level of sophistication," she said mockingly. "I would have been fine with a little church in Portsmouth, but that wasn't good enough for him. I did put my foot down about guests, though. My mother would have filled the grand ballroom!"

She paused, her smile fading as a faraway look came into her eyes. "Now, it's all...." Her sentence trailed off, unfinished, and there was a long silence between them until a shout of indignation came from Joel. Lisa had just splashed him, initiating a chase to the other end of the pool. Corrie turned to Jesse. "Where do you live?"

"Dover."

"Oh! Then you're not far from us. I'm staying in the dorms at UNH, but Joel has an apartment in Dover. I hope you'll see more of him when we get back."

Jesse was tempted to say he was already seeing somebody, but he just smiled and nodded noncommittally. "I hear Todd lives in Rochester."

Her grimace made it apparent she didn't care much for the town. "I keep trying to convince him to move out of that place. You should see the dump he's renting."

"Do you think you'll see much of him after this?" Jesse asked.

"Why not? We're still family. At least the way I see it."

That didn't appear to be the way Todd saw it. He was a bit flirtatious toward her when he joined them after he'd tired of swimming, but when he was alone with Jesse and Joel in the locker room after that, he muttered, "God! She's always giving me these goo-goo eyes!"

"*Goo-goo* eyes?" Joel asked, laughing. "What the fuck is a 'goo-goo eye'?"

"You know—she's all... panting after me."

"Who can resist all that charisma?"

Todd didn't seem to be in the mood for teasing. He looked disgusted. "Stuart just fuckin' *died*... and she's already chasing after me."

"Come on, Todd," Joel said a bit more gently, "you know this isn't a new thing. If she could've gotten away with it, she would have had *both* of you."

"Fuckin' sick bitch."

"Well, you asked for it with that threesome." Joel made a sour face.

Todd stripped out of his swim trunks and hung them in his locker. "I was just trying to show Stuart what a slut she was."

"Right," Joel said. "*You* suggest a threesome and *she's* a slut."

Todd removed his towel from the locker, but he didn't bother wrapping it around himself. In the small space, his ass was nearly pressed against Jesse's hip. "The difference is I know I'm trash. I don't pretend to be better than everyone else."

Joel rolled his eyes but didn't respond. Todd slammed his locker shut and stalked off to the showers. Jesse had stayed quietly in the background during this exchange, but now Joel looked at him and shook his head. Then he closed his locker and followed after Todd. There were only two showers, so Jesse wrapped his towel around his waist and sat down on the bench to wait for one of them to free up.

JESSE TENTATIVELY accepted an invitation to get together at Stickney's for dinner—just him, Joel, and Todd—but an hour later, when he was alone in his room trying to get back into *The Maltese Falcon*, Kyle called him on his cell. "Hey, kid. How do you feel about going out to dinner?"

"Sure!" The prospect of seeing Kyle before bedtime was far better than listening to Joel and Todd try to outdo each other for crude behavior.

"Do you mind if we go somewhere a little… less upscale than the hotel?"

Jesse laughed. "I'd be fine even if you took me to Burger King."

"I think we can find something nicer than Burger King. I'll pick you up at six, okay?"

Jesse called Joel to let him know he couldn't join them for dinner. When Joel asked what was up, he said, "I'm having dinner with my boyfriend."

There was a hesitation on the other end of the line. Then Joel said, "Cool. You'd be welcome to invite him along."

"Thanks. Maybe some other night." He could just imagine their reaction if he showed up at Stickney's with Kyle in tow.

KYLE CALLED back a few minutes before six and told Jesse, "I still don't want you to be seen with me. Can you come out to the parking lot?"

"This sounds like the scene where I foolishly allow myself to be lured outside at night so I can become victim number two."

"If I wasn't *more* paranoid than you are, I might be insulted that you've twice wondered if I'm planning on killing you. Especially since I'm pretty sure you spent the whole day hobnobbing with *real* murder suspects."

"There were only a couple of times they could have gotten away with killing me unseen."

He could practically hear Kyle growling over the phone. "Just get your cute butt downstairs, Jessica," he said, no doubt intending it to get under Jesse's skin. "I'll be watching for you, and I'll pull up as soon as you're out of sight of the door."

Jesse refused to let the "Jessica" jibe annoy him. He went downstairs and crossed the lobby, where one of the doormen opened the door to let him out into the ice-cold night air. Even bundled up in his ski jacket, hat, and gloves, he didn't relish leaving the warm lobby behind. But he hadn't walked far before he was out of the illuminated portico and Kyle's wagon pulled up. He jumped in on the passenger side and was pleased to find the inside warm and toasty.

Kyle leaned across the emergency brake and gave him a kiss. "Talk to any murderers on your way through the lobby?"

"Five or six—one of them might be innocent."

"I doubt it."

They drove to Gorham, which was only ten minutes from the base of the Mount Washington Auto Road, but thanks to the way the mountains forced everything to curve around, it was forty-five minutes from the hotel. Kyle took him to a Japanese restaurant called Yokohama.

"I don't know how authentic it is," he told Jesse, "but I like it."

It was fine with Jesse. He hadn't really been kidding about being okay with Burger King, if that was where Kyle wanted to take him. He just wanted to spend more time with the detective. And it turned out the food was pretty good, though unlike any Japanese or Chinese food he'd ever eaten. He also couldn't help noticing there were no Asians among the restaurant staff. He got the impression this was some kind of unique French-Canadian rendition of Japanese food.

"So," Kyle asked him while they were eating a very tasty version of fried rice unlike any Jesse had tasted before, "you might as well spit it out. What did you learn today?" He sounded mildly irritated, but his mouth was turned up in a wry smile.

Jesse glanced around them, but they were tucked in a corner with nobody near enough to overhear their conversation. "Joel claims the Lassiters—the parents, anyway—offered Stuart money to bail on the marriage."

Kyle hesitated a second before saying, "Yes, we know that. But how did *he* know it?"

"Stuart told him about it before they went to the summit. He says he told Stuart to take the money so they could run off together."

"Joel thinks Stuart wanted to run off with *him*?" Kyle asked skeptically.

"He says they were lovers. They'd been hiding it from Todd and Corrie."

"Why?"

Jesse shrugged. "I guess Stuart didn't think his brother would take it well. Todd seems to get along with Joel all right, but maybe the idea of his brother being gay would have freaked him out. He's kind of a macho asshole."

"I've noticed."

"I doubt Corrie would have been too pleased either. Though Joel claims she's actually more interested in Todd than she was in Stuart."

"If that was true," Kyle asked, "why wouldn't she just marry Todd instead?"

Jesse took another sip of his zombie, which came in a plastic tiki head the waitress had told him he could keep. "Todd would never marry her. He thinks she's hot, but he doesn't actually like her. On the other hand, Joel thinks she was hoping she could continue to have sex with Todd after marrying Stuart."

"Nice."

"Well," Jesse said philosophically, "she didn't know Stuart was *gay*, necessarily, but she might have sensed he didn't care much."

Kyle's scowl showed his opinion of that kind of marriage.

"There's something else," Jesse added. "I don't know if I believe him or not, but Joel claims Corrie is pregnant."

Kyle raised an eyebrow. "By Stuart or by Todd?"

"Who knows? Can they even tell the difference, when the fathers are this closely related?"

"A paternity test could," Kyle said, "but if Corrie wanted everyone to believe the baby was Stuart's and she was married to him, there wouldn't be much reason to doubt her word. The kid would *look* like Stuart, after all."

"Which would make sense, if she wanted to hide her affair with Todd from her parents," Jesse said.

Kyle grimaced and shook his head in disgust. Then he took a bite of his sweet-and-sour chicken, chewed, swallowed, and said, "I shouldn't tell you this, but I got some information tonight on Todd and Stuart's personal history—mostly about the death of their parents and how they ended up with Todd more or less raising his brother from the time they were teenagers. That's all I'm gonna say about it for now, but I need to make a trip down to Dover tomorrow, and I want you to come with me."

Jesse looked up from his zombie in alarm. "You aren't taking me back home, are you?"

Kyle gave him a long, evaluating look. Then he shrugged. "Do you want to go back home? I mean, we could just take both our cars, if you wanted to stay behind when I came back."

"No!" Jesse said quickly. Then he looked away from Kyle, embarrassed. Maybe this was a convenient way for the detective to wrap up their relationship. *Thanks, kid. It's been great. Look me up if you're ever in the area again.*

Kyle reached a hand across the table and placed it on Jesse's forearm. "I'm not saying you have to go home. And I'm sure as hell not saying I *want* you to go home. But you have to check out of your room by eleven thirty tomorrow, right? Where were you planning on going after that?"

"I don't know," Jesse said, his voice petulant. He hadn't wanted to think about it. Certainly, he couldn't beg his father for more time at the Mount Washington—it was far too expensive, and there were limits to how much of a brat he could be. "I guess I was thinking there might be a cheap motor inn nearby." Of course, he wouldn't be able to manage more than a couple of nights on the money he had in his wallet. And he'd probably have to live off the dollar menus at some fast-food joint.

Kyle sighed and seemed to be scrutinizing him carefully. At last he said, "I have to come back here, of course, but I was thinking of crashing at my house in Concord tomorrow night before I drive up here the next day. Would you like to spend the night with me?"

Jesse looked up into those serious hazel eyes and thought he saw a little anxiety behind Kyle's expression. They both knew staying alone at Kyle's might be it—their first time having real sex, as opposed to what had happened in the back of the Outback. Was he that worried about what it would be like to have sex with a man? Was he worried it might not be a good idea to get involved with Jesse after all? Or was he just worried that Jesse would turn him down? "Are you sure you want me to?"

"Oh yeah," Kyle said, his eyes narrowing, "I want you to. Are you sure *you* want to?"

Jesse laughed. "This could go around in circles for a while. Are you really, *really* sure you want to?" He leaned forward and looked Kyle directly in the eye. "*Fuck... yes.*"

Kyle exhaled heavily and gave him a lopsided grin. "Glad we got that settled." He glanced around at the restaurant. "Wesley, my partner, isn't real happy with all of this. I told him what was going on—about me being bi and dating you now. I think he handled it okay, though he thinks you're too young for me."

Jesse was still back at the "dating" part. Most of his friends hated the word. It sounded old-fashioned to them, and probably more to the point, it smacked too much of making a commitment. They preferred to "hang out." But Jesse liked the idea of commitment. "You really need to get off this kick about me being too young," he said. "It's not like I'm a fifteen-year-old virginal bride being married off to an old man in the 1940s, or whenever that shit was legal. I've graduated college and I'm trying to start a career. I'm incredibly attracted to you, and it's going to be a good long while before we have to worry about me waking up to your teeth on the bedside table in a glass."

Kyle cringed. "That's a pleasant image."

"Seven years isn't that big a deal, Kyle."

"Okay, okay," Kyle said with a smirk. "I'll try to shut up about it. But to get back to the point, I told Wesley about all this because he's going with us tomorrow."

"What?"

"We're still working on the case. So, yes, he's going to Dover with me to interview someone. I couldn't bring you along without telling him what was up with us."

Jesse didn't have a huge problem with Kyle's partner coming along for the ride, but he was thinking about tomorrow night. "He's not staying at your house, is he?"

Kyle grimaced. "For a threesome? No. He's got his own place. You and I will have the house to ourselves."

"Good."

17

WHEN THEY returned to the hotel, Kyle stopped the Outback in the parking lot within sight of the hotel entrance and told him, "I'll pick you up around nine tomorrow. Can you be in the lobby, waiting for me?"

"Sure."

They kissed, taking their time. Kyle was tempted to lure Jesse into the backseat again, but there would be plenty of time for groping—and a lot more than that—tomorrow evening. He settled for savoring Jesse's lips and tongue until he was panting into Kyle's mouth. God, that was a huge turn-on. But eventually Jesse pulled away, and Kyle let him.

"Good night," Jesse said.

"Night."

Jesse gave him a shy smile and a final quick peck on the lips and then climbed out of the wagon. Kyle watched him go, following his entire trek to the lobby of the hotel, making certain he made it safely inside.

Kyle had been agonizing the entire afternoon over whether to invite Jesse along on the trip. It was… irregular, to say the least, allowing a civilian to tag along on an investigation. Kyle had no delusions about the captain back in Concord thinking he was being at all professional. Hell, *Kyle* didn't think he was being professional. He only knew the thought of Jesse going back to Dover when things were just getting interesting between them made him nauseous. Jesse was the first person to spark something in him since Julie's death. He was terrified Jesse might just go back home and forget all about him.

On the other hand, if Jesse *was* likely to forget about him, maybe that would be for the best. Maybe he just had a thing for older guys, and Kyle fit the bill. The whole cop thing probably added to the sex appeal, considering Jesse's fascination with crime stories. If Jesse went back home and never called Kyle again, then it would probably be a good thing there was an hour drive separating them. Kyle would be less likely to make a fool out of himself, driving over to his house in the middle of the night and whining for Jesse to talk "just for a minute."

Ugh. Kyle had been called in on enough domestic disturbances of that sort. Even if they didn't get ugly, neighbors tended to call them in just to get the pathetic bastard to shut up and go home.

But what if Jesse was right for him? What if he was that guy who comes along just once or twice in a person's lifetime? Kyle didn't believe in the idea of One True Love—that there was just one person out there who was right for him, and that was it. What a miserable idea! What happened if that person died? Was he doomed to spend the next fifty to seventy years of his life alone and unhappy? Julie had been right for him. She'd adored him, and he'd adored her. He would miss her for the rest of his life. But if he let himself believe he'd never find love again, he'd end up killing himself.

Jesse felt like a second chance. Maybe that was just because he was gorgeous, showing an interest, and really knew how to kiss. The only thing Kyle knew for certain was that he wanted more time to sort this all out.

EVENTUALLY KYLE realized he'd been there a long time. He needed to get back to the hotel and get some sleep if he was going to be on the road most of the day tomorrow. He reached for the gearshift to back the wagon up, but something caught his eye and made him hesitate. There was someone in the bushes at the edge of the parking lot, deep enough in the shadows that he couldn't be seen clearly. But he was pushing his way through the bushes, and the swaying of the boxwood branches amplified his movements. Had he been there earlier? Had he watched Jesse walk to the hotel? Had he seen him getting out of Kyle's wagon?

Kyle took his hand off the gearshift and opened the door as quietly as possible. Then he slipped out and crept toward the bushes. As he approached, he rested one hand on his gun and called out, "Who's there?"

"Where?" a young man's voice answered.

"In the bushes."

"That's me." Joel Owens staggered out from behind one of the boxwoods, fumbling to zip up his fly. "Joel."

Kyle relaxed and took his hand off his gun. "So I see. What are you doing out here in the middle of the night, Joel?"

"I had to pee." From the way he was swaying on his feet, he was obviously drunk. He squinted at Kyle. "Oh, it's you."

"Where did you come from?"

Joel raised his hand and spun around, trying to orient himself. He stumbled a bit but finally pointed toward the nearby north entrance of the hotel.

"There are bathrooms inside the hotel, Joel. You shouldn't be peeing out here."

"You gonna arrest me?" Joel asked, sounding frightened and pathetic.

Kyle could certainly have fined him, but he wasn't particularly motivated to do so. It wasn't like the guy had whipped it out where people could see him. "Why are you wandering outside drunk, Joel? You're not even dressed for it." Joel was wearing a sweater, but it was a pretty cold night.

"Fuck it," Joel said. "Maybe I'll freeze to death. It would be better."

"Better than what?"

"Living without him."

"Stuart?" Kyle asked gently.

Joel nodded, and then his face crumpled up in a mask of agony as the tears came. It hit Kyle like a blow to the stomach, reminding him of nights he'd had after Julie's death, when drinking himself into oblivion had seemed the only way to stop the pain. He wasn't convinced yet that Joel was innocent, but what if this display of grief was just what it looked like? He stepped forward and placed a gentle hand on the young man's shoulder, not really intending more than that simple gesture of consolation. But Joel collapsed against him, and Kyle found himself holding him while he cried.

He waited it out, feeling self-conscious about how unprofessional this would look to anyone stumbling across them. But nobody came along the path at this time of night. At last, when Joel seemed to have cried himself out, Kyle said softly, "Let's get you inside before you catch pneumonia."

Joel allowed Kyle to lead him back to the hotel, one hand supporting him. When they entered the lobby, Kyle was so relieved to be back in a warm room, he relaxed and let go of Joel's shoulder. But Joel immediately drifted off and flopped down on one of the stuffed couches.

Kyle sighed but patiently took him by the elbow and helped him up again. "No dice, pal. I can't let you sleep it off in the lobby."

Unfortunately, it was pretty clear Joel was too drunk to find his way upstairs on his own, so Kyle kept a hold on his elbow and guided him to the elevator. Praying the young man wouldn't upchuck, Kyle nodded at the operator and said, "Fourth floor, please."

The old man raised his eyebrows and smiled at him as he pulled the handle.

Joel was leaning rather heavily against Kyle as they traveled up upward. He looked up into Kyle's eyes and said, "I give really good head."

"Everyone needs a hobby."

"You wanna try it?"

The elevator operator was looking away from them, too professional to acknowledge the inappropriate conversation going on beside him. Kyle was nevertheless incredibly embarrassed. He grimaced as the elevator door opened and shook his head. "Sorry. I think you should go back to your room and sleep... *alone*."

Joel looked like tears were threatening again, but Kyle led him down the hall. A few moments later, they were in front of the room Joel shared with Todd.

"You got your room key?"

Joel fumbled for the card in his blue jeans and handed it to Kyle, but before the detective could try it in the lock, the door swung open. Todd stood there in all his glory—or at least most of it—glaring at them. The only thing he had on was a pair of briefs, and Kyle had to admit Jesse's assessment was correct. Todd was gorgeous out of his clothes.

"What's going on?" he demanded.

"Your roommate is making a public nuisance of himself," Kyle said, giving Todd a wry smile. *And you're bucking for a public indecency charge*, he thought. Kyle hadn't checked the local ordinances, but a number of towns in New Hampshire considered standing in an open doorway inappropriately dressed to be a violation. But it wasn't his job to deal with local matters, and he frankly wasn't that much of a hard-ass.

Todd raised his eyebrows and looked at Joel. "He said he was gonna get a drink at the bar."

"I suspect he's had more than one."

Todd opened the door wider and gestured for Kyle to come in. The detective guided Joel into the room and sat him down upon his bed.

As soon as Kyle released his arm, Joel proceeded to strip off his sweater and shirt. He got a bit tangled in it, but Kyle didn't think it would be appropriate to help him undress. Fortunately, Todd closed the door and went to the bed to help Joel himself.

"I guess I'll leave you guys alone," Kyle said, growing uncomfortable as Joel undid the button of his jeans. "Just make sure he sleeps it off and doesn't wander—"

Too late. Joel shoved his jeans and underwear completely down past his knees, exposing himself.

"Jesus," Todd muttered, but he knelt and removed Joel's shoes.

Joel flopped backward on his bed to let Todd finish undressing him. He looked up at Kyle, pouting and spreading his legs as wide as the pants around his lower legs would allow. "Are you sure you don't wanna fuck me?"

Kyle wasn't a saint. Joel was cute, in his own way, and the detective felt his crotch stiffen at the sight of the young man lying there naked, begging to be fucked. But he had a much better offer waiting for him tomorrow night. "Sleep it off, Joel. I hope you don't get yourself into trouble someday, behaving like this."

He nodded at Todd, who rolled his eyes and actually smiled at him for once—or at least smirked. Kyle let himself out.

JESSE FELT a little guilty the next morning as he packed up his stuff to check out. The hotel had cost his father a good chunk of change, and he hadn't really accomplished much. Well, it had possibly gotten him a boyfriend. He was really excited about that, and his father probably would be too—especially since said boyfriend had a job and wasn't living in his parents' basement.

But he'd be lying if he said he hadn't wanted to solve the mystery. And leaving the hotel at this point felt like admitting defeat. He'd gotten to know the suspects a bit and learned more about them, but really, they just seemed like ordinary guys to him. He didn't like Corrie much. She was shallow and self-centered. But he actually did like Joel, his crude attempts at seduction notwithstanding, and Todd was okay—kind of a pig, but that didn't make him a killer. Jesse had had a roommate like that his freshman year. Topher was kind of a dick to girls, but he was cool to Jesse and not at all shy about nudity or sexual banter. He was the type of guy it was easy to fall for—straight, but so raunchy you never knew for certain if a few beers might tip him over the edge.

At any rate, Joel had been right. The only possible motives for killing Stuart seemed to have been preventing him from gold digging or revenge for dumping Corrie. Mr. Lassiter might be the primary suspect for the first motive, but his daughter was the primary suspect for the second. On the other hand, if Stuart had taken a payoff to leave, Mr. Lassiter had no reason to kill him. Which again pointed to Corrie, but was she really strong enough to grab a beefy guy like Stuart and shove him into a rock? On the surface, it didn't look like it to Jesse. Not unless she knew judo or something. She had the money to hire someone, of course. Or she could have manipulated someone into doing it—she certainly wasn't lacking in sex appeal. Some guy could have hiked up the mountain earlier, or taken the Cog up before the wedding party arrived, and then killed Stuart because he thought Corrie would love him for it. Or had she managed to pit brother against brother and motivate Todd to kill Stuart in a fit of jealousy? Then he would be free to marry her.

Except he really didn't show any sign of being interested in that. And if Joel was to be believed, Todd could have had Corrie any time he wanted, even after the wedding. Stuart wouldn't have prevented it.

Jesse was downstairs just before nine, but he didn't have to wait. Kyle was already in the lobby. Apparently he was no longer concerned about Jesse being seen with him, now that Jesse was leaving. Jesse checked out at the front desk, and Kyle insisted on taking the duffel bag as they walked through the enormous lobby, leaving Jesse with just his backpack. That was kind of cute but annoying. Jesse wasn't a frail young thing in need of a strong man to protect him. He'd carried a backpack up the mountain weighing twice what that duffel bag did. But he didn't want to begin the day with an argument, so he let Kyle play the macho protector.

When they'd stowed his bags in the back of the wagon, Kyle said, "Is your car parked here?"

"Yes."

"Have the valet fetch it," Kyle told him, "and then follow me. You can leave it at my hotel while we go down to Dover."

KYLE'S PARTNER was outside when they arrived at the Lodge, standing by the entrance with a small suitcase. Kyle pulled up near him in the wagon and stretched his arm out the driver's window to point at a parking space across from them. Jesse pulled his car into the space, locked it up, and went to join them.

He wasn't surprised to discover the other detective had grabbed the passenger seat. *Maybe I should have called shotgun,* he thought as he climbed into the backseat.

"Jesse," Kyle said. "This is my partner, Detective Roberts."

Jesse said, "Hey," to Roberts, but the detective barely glanced at him. He just gave a sort of noncommittal grunt.

Okay, then.

Roberts reached into his pocket and took out a folded piece of paper, which he thrust into Jesse's face. "You need to sign this."

Kyle gave his partner a sour look, but he didn't contradict him, so Jesse asked, "What is it?" The title on the top of the page said: "Scout Car Observer Program—Adult Release." "Didn't I already sign one of these?"

"This is another one," Kyle explained. "Civilians are supposed to fill one out whenever they ride along in a police car to observe our day-to-day routine. The first one you filled out only covered the night of the murder. Technically, this is all supposed to be taken care of in advance, but…."

"But that wouldn't be half-assed enough for *this* operation," Roberts muttered.

Jesse fished in his jeans pocket for the pen he always carried—he never knew when he'd be inspired to write something down—signed it, and handed it back to Detective Roberts.

Roberts grudgingly said "Thanks" and tucked it back into his jacket pocket.

They pulled out onto Route 302 and headed south toward Conway. Eventually, Jesse knew, they'd end up on Route 16, the highway he'd taken to get up into the White Mountains. That cut through Rochester on its way to Dover.

The ride was uncomfortably silent for several miles. Kyle attempted to engage his partner in conversation about their plans for the afternoon, but Roberts merely glanced at Jesse over his shoulder and refused to say much.

In Conway, Kyle pulled over at a gas station to fill the tank. He stepped out of the wagon to operate the gas pump, leaving Jesse alone with Roberts for the first time. To Jesse's surprise, the detective turned to give him an appraising look and said, "So… Kyle says you two are… you know…."

Jesse didn't know. Together? Fucking? Starting a band? He hated when people wouldn't just come right out and say what was on their minds. "Did he say we're dating?"

"Yeah."

"Then we are."

Roberts nodded, but there was something suspicious in his gaze, as though he thought Jesse was some kind of flimflam artist trying to take advantage of Kyle. Or maybe a gold digger. But if that was Jesse's game, he wouldn't have picked on a guy like Kyle. The detective wasn't starving, but he didn't exactly look wealthy.

"I'm cool with that," Roberts said. "You know, live and let live."

"Thanks," Jesse said.

If Roberts picked up on the sarcasm, he gave no sign. "You know he lost his wife a few years back, right?"

"Yes, he told me about Julie."

"He's been through a lot," Roberts went on. "And you're the first guy he's dated since she passed away—the first *anybody* he's dated."

God, kill me now. It was the "If you hurt him, I'll kill you" speech. In a way, it was kind of sweet that Roberts felt he had to look out for Kyle. But seriously? Jesse really didn't like being treated like some kind of gay Casanova preying upon poor, innocent Kyle.

"Look, Detective Roberts," Jesse said patiently, "I have no intention of hurting him. He's the one with all the second thoughts about this relationship. I *know* I like him. I know he's the most interesting man I've ever been involved with. I'm not going to break his heart. I'm just hoping he doesn't break mine."

Roberts huffed out a breath and looked out the window with a grim expression on his face. Outside, Jesse could hear Kyle putting the cap back on the gas tank. Roberts said, "Wesley."

"What?"

"If you're dating my best friend, you might as well call me Wesley. Just not when we're in front of… you know… the public."

Jesse restrained himself from laughing. "Wesley," he said.

THE REMAINDER of the trip took about an hour, during which time Jesse found Kyle and Wesley more talkative but unwilling to discuss anything about the case. The two detectives had clearly been friends for a long time, and they had a lot of favorite hangouts in Concord and Manchester. It became clear to Jesse that, if he planned on dating Kyle, he'd have to get used to Wesley being around all the time.

At one point, his cell phone buzzed, so he took it out of his pocket. It was Joel texting him: *dude! u checked out!*

Jesse thought about ignoring it. Wasn't he supposed to drop out of the whole mess, now that he'd left the hotel? But it went against his upbringing to snub people who hadn't done anything to warrant it, so he responded, *couldn't afford the hotel.*

where r u?

staying w/ teh boyfriend tonight

He thought about leaving it at that, but something prompted him to add, *back tomorrow.*

call me then?

k

Kyle would probably kill him for that, but Jesse did have to go back to the Lodge to pick up his car. Having lunch or something with Joel wouldn't compromise the investigation, would it?

THEIR ROUTE took them through Rochester just before they reached Dover, and to Jesse's surprise, Kyle veered off the main road onto a side street. After several turns, he pulled up to the curb of a narrow street bordered by rundown houses. Most had been divided into two or more apartments, judging from the doors, and the yards were overgrown and full of broken toys and cheap, rusty charcoal grills.

"Is this where Todd and Stuart's apartment is?" Jesse asked, since that was the only thing he could think of. He knew it was in Rochester somewhere, and most likely not in a good neighborhood.

But Kyle shook his head. He was looking past Wesley out the passenger-seat window. Jesse turned to see an ugly brown tenement with the hideous asphalt shingle siding once used on so many houses, now disintegrating with age. One of the street-side windows was cracked but had been patched with duct tape. "It's not where they live now—or Todd, anyway. It's where they lived for a few years as teenagers."

"Are we going inside?"

Wesley turned to give him a sour look, so he quickly amended that to, "I mean, are you two going inside?"

"Nobody's going inside," Kyle replied. "Other people live there now. None of the neighbors from that time are here either."

"Then why did we stop?"

"I just wanted to see it," Kyle said. He looked at Jesse and seemed to weigh something before he went on. "It may not have anything to do with what happened to Stuart, but when he and Todd were teens, their parents died. Pretty horribly."

Jesse glanced out the window at the tenement again, as if it might show him what Kyle meant. "How?"

Wesley redirected his sour face at Kyle.

But Kyle shook his head in response. "I don't see why not. It's ancient history, and it was in a bunch of newspapers, so it's public knowledge if he wants to spend five minutes looking it up."

And then he told Jesse the whole story.

19

KYLE HAD little reason for stopping in front of the Warrens' old apartment other than morbid curiosity. But there was another reason he'd come through Rochester. The investigation agency hired by the Lassiters—Rochester Investigations, Inc.—had their office on a side street near the main drag. When he'd contacted them yesterday about the report faxed to the department by McDonnell, he'd been told that Richard Winchester, the investigator who'd taken the Lassiter case and written up the report, was out of town until today. So he'd arranged for a meeting at 4:00 p.m.

That gave them almost four hours to kill. He'd been adamant about getting out of the hotel early because he wanted time to speak with the only civilian he'd been able to track down who might still remember what happened seven years ago—Estelle Moore, Todd and Stuart's grandmother. So he drove through the side streets until he located the agency, marked it in his memory, and then continued on toward Dover, a little over ten miles away.

Since the death of her husband three years earlier, Mrs. Moore had resided in an assisted living community on Back River Rd. It resembled a large hotel.

"You stay in the car," Wesley ordered Jesse as soon as they'd parked.

Kyle rolled his eyes at him. "It's freezing out here."

"So leave the engine running."

Kyle had no idea how long this would take. He understood Wesley not wanting Jesse to tag along, now that they were on official business, but the place had to have a lobby he could sit in. He asked Jesse, "Do you have a Kindle or something?"

"No, but I can bring my book."

"You can sit in the lobby while we do what we came for."

Wesley glared at him but didn't argue. He slammed his door a little harder than necessary when he got out of the wagon, though.

Jesse retrieved *The Maltese Falcon* from his backpack and followed them into the building. The entryway opened into a small lobby with a restaurant-style dining room off to the side. The place looked nice. If Kyle was ever forced to move into an assisted living community, he hoped to land in a place like this, rather than the hospital-style nursing home his own grandmother had passed away in.

The receptionist had the three men take a seat while she called up to Mrs. Moore's room, and a few minutes later, a surprisingly small—considering how tall her grandchildren were—elderly woman came down in the elevator. She could have been anyone's grandmother, smiling sweetly, wearing pastel pink slacks and a fluffy lilac sweater, her white hair drawn up in a tidy bun. Kyle had called yesterday and arranged to meet, so she wasn't surprised to see him. She crossed the lobby and looked at both the uniformed detectives as they stood to greet her.

"Detective Dubois?"

She didn't seem inclined to shake hands, so Kyle simply smiled and nodded. "Good afternoon, Mrs. Moore." Jesse stood to be polite, which wasn't unreasonable, but it put Kyle in the position of having to introduce him. "This is our friend, Jesse Morales. We're just giving him a ride home, so he'll be waiting out here in the lobby."

Jesse smiled at her.

"The staff says we can take over one of the lounges," Mrs. Moore said.

"Yes," the receptionist said. "Estelle, why don't you show your friends to the lounge, and I'll have Marty bring you some coffee."

"Thank you, Marie." She glanced at Jesse and then back at Kyle. "Is there some reason your friend can't join us for coffee?"

"I'll be fine waiting out here," Jesse said quickly. Wesley was glaring at him like a pit bull again.

But Mrs. Moore would have none of it. "Not at all," she said, turning toward the dining room. "This way, please."

Kyle, Wesley, and Jesse exchanged looks, and Kyle shrugged. When they followed Mrs. Moore, Jesse tagged along. It wasn't strictly illegal for him to listen in, but Wesley was right to be annoyed. The chief wouldn't be at all happy to hear they had a civilian following them around when they were on duty. Kyle hadn't thought it would be that big a deal to bring Jesse along on the trip for company, but maybe it hadn't been such a good idea after all.

They walked through the dining room and underneath a massive stairwell that led up to the second floor, then turned toward a corner nook where some couches and chairs were set up around a coffee table. Technically, it wasn't a separate room, but it was far enough removed to provide some privacy.

Mrs. Moore took one of the chairs and Wesley sat on one of the couches, with Kyle taking the one opposite. Jesse sat beside him. Kyle was intensely aware of the fact that he was conducting official business with someone he was dating sitting by his side. It was unsettling, to say the least. Julie had certainly never come along on investigations. The thought would never have crossed his mind, nor hers. He didn't think Jesse would do or say anything to put him on the spot, but it was still nerve-racking.

"Now, you said on the phone you had some questions about what happened to my daughter and son-in-law seven years ago?"

"That's right, ma'am."

She brushed her lap with her hand and crinkled her forehead. "I can't imagine why anyone would want to go digging around in all that again. It was… horrible."

"Yes, it was." Kyle shifted uncomfortably and said, "I'm afraid I have some very bad news. One of your grandchildren—Stuart—was killed this week, hiking on Mount Washington."

"Oh." The old woman blinked and seemed to be staring hard at the cloth runner on the coffee table between them with its print of a New England winter scene. "The poor boy."

She was silent for a long time, and Kyle gave her a moment to digest the news. A young man arrived, carrying a tray with a coffee carafe, four cups and saucers, and cream and sugar. He set it down and murmured, "There you go, Estelle. Do you need anything else?"

"No, Marty. Thank you."

The man left, and Mrs. Moore busied herself pouring coffee for the four of them. She set the carafe down and said, "Please help yourselves to cream and sugar."

"Thank you," Kyle said.

"I'm… sorry to hear about Stuart," she said, lifting her cup close to her face. "But after seven years without a word from him or Todd… well, I'm afraid I can't say we were particularly close. It saddens me, of course, but… they never even responded when I sent them the news that Howard—their grandfather—had passed away."

"I understand. But we're trying to piece together exactly what happened when Stuart was killed, and I was hoping you might be able to help us."

"I don't see how, but I'll be happy to answer any questions I can."

Kyle withdrew his notebook from his jacket pocket and flipped it to a blank page. "I've read the report from the Rochester Police Department, but I'd like it if you could tell me what you know about that night, and how the boys came to live with you and your husband."

She pursed her lips as if she'd just tasted something unpleasant. "Joe Warren, my son-in-law, was *not* a good man. He was rather horrible, in fact. Mean-spirited and bitter, even as a young man. We warned Michelle to stay away from him, but… well, I'm afraid she was a bit self-centered. We spoiled her."

"The report indicated that the boys were physically abused."

Mrs. Moore took a sip of her coffee, and Kyle noticed her hand was trembling. She lowered the cup to her lap. "We didn't know. Not at first. We saw them so rarely—Christmas… sometimes Thanksgiving. When the state took the boys away… we were just as shocked as anybody else would have been. Please believe me."

She gave Kyle a pleading look. He wasn't sure if he did believe her. It was easy for people to turn a blind eye, especially when it concerned family. Had she and her husband ever noticed bruises on the boys and dismissed them as teenage roughhousing? At this point, she might not even know—not anymore. It was too long ago, and it was easy to edit the past, make it more palatable to remember.

But he nodded to appease her, and she continued, "I would be lying if I said Michelle was a better parent than Joe. As far as I know, she never struck them, but...." She exhaled sharply and shook her head. "She was mean to them. Especially to Stuart. I don't know why, but she just... she never seemed to lose a chance to belittle him. I tried talking to her about it, but she told me he was a troublemaker, and she knew what she was doing...."

"*Was* he a troublemaker, as far as you could see?" Kyle asked.

She sighed and shrugged. "He was a teenage boy. They both were. And they'd been caught shoplifting and vandalizing property over the years." She made a sour face. "It's not as if they had decent role models in their lives."

The fact that Joe Warren had been a cop really rankled Kyle. He knew police officers were just as vulnerable to problems in their personal lives as anyone else—alcoholism, divorce, and suicide were big problems in the profession—but beating up children was despicable, no matter how you sliced it. And for an officer of the law, sworn to protect the public, to go after his own kids....

"Mrs. Moore," Kyle said, flipping back a page in his notebooks to consult what he'd jotted down back at the hotel, "the police report said your daughter had filed for divorce."

"Finally!" the old woman exclaimed. "If only she'd done it sooner! I spoke to her about it just a few months before... it happened. She called me after one of their almost constant fights, determined to come stay with us, because she said she'd finally had enough. Joe was drinking again, just as bad as before, and they were fighting so much he was sleeping on the couch."

"Did she come to see you?"

Mrs. Moore frowned. "No, of course not. I told her she'd be welcome—and she could bring the boys—but I never really expected her to come. This wasn't the first time she'd threatened to leave him, and I didn't expect it to be the last time."

"The report says she began going out to bars at night, sleeping with other men."

"I wouldn't know anything about that," Mrs. Moore said curtly. She set her unfinished coffee down on its saucer on the table. "I suppose it wasn't out of character. She wasn't afraid of him, despite his temper. I think she enjoyed egging him on."

Charming. Like poking at a bear with a stick and then being surprised when it ripped your head off. "Did you think Joe was capable of murder?"

"I suppose I never thought he'd go that far," she replied, her shoulders slumping a bit. "Michelle thought she could handle him, and I wanted to believe she was right."

Kyle decided to fast-forward. She hadn't been present during the murder/suicide, and he already had the police report. "So the boys came to live with you and your husband."

"Yes."

"And how was that?"

She looked at him curiously. "What do you mean?"

"I mean, did you and your husband get along with the boys?"

"Oh. No, not really." She raised her eyebrows. "Todd was… well, very angry. Not that we blamed him. But he didn't want to listen to anything we told him by that point. And he was older. It was too late for us to undo the damage his father—and I suppose Michelle too—had done."

"What about Stuart?"

An odd expression came over the old woman's face, as if they'd somehow stumbled onto something that disturbed her to talk about—and that after discussing her own daughter's murder. "Stuart was… strange."

"Strange?"

"He didn't… seem to care… about *anything*. He was polite and not particularly disobedient—except when Todd talked him into things. At times, he could even be charming. Much more so than his brother. But… well, Todd cried at the funeral, and when we got home, he punched a hole in the wall of his room." Mrs. Moore shook her head. "We didn't *like* that, of course, but at least it was a normal human reaction."

"How did Stuart react?"

"He didn't! He didn't seem upset at all. He acted *bored* at the funeral, and when we came home, he just wanted to watch television as if nothing had happened."

20

JESSE FOUND what Mrs. Moore said about the Warrens to be interesting, but he wasn't sure what it accomplished as far as the murder investigation was concerned. This opinion seemed to be confirmed when he was back in the wagon with Kyle and Wesley, heading to Rochester.

Wesley seemed irritable. He sat in the passenger seat with his arms folded across his chest and muttered, "Well, *that* was useful."

Kyle frowned but remained silent.

Jesse thought it was interesting that Stuart's grandparents had apparently been so disturbed by his lack of feeling about his parents' death—the way Mrs. Moore had described it, they'd regarded him as some sort of sociopath—that they didn't protest when Todd wanted Stuart to come live with him, even though he was still well under eighteen. Interesting, but not illuminating. If Todd had been the one murdered on top of the mountain, Stuart's odd behavior at the time of his parents' death might indicate he was cold-blooded enough to murder his brother. But since he was the one killed, any supposed sociopathy on his part seemed irrelevant.

Kyle stopped at a McDonald's drive-through so they could all grab something to eat. Then he drove back to Rochester and parked the wagon on the street in front of the detective agency. Once again, Kyle defied Wesley by telling Jesse he could come inside. "Just try to stay in the background."

"Jesus Christ!" Wesley snapped. "Why don't you just give him a plastic junior detective badge? Then maybe you can get him his own desk back at the station!"

"I tried to stay in the background with Mrs. Moore," Jesse said defensively. "It wasn't my fault she invited me in."

"You were fine," Kyle said.

But Wesley wasn't mollified. "This is totally unprofessional and you fucking know it." When Kyle refused to answer, he sighed and said, "Fine. But not one goddamned word about Sparky the Wonder Boy goes on the reports, or I'll wring your neck."

Sparky? Jesse thought, trying not to smile. Well, at least it wasn't "Jessica."

"Of course not," Kyle said. "I'm not a fucking idiot."

"You *are* a fucking idiot, and you're thinking with your dick!" Wesley glanced at Jesse in the backseat. "No offense."

"None taken."

Kyle looked as if he might say something, but Wesley opened his door and hopped out, slamming it behind him. Kyle growled and got out of the wagon. Since nobody had expressly ordered him to stay behind, Jesse followed them.

The office of Rochester Investigators, Inc. was small, with just three desks, a couple of chairs for clients, and a small nook containing a microwave, a toaster, and a coffeemaker. There were two men present who introduced themselves as PI Taylor and PI Winchester. Winchester was apparently the one they'd come to see, because as soon as they were introduced, Taylor excused himself and went out.

"Have a seat," Winchester said, taking up a position behind one of the desks. He glanced at Jesse and asked Kyle, "Who's the kid?"

Kyle dragged one of the two free chairs up in front of the desk and nodded at Wesley to do the same. Jesse sat nearby in a chair by the water cooler. "He's a friend—Jesse Morales. I hope you don't mind me bringing him, but he writes detective novels, and he's never met a PI before."

"Is that so?" Winchester said, looking delighted. "Well, I'll be happy to answer any questions you have."

Jesse smiled and said, "Thanks," though he knew Kyle and Wesley wouldn't be too happy with him derailing the conversation.

Fortunately, Kyle took control and prompted the PI to talk about a report he'd brought with him. Jesse hadn't been told what it was about, but he soon gathered that it was information the Lassiters had paid the agency to collect about the Warrens, presumably to reassure themselves their daughter wasn't marrying a psychopath. Unfortunately, the report hadn't really assuaged their fears. But there was little Kyle and Winchester talked about that Jesse hadn't known already. What he hadn't gleaned from his conversations with Joel and Todd, he had certainly gotten from Kyle's interview with Mrs. Moore.

Winchester had been the PI on the case, and Kyle had apparently hoped he'd have more detail than was in the report. But the investigator disappointed him. "I'm sorry," he said, spreading his hands. "That's all I got. The kids aren't exactly angels. I doubt I'd want *my* daughter to marry one of them. But it's all petty shit. Nothing big."

Kyle tapped his pen against his notepad a few times and then folded the pad shut. "I'm not sure what I was hoping for. But thanks for your time."

"No problem." Winchester glanced at Jesse and then back at the two detectives, his mouth open as if he wanted to say more. Then he leaned forward in his chair and lowered his voice. "This probably isn't any use to you, if you're investigating the Warrens, but I discovered one thing that Mr. Lassiter told me to strike from the report. He was pretty pissed off that I'd uncovered it."

That seemed to catch Kyle's attention. He hesitated in the act of putting his notepad back into his jacket pocket. "Yeah? What was that?"

Winchester grinned at him. "Say you'll get a warrant if I don't spill."

"I'll get a warrant if you don't spill," Kyle deadpanned.

Winchester held up his hands in mock surrender. "Well, I guess I gotta, then." He put his hands down on the desk again. "Their boy, Ryan. He spent a year at Silver Hill Hospital down in Connecticut."

"A hospital?" Wesley asked.

"A *psychiatric* hospital," Winchester said, almost gleefully.

Kyle looked thoughtful. "What was he being treated for?"

"Have you seen his younger sister? Corrie?"

"Yeah…," Kyle said hesitantly.

"She's a knockout, isn't she?"

"She's a good-looking girl."

"Well," Winchester said, "It turns out Ryan thinks she's pretty good-looking too."

Jesse couldn't stop his eyes going wide at that, and Winchester turned to him, laughing. "Oh yeah." He looked back at Kyle. "The pervert's been hitting on her for years. She's been able to brush him off because he wasn't being too overt—creepy comments, 'accidentally' leaving his bedroom door open when he's undressing, inappropriate touches. But about a year ago, he tried to force himself on her. So they arranged to send him away for a while, and nobody ever talks about it. He just got out of an institution down in Florida."

"Isn't that nice?" Wesley commented grimly.

"Isn't it, though? Like I said, it probably doesn't help you any, but...."

"No," Kyle said, "that's... that's actually useful. How do you think Ryan felt about Corrie marrying Stuart?"

Winchester snorted. "Are you kidding? It was hearing about her engagement that pushed him over the edge."

21

AFTER THEY left Winchester, Kyle drove to the state police station in Concord so he and Wesley could attend to some things—including dropping off the paperwork for Jesse's ride-along. He allowed Jesse to follow them inside and got him a visitor ID but kept a close watch on him the entire time. Not that Kyle really expected Jesse to wander off and get into trouble, but he didn't need the shit it would bring down if someone caught Jesse in a hallway or a room by himself. Of course, Wesley watched him like a hawk too. Jesse couldn't have slipped off by himself, even if he'd wanted to.

For his part, Jesse seemed to be fine tagging along after Kyle and sitting quietly nearby while Kyle took care of some stuff on the computer. He did comment, briefly, "God, I wish I could take some pictures of this place for future reference!" That got him a glare from Wesley, though, so he quickly added, "Not that I would do that."

Afterward, the three of them went to dinner at a pub downtown called the Barley House. Then Kyle dropped Wesley off at his apartment and drove to the quiet neighborhood at the outer limit of the city where he lived.

His house was a small ranch with light green siding and dark green shutters. It was cute and pleasant, situated on a postage-sized patch of lawn in a suburban neighborhood. It even had a picket fence in front. It had seemed small when he and Julie first bought it, but they'd made it their own. Now he thought of it as home and couldn't imagine living anywhere else.

Jesse looked at the house with interest as Kyle activated the garage door and pulled into its illuminated interior. Kyle used the remote to close the garage door behind them, shut down the engine, and opened his door.

"Do you just want to go directly to bed?" he asked, noticing the way Jesse's eyelids were drooping. "To sleep, I mean?"

Jesse stretched. "What time is it?"

"About nine o'clock."

"Oh Jesus! I never go to bed this early. Just get me a cup of coffee and I'll be fine."

Kyle smiled and leaned forward to give him a quick kiss. "Coffee it is. As soon as we get your stuff inside."

They unloaded Jesse's bags from the back of the wagon, and Jesse carried them while Kyle unlocked the door leading into the house.

When Kyle flicked the kitchen lights on, Jesse exclaimed in delight, "It's clean!"

It was. Not spotless—there were some coffee cups in the sink and an open newspaper on the table next to a plate with crumbs on it. But the stovetop was wiped clean and the counters were clean and uncluttered.

Kyle raised an eyebrow at him. "What did you expect?"

"A pit," Jesse replied. "Maybe I've just been in college too long, but every time a guy takes me home, his place is nasty. One guy even used his kitchen sink as a urinal."

Kyle shuddered. "I'd kill myself if I had to live someplace that disgusting. Speaking of which, would you mind taking off your shoes?"

"Oh, sure." Jesse slipped his shoes off as Kyle did the same.

"Sorry. It was Julie's thing. I got into the habit."

"It's fine."

"I don't know if you think sharing slippers is gross, but you'd be welcome to borrow a pair of mine, if you want."

"Sure."

Kyle opened a closet door and retrieved two pairs of leather moccasins. He handed one to Jesse and slipped into the others himself. Then he directed Jesse to a seat at the table while he set up the coffeemaker.

"We can go into the living room," Kyle suggested while the coffee was brewing.

The living room was small and tidy, like the kitchen. It was beige carpeted and held a brown stuffed sofa and chairs, bookcases full of paperbacks, and DVD racks full of the sappy movies Kyle and Julie had loved. Not much had changed in the room since Julie's death except for the large HD television Kyle had given himself last Christmas.

Kyle walked across the room to snatch a picture frame from a small table. He opened a drawer in the table and was about to put the picture in it when Jesse stopped him. "Is that her?"

Kyle hesitated, the picture still in his hands. "Yeah," he said. He didn't know if having the picture out when his new boyfriend visited for the first time was tacky or not. "I'm sorry. I didn't know I'd be bringing… someone over, the last time I was here."

"Can I see?"

Kyle nodded, and Jesse came over. "She's lovely," Jesse said, smiling at him.

She had been. Not stunningly beautiful, perhaps, but her face had been sweet and charming, with short, light brown hair and emerald green eyes. The first time Kyle had looked at her, sitting on the lawn in front of their dorm, he'd thought she looked like someone who would be fun to know. And he'd been right.

"You really don't have to hide the picture," Jesse said.

Kyle gave him a shy smile and then slid the picture into the drawer and closed it. "Thanks. But I think I need to put it away. At least for now."

He went back into the kitchen for a few minutes while Jesse sat down on the couch. Then he returned with two mugs of coffee and sat down beside the young man. Jesse took his cup and sipped it, leaning forward to look at the DVD rack.

"You see anything you wanna watch?" Kyle asked.

"Not tonight," Jesse replied. "I was just curious what you liked. Do you really watch all these romantic comedies?"

Kyle thought about denying it. If it had been Wesley asking the question, he might have punted, claimed all the movies were Julie's, and he just hadn't felt like getting rid of them. But Jesse didn't make him feel like he had to hide. "I guess so. They cheer me up."

"And romance novels!" Jesse exclaimed as he glanced up at the bookshelves.

Unfortunately, Kyle found that more embarrassing than his taste in movies. "That's… um… not something I'd like to get around."

Jesse laughed. "You don't want Wesley finding out, you mean."

"No. I'd never live it down."

"I won't tell him," Jesse said, leaning over to kiss Kyle on the mouth.

His lips were soft and warm and tasted of coffee. He broke the kiss just long enough to take another swig of his coffee and set the mug on the coffee table. Then he pulled Kyle in for another. This one was longer and more passionate, and as their bodies shifted on the couch, finding a way to fit together, Kyle thought he felt a distinct hardening in the crotch that pressed into him.

He came up for air and gasped, "We don't have to do this tonight if you're tired."

"Are you kidding me? I've been waiting three days for this."

"Do you die if you go more than three days without sex?"

"I might." With that, Jesse pulled him in for another long kiss.

Eventually, the knowledge that his bed would be a much more comfortable place to do this filtered through to Kyle's brain at about the point he was considering ripping Jesse's T-shirt off. He didn't bother to say anything. He simply stood, took Jesse by the hand, and led him down the short hallway to the bedroom.

But when Jesse moved to take off his shirt, Kyle stopped him. "Please, let me do it. I know this is going to sound a little weird, but… I've only ever slept with women. Your body is completely uncharted territory for me."

"You've got your own," Jesse teased.

"I'm bored with mine. I want to explore yours—every bit of it. And I want to take my time."

"I'm all yours."

God, that sounded good.

They stood together while Kyle caressed and kissed Jesse's face, reveling in the softness of his lips that wasn't all that different from a woman's, and in the coarseness of the stubble on his cheeks, so distinctly male. He slid his hands up along the taut muscles of Jesse's abdomen underneath his sweater and T-shirt and then pushed up to slide them both off in one smooth motion. He tossed them onto the chair and went back to caressing Jesse's chest and stomach. His skin was amazingly smooth, yet the muscles underneath were firm and hard. Not bulky—Jesse was no bodybuilder. But he was in good shape, and Kyle found that incredibly sexy.

He wrapped his arms around Jesse's back and pulled him close so he could lick a nipple. He heard Jesse draw in a hiss of breath as the nipple hardened. Yes, a woman's nipple did that too, but not, in Kyle's experience, so delicately. He tasted the other to make sure it worked the same way. It did. And it elicited a moan of arousal from Jesse, who ran a hand through Kyle's hair.

The hard bulge at Jesse's crotch called out to Kyle, and he longed to caress it, peel away the layers of jeans and underwear, but he refrained. That was for later. He knelt before Jesse as if he were worshiping him— which he practically was—and planted a soft kiss on the faint trail of black hair leading from Jesse's navel down into the waistband of his jeans. Then he slid his hands down the curves of Jesse's lower back and ass, lingering only a moment before continuing down the back of his legs.

"Sit down now," he said gently.

Jesse sat down on the edge of the bed, and Kyle removed his sneakers and socks. Feet didn't do much for him, but he stroked Jesse's gently and kissed the top of each one. He lowered them to the carpet and lifted his head until his face was once again at the level of Jesse's crotch.

"Lie back."

Jesse complied. Kyle undid the button on his fly then, and slowly drew down the zipper. He slipped his hand inside to cup the hard shaft that strained against Jesse's white briefs. He gave it a squeeze, causing Jesse to moan again and writhe deliciously on the bed. Kyle reluctantly pulled his hand away, just long enough to reach down and grasp the jeans at Jesse's ankles and drag the pants off his body.

He tossed those aside and felt his way back up Jesse's legs. They were *definitely* not female—the young man's legs and arms were muscular and rather hairy, even though his chest was mostly smooth. And then Kyle was confronted with Jesse's crotch. His cock and balls were still concealed from Kyle's view by a layer of white cotton, but very little was actually hidden. Kyle could see the contour of Jesse's hard cock, its size and bulk and even the fact that he was circumcised. Kyle could smell the musky scent of Jesse's sweat and feel the heat radiating from between his legs as he moved his face nearer.

He brushed his lips against the tip of Jesse's cock through the cotton, and Jesse grunted, grabbing the bedspread in his fists on either side of his body. Kyle could feel a damp spot at the slit, and for the first time in his life, he tasted another man's precome on his lips. The flavor was almost sweet, and it drove him over the edge. He grabbed the band of Jesse's underwear with both hands and yanked them down. Jesse's cock bounced up from its confinement and slid along Kyle's cheek, painting a streak of precome across it.

Kyle was tired of fucking around. He needed that cock in his mouth. Jesse gasped when he engulfed the head of it between his lips and then parted his teeth to allow several inches of it to slide along his tongue. He'd been thinking about this moment all day long—what it would feel like to take Jesse into his mouth. At this moment, there was no denying he was having sex with a man. He was taking a man inside himself, tasting the salt and musk of Jesse's sweat, feeling the solid mass of his cock sliding into him. He could feel the wiry black hairs around the base of it tickling his nose and smell its scent. It wasn't an enormous cock, though it wasn't small either. It seemed about right for Jesse's body. But it felt huge in Kyle's mouth.

He wanted to take it all in, but his gag reflex gave him a little trouble, so he sucked and licked, sliding it farther along his tongue, then backing off a bit until Jesse said, "No, don't make me come yet."

Part of Kyle wanted that to happen. He wanted to feel Jesse's cock squirt into his mouth and taste another man's come for the first time. But he relented and slid the cock out of his mouth.

"Do you mind if I undress myself?" he asked Jesse, who lay spread out before him.

"No! Do it before I go out of my fucking mind!"

Kyle chuckled and stripped quickly, hoping Jesse wouldn't be disappointed by what he saw. From the way Jesse stared at him, panting, his hard cock twitching, that didn't seem to be a problem. When he freed his own cock, his boxer briefs were practically saturated in the front with precome.

"Do you want to fuck me?" Jesse asked.

Kyle felt a visceral tug in his gut at the words. Hell yes, he wanted to fuck him. "You've done it before?"

"Sure. I love it."

"Do you have protection?" Kyle was ashamed to realize he'd totally forgotten to pick up condoms and lube. He was green, but he should have had that much sense.

Fortunately, Jesse had sense enough for both of them. He rolled over and squirmed across the bed, giving Kyle a magnificent view of his smooth, pale ass. He reached down into his backpack on the other side of the bed and produced a box of condoms and a small tube of KY.

"Do you want to prep me," Jesse asked, "or does the idea of sticking your fingers into a guy's butt gross you out?"

"I want to do it."

So he did, while Jesse lay on his back and squirmed with pleasure, stroking Kyle's throbbing, sheathed hard-on with a lubricated hand. He knew the routine from the gay romance novels he'd read—one finger, two fingers, three fingers, all very slowly and patiently. It was hard to be patient, but it clearly felt good to Jesse, and that was an enormous turn-on.

At last, Jesse said, "Okay, let's go."

He lifted his legs up in the air and guided Kyle to kneel on the mattress between them. Even after all the prep, Kyle still found it a little hard to penetrate Jesse's sphincter, and Jesse made some faces that were hard to read—was he in ecstasy or in pain? Fortunately, Jesse kept muttering encouragement, so Kyle pushed a little harder. When Jesse's body opened to receive him, he felt a rush of warm softness engulfing his shaft, literally sucking him inside until his pubic hair was pressed up against Jesse's ass.

"Oh fuck!" he gasped. "That feels amazing." He looked between Jesse's legs to find him smiling sleepily back at him. "Are you good?"

"I'm beyond good. See if you can lean forward without slipping out."

Kyle did as he was instructed, resting the bulk of his body against the underside of Jesse's legs. Jesse's hips rotated with the motion to keep

Kyle's dick embedded inside him. The maneuver seemed to bend him nearly in half, but he didn't appear to be in pain.

"Fuck me," Jesse said softly.

Kyle wanted to kiss while they fucked, but that wasn't really easy to do in this position. He managed to get a few kisses in with Jesse lifting his head to meet him halfway, but for the most part, they just looked into each other's eyes as Kyle pumped in and out of Jesse's ass. He popped out a couple times, in the beginning, until he figured out exactly how far he could withdraw before Jesse's body pushed him out, but eventually he found a motion that felt natural and easy. As the pressure built up in his loins, he felt something he hadn't expected to ever feel again—not since Julie's death. It was a sense of joining, as if he could feel Jesse's spirit merging with his through the linking of their physical bodies, until his entire abdomen and chest seemed to have a warmth pooling in it and swirling around.

It's too soon for that, he thought. *We barely know each other*. The attraction between them was incredibly strong. He couldn't deny that. But that was just sexual. Or mostly sexual, anyway. Perhaps there was something more. The only thing he was certain of was that it felt amazing. He rode the feeling until he exploded deep inside Jesse, his right hand stroking Jesse until the young man erupted between them.

They stayed connected for a long time after their orgasms, looking into each other's eyes, neither saying a word.

22

JESSE HADN'T wanted that moment to ever end with Kyle deep inside him, looking down at him as if he were seeing into his soul. The prelude to actually having sex—he wasn't sure if it could properly be called "foreplay," all the caressing and licking and nuzzling as Kyle explored his body—had been a little frustrating, though still really hot. And Kyle had needed some coaching on the sex part, which was amusing, considering how much older he was. Obviously, anal hadn't been part of his sexual repertoire until now. But once he'd gotten in there….

Jesus. That was the best sex Jesse had ever had in his life. Not because Kyle had instantly turned into a porn star—though he was fucking awesome—but because it was the first time Jesse had ever felt so deeply connected to another man during it. Certainly, he'd enjoyed it with other men, but he'd never felt that powerful tug in the depths of his chest, the yearning to somehow bring their bodies as close as possible, to merge them together.

When Kyle finally softened and pulled out, Jesse felt the loss of connection like a wound. He made a low, guttural noise in protest, but Kyle gently pulled his legs down out of the way so he could lay his body full-length upon Jesse's. His skin was hot and damp with sweat, but it felt comforting and embracing to Jesse as Kyle covered him and kissed him tenderly.

"That was amazing," Kyle whispered. "If I sucked, just wait until morning to tell me. That's all I ask. I want to bask in it for tonight."

Jesse giggled. "Stop that. You didn't suck. Well, you *sucked* me, of course—"

"I think I need to work on that one."

"You'll have plenty of time to practice," Jesse told him, "because I loved every minute of it, and I want you to do it again. Many, many times."

"It's almost three o'clock in the morning."

"It doesn't have to be tonight."

Kyle smiled at him and kissed him on the tip of the nose. "You're sure, then? That you want more of this?"

"Absolutely," Jesse said, serious now. He looked into Kyle's eyes, not sure what to say that wouldn't sound needy or pathetic.

Kyle seemed to understand. "It's really late, kid, and we're both tired. Let's go to sleep, and tomorrow we can talk about where we want this to go."

Jesse reached up with his right hand to caress the side of Kyle's cheek, feeling the rough razor stubble that had replaced the clean-shaven look he'd had that morning. "Okay."

IN THE morning, Jesse woke to find himself cocooned in Kyle's arms, his back nestled against the detective's chest and stomach, and his ass firmly planted in Kyle's lap. Kyle's morning erection had managed to wedge itself between Jesse's butt cheeks. He felt safe and protected, and he liked that feeling. He hoped there would be a lot more of it in his future.

He lay there as long as he could before he finally decided wetting the bed wouldn't be a great way to start the morning. So he extricated himself from Kyle's embrace and ran down the hall to the bathroom. When he returned, Kyle was awake, peering up at him through sleep-heavy lids.

"You kept me up too late," he grumbled.

"You got laid," Jesse reminded him.

Kyle smiled and stretched, looking Jesse's naked body up and down lecherously. "Oh yeah. That part was nice."

Jesse climbed back onto the bed and slipped under the covers. Kyle immediately pulled him into a warm embrace. The unmistakable heat and firmness of a naked man's body pressed up against his own instantly made Jesse hard, and they ended up nuzzling wordlessly for several minutes while they caressed each other to climax.

"Unfortunately," Kyle said as grabbed his underwear off the floor and wiped come off his stomach with it, "I don't really have the option to spend the day in bed, doing nothing but making love to the most beautiful man I've ever laid eyes on."

Jesse felt his face flush at the compliment. "Why not? Can't you call in sick?"

"I have a murder investigation," Kyle replied. "And I can't keep everyone sequestered at the hotel indefinitely. They're all slated to check out on Sunday, and I can't keep them there without a reason."

"One of them killed Stuart. Isn't that a reason?"

Kyle shook his head. "I have to have something more definite than that if I want to prevent them from returning home. They agreed to finish their stay, but I certainly can't order them to pay these outrageous hotel fees a day longer than they're willing to."

He was lying on his back, and Jesse sat up on his haunches beside him, unintentionally spreading himself wide. Kyle lazily reached out his right hand and slid it underneath Jesse's ball sac, tickling it with the hair on his forearm. A moment later, Jesse felt a thrill go through him as Kyle's finger lightly prodded his entrance.

"Do you think it's disgusting for a guy to lick another guy's asshole?" Kyle asked.

Jesse laughed. "God no! I love it when guys do that to me. Or were you asking me to do it to you?"

"Me to you," Kyle said, giving him a wry smile. "Though I'm willing to try it the other way too." He glanced at the clock on the night table and sighed. "Unfortunately, it'll have to wait 'til later. We need to get breakfast and head over to Wesley's."

ALTHOUGH JESSE would have been fine with some cereal and a cup of coffee—he'd just spent the last four years in college, after all—Kyle insisted upon making pancakes and bacon. He was a surprisingly good cook. The pancakes were light and fluffy and perfectly browned, the bacon was crispy without being burnt, and he knew how to make a good cup of coffee.

While they ate, Jesse tentatively asked, "So what bearing does it have on Stuart's murder—the death of his parents?"

He half-expected Kyle to slap him down for prying into the investigation again, but Kyle looked at him thoughtfully while chewing a mouthful of pancake. Then he swallowed and said, "It could be a coincidence. Sometimes people happen to lead lives filled with tragedy, just one horrible thing after another. And there's no reason for it. They're just unlucky."

"You don't think seeing his parents die that way made Todd into a dangerous psychopath, do you?"

Kyle shook his head. "That's pop psychology. Sure, I'd expect both him and Stuart to have some issues after something like that. But it's a pretty big leap to go from witnessing your parents' death to killing people yourself. Granted, they had a rough upbringing in general—the parents were abusive. But I can't count how many survivors of childhood abuse I know who *aren't* murderers."

"What about creepy Ryan?"

Kyle stood and walked to the stove, then retrieved a plate of pancakes from the oven, where he'd been keeping them warm. "What about him?"

"Apart from the whole crushing on his sister thing—which is nasty—does he have a motive to kill Stuart?"

"Jealousy?"

"I suppose that depends on whether Stuart took the money or not. If he rejected it, Ryan might have been motivated to kill him. But I'm thinking he took the money, and Ryan knew that."

Kyle came back to the table and used a spatula to drop three more pancakes onto Jesse's plate, saving the remaining two for his own plate. "What makes you think that?"

Jesse wasn't sure if he could eat three more pancakes, but he didn't want to insult Kyle by refusing them, so he slathered them with maple syrup. "There was no reason for him to be up on the summit—and lie about it to you—unless he was up to something."

"Like murder?" Kyle asked, giving him a wry smile. He set the empty plate down on the stovetop, then returned to the table and sat down.

Jesse was mildly irritated at being teased again, but he let it slide. "Probably not. I think Ryan was the delivery boy. There was no other reason for him to be at the summit. So if anybody knew whether Stuart took the money or not, it would be him."

Kyle took a bite of pancake and sat there for a long time, chewing. When Jesse tried to look him in the eye, Kyle looked down at his plate and poured a little more syrup on the pancake he was eating.

"You found the money on Stuart's body, didn't you," Jesse said coolly.

"Why would you think that?"

"Because you just put way too much syrup on your pancakes," Jesse replied, "and you won't look at me. You're hiding something."

Kyle growled and pushed his plate away. "Jesus. Will you stop? I can't discuss the case with you."

"If you hadn't found the money, you'd have no way of knowing whether Stuart refused it, or if he took it and the killer took it off his body."

"Fine!" Kyle snapped. "Yes, we found the money on him. But you keep that to yourself. Understand? I know you were texting somebody yesterday while we were on the road—probably Joel or Todd."

"Joel."

"Did you already talk to him about this?"

"No, of course not."

Kyle frowned and leaned forward, dropping his fork on his plate. "Are you planning on seeing him when we get back to the hotel?"

"He wants me to call him," Jesse admitted. "But it's not like I'm *interested* in him, if that's what you're worried about."

"That's not what I'm worried about, and you know it. Goddammit, Jesse! One of those people at the hotel is a murderer. Even if it's not Joel, you're putting yourself in danger if you keep going back there. Don't you get that?"

He wasn't having trouble looking Jesse in the eye now, and it was taking all Jesse's willpower to meet his gaze without flinching. "Are you forbidding me to talk to him?"

Jesse wasn't even sure why he was so determined to stay in touch with Joel. Maybe it was just stubbornness, digging in his heels because he knew Kyle *wanted* to order him to stop. They both knew he couldn't really do that, but Jesse could tell Kyle was beginning to get angry about it. Was it worth having a confrontation over?

Fortunately, the conversation was interrupted by Kyle's cellphone. He growled and left the table to fetch the phone from his jacket pocket. "Hey, Wes."

KYLE HAD already learned it was pointless to tell Jesse to stay out of the investigation. It wasn't exactly that Jesse had a death wish, but he didn't seem to have much comprehension of the danger involved. Despite Jesse's reassurances on the matter, Kyle felt certain this was one area in which age *did* make a difference. Certainly experience did. Kyle had dealt with enough violent people in his eight years on the force to know that someone who'd killed once wouldn't find it hard to kill again.

But he didn't bother to start the argument up again after he'd spoken with Wesley. Jesse wouldn't listen. The best Kyle could do was try to keep an eye on him.

He went into the bathroom to shower while Jesse finished his pancakes, but he hadn't been under the spray long before he heard the bathroom door open.

"It's Jesse. Please don't panic and kill me with your bare hands."

Kyle laughed. "I'll try not to."

A moment later, the rippled-glass door slid open and Jesse stepped into the tub, completely naked and breathtakingly beautiful. Kyle felt himself hardening almost instantly. "Mmm," he murmured appreciatively, stepping forward and placing soapy hands on Jesse's hips, "I can think of other things I'd like to do with my bare hands."

"You wanna frisk me?"

Kyle smirked at him and reached for the bar of soap. Without saying a word, he worked up a lather, set the bar aside, and then began to slide his hands along Jesse's torso. Jesse's eyes fluttered closed, and he moaned as Kyle explored every inch of his smooth skin once more, and his dick hardened even before Kyle reached down to stroke it.

I'll never get tired of this, Kyle thought.

He brought Jesse to climax and then allowed Jesse to do the same to him. Unfortunately they didn't have time for much else, but it was definitely the most fun Kyle had had in a shower in a very long time.

THEY PICKED up Wesley about an hour later. He saw Jesse sitting in the back seat again, and his eyes narrowed in irritation. "You're coming back with us, I see."

"I have to," Jesse said. "My car is in the Lodge parking lot."

"Don't be a dick, Wesley," Kyle muttered.

Wesley raised his hand to ward them off. "I'm just wondering where he's gonna sleep tonight, is all."

Kyle had been thinking about that. "He can get a room in the Lodge. I'll pay for it, if it's just a night or two."

"You don't have to do that," Jesse insisted. "I can pay for it myself."

Kyle wasn't sure how much money Jesse had, though he was inclined to doubt he had much. Should he insist on paying? Or would that just insult him?

Wesley sighed and shook his head. "Look, I've been thinking about it, and… Jesse can stay in our room if he wants to. I mean, as long as you guys don't start boning when I'm there or anything."

Kyle raised his eyebrows, uncertain if this concession would be all that appealing to Jesse, but Jesse just smiled and said, "It'll be hard to restrain myself, but I think I can manage."

"And no running around naked either," Wesley warned.

"Yes, sir."

Kyle kept his eye on the road as they pulled out of Concord and restrained himself from saying anything. He supposed it would be worth it to save a few hundred dollars.

Maybe.

THE REMAINDER of the trip was uneventful. Wesley refused to discuss any details of the case in front of Jesse—which was correct, of course. Kyle was beginning to have a hard time remembering not to do that, so it was probably good having Wesley along to shut him up. But there wasn't much the three of them really had in common, so conversation tended to fall flat except when they talked about stopping for lunch. But even that fizzled when they decided it wasn't worth taking the time to stop, since they'd be back in Bretton Woods by one o'clock and could hit Fabyan's then.

At some point Jesse's cell phone buzzed, and he started texting back and forth with someone. Kyle suspected it was Joel, which irritated him, but he said nothing. Wesley would totally flip out if he found out Jesse was conversing with one of the suspects, and Kyle didn't need Jesse and Wes at war with each other. He'd try to get Jesse alone later and find out what was going on.

He finally got his chance when they'd pulled into Fabyan's and sat down for lunch. Wesley excused himself to go to the bathroom, and Kyle took advantage of the moment of privacy to ask, "That was Joel texting you in the car, wasn't it?"

"Yes," Jesse admitted.

"What are you planning?"

"He and Todd and Corrie are getting together tonight for a kind of farewell party in Stuart's honor," Jesse replied. "After all, they're going home tomorrow, unless you say they can't." Kyle knew he didn't have any good reason to prevent them from leaving. Jesse continued, "They figured they'd invite me since I've been hanging out with them the past few days."

"I don't think that's a good idea," Kyle told him.

Jesse nodded. "I know you don't. But I'll be safe enough with all of them there. And they'll be drinking. If they're ever going to be off their guard, it will be tonight."

Kyle frowned at him, but there wasn't time to say anything else because Wesley returned from the bathroom at that moment. "What's up?" he asked Kyle. "Why are you looking all pissed off?"

Kyle did his best to reset his expression to neutral. "I'm not. I'm fine."

AFTER LUNCH, they went back to the hotel and settled Jesse in. It didn't take long since all he had to do was toss his backpack and duffel bag in a corner. He stretched out on Kyle's queen-sized bed with his book, wearing just his jeans and a hunter green T-shirt, and Kyle wanted nothing more than to tear those clothes off his lithe body and make love to him. But of course, Wesley was right there in the room with them, watching TV. So Kyle forced himself to focus on filling out a report of what he'd learned from Mrs. Moore and PI Winchester the day before.

The frustrating thing was, looking over what they had so far, Kyle knew he didn't have enough to pin Stuart's murder on anyone. All he had was a bunch of possible motives—none of which were very satisfying, as far as he was concerned—and a bunch of people who had the opportunity and means of committing the crime.

Todd might have been jealous of Corrie, though that seemed unlikely, or he might have known about the money and wanted it for himself. Joel might have wanted the money for himself—unlikely, if he really loved Stuart—or perhaps he was afraid Stuart was going to go through with the wedding, after all. Then he might have done it out of jealousy or feelings of betrayal. Ryan might have thought Stuart couldn't be trusted to take the money and run, so he wanted to make sure Stuart couldn't back out of the deal. Again, that seemed rather unlikely.

Or Corrie might have wanted to kill Stuart because he was backing out of the wedding. That seemed a likely motive, if she was really pregnant with Stuart's baby, or even if Kyle accepted Joel's theory that Corrie wanted to keep Stuart in her clutches so Todd would stick around. But was she physically capable of grabbing a guy Stuart's size and bashing his head against a rock? Maybe if she was quick enough. But it didn't seem likely.

No matter how he sliced it, Kyle had to admit he needed more information. And Jesse's plan to go to the party that night seemed like a way to get it. Not necessarily a *good* way. It was dangerous, and Kyle didn't want him involved any more than he already had been. But he seemed to have their confidence, and if they were relaxed and drinking, maybe one of them would let something slip.

Or maybe one of them will get violent.

His thoughts were interrupted by Wesley shutting off the TV and standing up to stretch. "That's it. I'm bored out of my fucking mind. Unless you've got any other brilliant ideas, I'm gonna go down the road and get a beer." He looked pointedly at both Kyle and Jesse. "I'll be gone an hour. So do what you want. But I expect everyone to have clothes on when I come back in that door."

Kyle gave him a sour look and muttered, "Yes, Mother," but he was actually delighted to hear Wesley was going to give him and Jesse some time alone. Jesse just gave Kyle a wicked smirk.

Wesley was in his boxers, so he took a couple of minutes to scrounge up the clothing he'd shed on the floor beside his bed and slip back into it. Then he grabbed his coat and headed out the door.

"Have fun, boys."

When the door had closed behind him, Jesse asked, "Should I tell him his balls keep flopping out when he's in his boxers?"

"I'm sure he knows," Kyle replied, grimacing at the image that brought to mind. "He's just never cared because to him I'm just another guy. I'd like to keep it that way, so don't make him start feeling self-conscious."

Jesse laughed. "Sure."

Kyle stood and began unbuttoning his shirt as he walked to the bed. "He's just trying to be nice."

"So I gather you'd like to take advantage of his generous offer of fuck time?" Jesse put his book on the nightstand and rose to his knees at the edge of the mattress.

"Fuck yes. I'm already hard as a rock."

"Really?" Jesse asked innocently, leaning forward to slide a hand down Kyle's abdomen and then inside his waistband. "Let me see." He was prevented from sliding all the way down by the belt, so Kyle undid it. He felt a wave of ticklish pleasure as Jesse continued to slide his hand down into his underwear and through his pubic hair. Jesse's fingers coiled around the base of his hard dick and squeezed it. "There it is!"

Kyle moaned and lowered his face to nibble Jesse's earlobe while he slid his hands up and under the sides of Jesse's T-shirt and along the hot naked flesh he found there. He moved around to Jesse's smooth, muscular back, and then lower into his jeans and underwear to cup his ass. With a grin, Jesse undid the button and zipper of his jeans and shoved them down to his knees.

"Why don't you lie down on the bed?" Kyle whispered into his ear.

They both wrestled out of their clothes as quickly as possible, tossing them haphazardly onto the floor. Jesse lay back on the bedspread, every inch of his smooth, amber skin exposed. Kyle got himself tangled in his pants legs and felt like an idiot for a minute while he fought to separate his socks from his jeans. Eventually he managed to get everything off and neatly draped across one of the chairs. He approached the bed, stark naked and feeling self-conscious about the erection bobbing in front of him as he walked. But Jesse didn't seem to think it looked goofy like that. His eyes were fixed on it, longing written on his beautiful face, his mouth slightly open as he unconsciously licked his lips.

God, that was hot.

Jesse's own erection jutted up in the air from his prone body, and Kyle knew he had to taste it before doing anything else. He climbed onto the bed but stopped halfway up his lover's body, kissing the inside of Jesse's thighs gently, making them tremble. Jesse moaned quietly as Kyle's lips found his ball sac, and his tongue darted out to taste the salty musk of the skin there. It was clean, of course—the scent of the hotel body wash from Jesse's shower still lingered—but Kyle knew it didn't take long for a man's scent to reassert itself, and he was delighted by it.

He discovered that each testicle jumped a little as he licked it, and he amused himself by alternating licks until Jesse's scrotum had tightened with arousal too much for that little game to work anymore. Then Kyle slid his tongue up the underside of Jesse's cock, loving the way it made the shaft twitch and the faint whimper his attentions elicited deep in Jesse's throat.

He took Jesse into his mouth and managed to slide the hard cock deeper in than he'd done the day before. But his gag reflex prevented him from taking it all the way inside. *I'll have to ask Jesse to give me lessons*, Kyle thought. He didn't appear to be doing too badly, though. Jesse was writhing on the bed and digging his fingers into the bedspread like claws.

Kyle was torn between wanting to continue sucking him, wanting to move up his body and suck other things, wanting to kiss him, or wanting to do what he'd been fantasizing about ever since that morning. But when he thought about exploring Jesse's ass, a powerful jolt of sexual desire surged through his hard cock.

Guess that's the tiebreaker.

Kyle let Jesse's cock slip out of his mouth, causing Jesse to whimper again—*God, I love that!*—and sank down past Jesse's balls to lick underneath them. What was it called? The taint. That was it. Kyle licked along the taut muscle leading from the balls to the crease of Jesse's ass, but was frustrated that Jesse's asshole was just out of reach. He slid his arms underneath Jesse's thighs and lifted up, encouraging him to fold his legs up and rotate his hips, exposing his tight, perfect little puckered hole. It was small and pink, nestled in between two pale, smooth ass cheeks.

Kyle leaned forward and slid his tongue over the opening. He paused for a moment to determine if the taste turned him off, but it didn't—not at all. The muskiness was stronger than that of Jesse's ball sac and perhaps a bit different, but not at all unpleasant. Which was good, because Kyle was even more turned on than he'd been a moment before. He dove in again and was rewarded by a low moan. As Kyle continued to lick his puckered hole, Jesse made more soft noises and bucked in his arms. It drove Kyle wild that Jesse responded so well to him, and that drove him to probe deeper until he was startled by several quick jerks of Jesse's hips and a breathless gasp of "No!"

Afraid he might have done something to hurt him, Kyle raised his head up over Jesse's crotch just in time to see his cock erupt all over his belly. *Fuck yeah!*

"Yes," Kyle groaned as he shoved his face forward to lap up the thick white come squirting out of Jesse's dickhead. He'd never tasted another man's come in his life and he wasn't absolutely certain it was safe to be lapping up Jesse's like this, but he wasn't able to control himself. It tasted amazing and smelled so hot he was ready to squirt his own onto the bedspread. By the time Jesse had finished coming, and Kyle was done licking it all up, his face was practically covered in it.

"I'm sorry," Jesse said breathlessly. "I didn't want to come so fast."

"That was fucking amazing! I haven't been that out of control in...." Kyle couldn't actually remember if he'd *ever* let himself get that raunchy.

"Did you come?"

"Not yet."

"Roll over," Jesse insisted.

He moved around so they were in a sixty-nine position, which was fine with Kyle. He continued to suck gently on Jesse's softened dick, milking the last traces of come out of it while Jesse took his painfully hard cock into his mouth. It didn't take long for Kyle to shoot. Jesse was a much better cocksucker than he was, taking his shaft deep into his throat and caressing it with his tongue. Kyle squirted again and again into Jesse's throat, and the young man swallowed every last drop.

Kyle was a little reluctant to make out with Jesse, considering where his mouth had just been, but Jesse didn't seem to care. He crawled up Kyle's body until they were face-to-face again and started kissing him without hesitation. Kyle gave in and kissed him back.

Eventually, Kyle pulled away and said, "Not that I want to break this up, but are you still planning to meet with Joel and company tonight?"

"I guess so," Jesse said slowly. "I mean, I could learn something important, right?"

Kyle didn't want to agree with him. He didn't want to sound as if he was encouraging it, or even condoning it. "I'd rather you didn't."

"I know," Jesse said. "But I'm going to."

Kyle frowned at him and let out a long, irritated sigh. "Well, then, you might as well head out. If you wait until Wesley gets back, you'll have to deal with him flipping out on you."

"Do you want to put a wire on me?" Jesse asked.

Kyle knew he was kidding, but if he'd been able to force Jesse to wear one, he would have. "Sure," he replied sarcastically, "I'll just pull the one out of my ass and stick it up yours." Jesse grinned at that, and Kyle added, more seriously, "We'd have to set that up in Concord, and there isn't time." He kissed Jesse's forehead. "Take your cell phone, and call me if you get into trouble. I'm two minutes away."

24

JESSE TEXTED Joel just before getting into his car and received the response *cum up to the room.*

Jesse wasn't sure if the misspelling of "come" was intentional or not. Knowing Joel, it probably was. But Jesse ignored it.

He made the short trip across Route 302, and within a few minutes, he was knocking on the door to Joel and Todd's room. He could hear music coming from inside—"Mexican Moon" by Concrete Blonde—and a second later, the door flew open. Joel beamed at him, already slightly drunk, judging by the way he was leaning against the door. He had a drink in one hand that might have been a screwdriver. "Jesse! The other gorgeous man I can't sleep with!"

"Try getting him drunk!" Todd called from somewhere behind him.

As Joel ushered him inside, Jesse discovered the three of them weren't the only ones in the room. Corrie was stretched out alongside Todd on his bed—both fully clothed—and, surprisingly, Ryan was also there. He was seated in one of the old-fashioned upholstered chairs, looking decidedly uncomfortable, but he had a beer in his hand, at least. There was a stockpile of alcohol and drink fixings on the desk beside him—beer, vodka, rum, tequila, coke, orange juice, cranberry juice, and a bucket half-full of ice.

"You already know Corrie," Joel said, closing the door behind them. He made a dismissive gesture in Ryan's direction. "And that's *Ryan*." The way he hammered the name made his low opinion of the guy clear.

Ryan scowled at him. "Fuck you, Joel." He glanced back at Jesse with a puzzled expression, and Jesse suspected he was trying to recall where he'd seen him before. This was the first time they'd met face-to-face since bumping into each other on the summit. Jesse decided it was probably better if Ryan didn't remember him, so he avoided making eye contact.

"Everybody play nice," Corrie said. "We're supposed to be saying good-bye to Stuart, not fighting."

"He didn't even *like* Stuart," Joel complained, waving his drink like a parody of Bette Davis and sloshing some on the carpet. "He was all jealous of him."

Ryan glared at the carpet, his face turning red. But Corrie merely clucked and told him, "Sit down, Joel."

He flopped down on the edge of his bed, nearly spilling his drink again, and then patted the mattress beside him. "Come on, Jesse. Grab a drink and sit with me."

Jesse had no intention of getting drunk surrounded by the four main suspects in Stuart's murder. Or getting drunk and snuggling up with Joel, for that matter. But he couldn't just stand there staring at everybody. So he grabbed a beer off the desk, figuring he'd be able to sip it slowly and stay sober. Then he sat down on Joel's bed.

Joel immediately tried to lean against him, but Jesse held up his empty hand and said gently, "No."

Joel sighed and downed the remainder of his drink.

THE "PARTY" wasn't really much of a party, from Jesse's perspective. Everyone was pretty maudlin. Corrie appeared to have come up with the idea of toasting Stuart on what would have been their wedding night, so she was the one who kept trying to reminisce about him. She told stories about the day they'd met, with Joel grudgingly supplying a few details she was fuzzy on, and about the first time Stuart took her to meet Todd. Todd grunted in acknowledgement of how hostile he'd been to her, but that was about it. The stories were mildly interesting to Jesse—he was always interested in hearing about people's lives, and of course Stuart's was of particular interest to him—but pretty average. Everybody had stories like that, more or less.

The guys were mostly just drinking. Corrie was trying to nuzzle up to Todd while she talked, and he was tolerating it without particularly paying attention to her. Ryan kept stealing glances at the two of them, which Jesse found worrisome. However, Todd could certainly take care of himself if Ryan got violent after a few drinks.

And of course, Joel was pushing Jesse to finish his beer and move on to harder liquor—no doubt hoping Jesse would be more cooperative after a few drinks. Jesse wasn't worried. He'd fended off guys like Joel before.

But the simple fact was, it was a dull party. Jesse was becoming convinced he wouldn't learn anything useful when Ryan finished his third beer, gave Todd a look that could have melted tungsten, and then announced, "Well, this has been fun, but—"

"You can't leave yet," Corrie interrupted. "We have to go to the *catacombs*." She said the last word in a goofy "spooky" voice that made everyone turn to look at her, which she'd no doubt intended.

Joel giggled, and Jesse got the impression he was in on the joke. But clearly the other two guys weren't. They both looked baffled.

"Catacombs?" Todd asked.

"What catacombs?" Ryan asked impatiently. "You mean the Cave downstairs?"

"No," Joel said. "The catacombs *upstairs*." He pointed up to the ceiling. All eyes followed his finger, but Todd and Ryan still looked confused, and Jesse had no idea what Joel was talking about either. Did the hotel have an attic?

Corrie laughed and leaned forward, her blue eyes widening with excitement. "He says it's like a ghost hotel up there."

"A ghost hotel?" Todd asked. He didn't sound enthusiastic about the prospect of exploring.

Joel climbed unsteadily to his feet and took Jesse's hand. "Come on. You'll love it." He turned to the others. "We're gonna play a game!"

KYLE GREW less and less convinced Jesse's plan was a good idea as the hotel clock crept up on 8:00 p.m. He'd had no choice but to tell Wesley what was going on when his partner got back from Fabyan's—there was no way to hide the fact that Jesse had gone *somewhere*, and there really wasn't anywhere for him to go except the Mount Washington.

Wesley had been understandably pissed. "Jesus H. Christ, Kyle! Where the fuck is your head? He's gonna get himself killed, and *we're* gonna be held responsible because *you* let him go over there!"

"Getting a reprimand from the department is hardly the first thing on my mind," Kyle snapped. "I like him. He might end up being my boyfriend. I sure as fuck don't want somebody wringing his neck!"

"Then why didn't you stop him?"

"Because, one, he's has every right to hang out with Joel. I can't arrest him for making friends with a possible murderer, as much as I'd like to. And two, he's got it into his head that they'll let something slip if they're drinking and relaxing. He might be right."

"He might already be *dead*," Wesley snarled, undoing his belt and dropping his jeans to the floor. He kicked his way out of them and flopped down onto his bed in his boxers. When Kyle didn't respond, he grabbed the remote and turned the TV on.

They fell into an uneasy silence for a while, watching some gorefest cop show Kyle had never seen before and didn't particularly want to see again. When the hell did TV shows turn into horror movies? He'd certainly seen a lot of shit on the job, but this show really reveled in it. It was disgusting.

He finally couldn't stand it anymore. "I'm going over there," he announced.

Wesley sighed and shut off the TV. Then, without a word, he stood up and fished around on the floor for his jeans.

I should have done this right away, Kyle thought. There was no reason to trust he could get to the hotel in time if Jesse ran into trouble. He might as well hang out in the observatory on the main floor. Then he could rush upstairs if he had to.

He glanced at his phone, but of course, Jesse hadn't called.

Why the hell didn't I just tie him to the bed?

THEY HAD to smuggle the alcohol under their jackets as they walked through the halls, especially past the friendly old elevator operator who smiled and nodded at them as they passed him in the rotunda. Joel led them around the corner, where there was an alternate elevator guests could operate themselves.

Only when Jesse, Todd, Corrie, and Ryan were inside with him and the doors were safely closed did Joel say in a hushed voice, "Yesterday, I got bored and decided to do some exploring. I thought the fifth floor would be the ritziest floor in the hotel, since it's at the very top, but I was wrong."

He pressed the button, and the elevator quietly moved up two floors. The door opened, and Corrie audibly gasped.

What greeted them could have been the set of a horror movie.

It did look like the other floors of the hotel in many ways. The hall carpet was a similar green-and-gold pattern as the ones on the other floors, and the hallway stretched off in both directions, with doors on both sides that presumably led to hotel rooms. But the lighting was dim and had an eerie bluish tinge to it. In fact, there was only one light Jesse could see when the door opened—a wall sconce near the elevator with a single bright blue light in it, aimed upward. But the creepiest element was the wall in front of them, where an enormous section of plaster had crumbled away to reveal broken wooden slats. The carpet was covered in plaster and dust.

The wealthiest guests of the hotel certainly weren't staying up here. Nobody was staying up here. The floor was abandoned and in ruin.

"The whole floor is like this," Joel informed them as he stepped out of the elevator into the desolate hallway. Jesse and the others followed him. "There are holes in the walls and the floors, and most of the rooms don't have doors on them. Judging from the stepladders and other equipment lying around, I'd say they're still fixing it up."

"They supposedly renovated the entire hotel a few years ago," Corrie said, taking Todd's arm as if he'd protect her from whatever monsters might be roaming these hallways.

"Then they haven't gotten to this floor."

"It's weird that they didn't close it off."

Joel shrugged, unconcerned. "Maybe they expect their clientele to be sophisticated enough not to go into an area obviously not open to the public. But they didn't count on the drunk dudes from Rochester."

Todd snorted and gave Joel a high five.

"Seriously," Ryan said, "I don't think they want us up here." He was echoing Jesse's thoughts, but Jesse had no intention of shutting this little excursion down. He suspected things were just about to get interesting.

Still, he fingered his cell phone in his jacket pocket to reassure himself that Kyle was close by.

"Fuck that!" Todd said. "Let's look around."

He didn't wait for the others to agree but started walking down the hallway. Corrie went with him, still clutching his arm. Ryan sighed melodramatically and followed them.

"This'll be great!" Joel said in a gleeful voice to Jesse, then grabbed him by both shoulders and propelled him down the hall after the others.

THE ROOMS were pretty boring, actually. They were all the same—empty and in roughly the same state of neglect. Some had more plaster falling off the walls than others. In some, the carpets were torn up; in others they were there, but stained and mildewed.

"Make sure to walk softly," Joel reminded them, "and keep your voices down. Otherwise someone might send someone up to look for rats."

"Talking rats," Ryan muttered.

"Exactly. With unpleasant dispositions."

Ryan flipped him off but didn't even bother turning around.

When they'd reached the far end, Joel said, "Let's camp out here for a bit so we can play the game."

There were two rooms nearby. One had a carpet, but by unspoken consent, they avoided it and chose the room with a bare wooden floor. It was getting chilly, since all the radiators up here were turned off, and sitting on wood would be colder than sitting on a carpet, but it was probably still healthier to avoid whatever mold might be growing on the carpet. They sat in a circle, huddled in their jackets, and placed all the bottles of alcohol in the center. Nobody had been motivated to grab the coke or orange juice, so they were stuck with straight shots of vodka, rum, and tequila.

Joel dug into his jacket pocket and produced a thick, squat candle that looked like something from one of the gift shops. There was a Mount Washington Hotel image wrapped around it. He placed it on the floor in the center of their circle and lit it with a plastic disposable lighter.

"Are we going to tell ghost stories?" Corrie asked.

"In a way," Joel said, sitting back on his butt and giving her a knowing smile. The candle illuminated everyone's faces from below, reminding Jesse of the cheesy lighting in a lot of old black-and-white horror movies. "We're gonna play Truth or Dare."

Ryan groaned. "Lame."

"You'll like this version," Joel said. "'Cause I made up new rules."

"All the guys have to get naked and fuck you?" Todd asked, sneering at him.

"Sounds good to me," Corrie said. "I'll be happy to watch."

"Close!" Joel said. He looked around at everyone and continued, "We've all been avoiding saying it, but… we're not fooling ourselves. We know the truth."

Ryan sighed impatiently. "What truth?"

"That Stuart didn't just die up there on the mountain. He was murdered. And the chances of it being some random hiker he bumped into are almost nonexistent."

Everyone was looking uncomfortable now. Jesse felt the increase in tension like a buildup of static electricity. He wished he could dial Kyle on his cellphone and just let the detective overhear whatever it was Joel was driving at, but he hadn't thought to arrange it ahead of time. Kyle would pick up and speak into the phone, and everyone would hear him. Jesse's phone could record, of course, but he couldn't start the recorder without looking at it.

Corrie said, "It's still *possible* it was a stranger. Someone could have been trying to rob him."

"No," Joel replied, shaking his head. "It was somebody who knew him. It almost always is, right, Jesse?"

Jesse was startled at being included in the conversation, but he quickly said, "Um… statistically, yes. It's almost always somebody who knew the victim."

"And that means, excluding Mr. and Mrs. Lassiter—and Lisa, of course—it had to be one of us sitting here… right now."

A chill seemed to ripple through the five of them as they all glanced down at the candle, as though not wanting to be seen accusing anyone with a look. But then Todd said angrily, "Why exclude the Lassiters? They hated him!"

"They did not!" Corrie said defensively.

"Shut the fuck up about my parents!" Ryan snarled.

But Joel reached out to put a hand on Todd's arm, which may have been the only thing preventing him from tackling Ryan at that moment. "Keep your voices down!" he hissed. "I'm sorry, but… Todd's right, Corrie. Your parents just put up with Stuart to make you happy. But unless they snuck up the mountain when nobody was looking, they couldn't have done it."

"Then neither could I," Ryan said quickly. "I was in Concord all day."

"No." The word echoed in the empty room before Jesse was aware *he* was the one who'd said it. Still not sure it was a good idea, he continued, "You were on the summit that day. I saw you on the observation deck."

Ryan looked him in the eye, surprise gradually giving way to anger in his expression. "That's where I know you from," he said grimly.

"Ryan?" Corrie asked. "What's he talking about?"

Ryan calmly reached out to snag the bottle of tequila. He unscrewed the cap and took a healthy swallow before he answered his sister. "Yeah, I was there."

Joel cackled gleefully. "This is great!"

"Why were you there, Ryan?" Corrie asked, her voice low and menacing.

"I didn't kill him!"

"No, no! Not yet!" Joel interrupted. He put both hands flat on the floor on either side of the candle, leaning forward so the light illuminated his drunken smile sharply. "We have to play the game!"

"What game?" Todd growled, his eyes locked on Ryan.

"We start with everyone answering the question 'Did you kill Stuart?' If you don't say yes—and seriously, I doubt anyone will confess immediately—then you have to take a swig of something and accept a dare. I make up the dares, and they're going to be raunchy."

"Why do you make up the dares?" Corrie asked.

"Because it's my game. But don't worry. The next round, everybody gets the chance to ask a question. All the questions have to be related to the murder. And everyone takes a drink after each question they refuse to answer."

"This is stupid," Ryan said.

"Are you chicken?" Todd asked.

The two exchanged a long, challenging look, and Ryan finally said, "Not me."

"What happens if someone confesses?" Corrie asked Joel.

Joel took a drink from the rum bottle, his face contorting as the liquor burned its way down his throat. "Uh-uh. That's cheating. You'll find out what the prize is at the end of the game."

"What about Jesse?"

"No, he's not the prize."

Corrie laughed. "I mean, you don't think *he* did it, do you?"

Joel turned to look at Jesse, and the expression on his face suddenly didn't seem drunk at all, but shrewd and cold. "No. I have a whole different set of questions for Jesse."

Shit. Jesse wondered if Joel might be onto him, after all. Maybe it would be a good idea to just say he wasn't interested in this game and see if he could get out of there. If Joel would *let* him get out of there.

But before he could make a decision, Todd said, "Fine. Start the game."

Joel laughed like a drunken maniac again, and any trace of the clarity he'd seemed to possess a moment ago was gone. "Okay, okay! First question." He held out the bottle of rum to Jesse. "Are you with the police?"

Jesse felt his blood go cold. But he replied without hesitating. "No." After all, "with" in this context generally meant "working for," and he wasn't doing that.

"Of course not," Joel said, his voice mocking. He pushed the bottle at him again. "Come on. Anyone who says no has to drink and do a dare."

Jesse took the bottle and drank from it. The rum clawed its way down his esophagus, and he wondered if the prize at the end of the evening was going to be everyone puking in the bathtub together. Of course, he knew what Joel was hoping. People would get drunk enough to let their guards down, and then one of them would slip up and confess. Either that, or Joel was the killer, and he was planning on killing all of them when they were passed out. Jesse repressed a shudder at the thought.

"Now for the dare," Joel said happily. "It's the same for everybody this round. You have to kiss everyone in the room on the lips."

Ryan scoffed at that. "You seriously expect me to let him kiss me? You think I'm gonna let *Todd* kiss me?"

"Pussy," Todd said. There was a glint in his eyes, as if he'd be willing to do anything on a dare.

"Yes," Joel said. "This way, everyone gets to kiss at least one person they'd like to kiss—I'm willing to bet Jesse wouldn't mind kissing at least one of the guys here"—he looked a bit petulant as he said that—"and everyone gets to kiss… a murderer."

"You're sick," Corrie said. But she was smiling. Jesse suspected she liked the idea of being this close to a killer—assuming she wasn't one herself. Even though Joel was about to force her to kiss her twisted brother.

Joel looked Jesse in the eye. "Chicken?"

"I didn't say that," Jesse replied. "I'll kiss everyone. But if you start telling me to put my mouth in… other places… I may have to bow out. I have a boyfriend, remember."

"Don't worry," Joel said, smiling. "We'll get to the boyfriend soon enough."

"SO ARE you just gonna run up there and bust his cover?"

Kyle looked around the lobby of the Mount Washington, full of young skiers at the moment, relaxing in front of the fireplace or laughing and talking with their friends. It was ridiculous to expect Jesse to be sitting down here, but he was still disappointed he wasn't there. "No," he answered Wesley, glancing down at his cell phone, "not unless he calls."

The cell phone was obstinately silent.

Wesley sighed and walked away from him into the Conservatory. Kyle followed, hoping Jesse might be hanging out in that room. No such luck. Just more skiers and an elderly couple sitting by the windows, watching the moonrise and talking quietly over coffee.

One of the waitstaff approached them and asked, "Can I get you something from the bar?"

Kyle started to shake his head, but Wesley interrupted, telling the young woman, "Just a Coke for me. My friend will have a Corona."

"I shouldn't be drinking," Kyle said.

Wesley waved the young woman away with a knowing nod. Then he flopped down in one of the wicker love seats near the window. "What you need is to relax. It's just one beer. You're not gonna be too drunk to run to the rescue—I guarantee it."

Kyle sat down beside him, grateful the love seat was large enough to put some space between them. He was fond of Wesley, but he didn't want to sit in the guy's frigging lap. "All right, Mom." At least they weren't in uniform—or, in fact, on duty—so he wouldn't be violating regulations by having a drink.

He placed his cell phone on the coffee table in front of them so he could grab it the second it rang.

EVERYONE ANSWERED no to the question about murdering Stuart, of course, so the first round involved a lot of kissing. The biggest surprise for Jesse was that Todd turned out to be a great kisser. Joel's kiss had been drunken and sloppy, not surprisingly, and Corrie's had been chaste, probably because she knew Jesse wasn't at all interested. Ryan barely pecked him on the lips and insisted upon making a face afterward—*Fuck you very much.* But Todd grabbed him and went to town, even slipping him some tongue. Jesse had to admit it stirred his blood, despite being creeped out by the possibility Todd could be the killer.

When Todd finally let him up for air, he had a triumphant smirk on his face, but Jesse couldn't say he cared. It was amusing to watch Todd give everyone else the same treatment. Joel whimpered with desire, and Ryan looked like he might pass out.

"Now for the next round," Joel said. "This part is called 'Why I think you did it.' First, I accuse someone. If he or she can come up with a good reason why that's invalid, I have to take a drink. If not, they have to take a drink. But then they get to accuse somebody."

"Just because someone can't prove they didn't do it doesn't mean they did," Corrie pointed out.

"True," Joel admitted. "But we're still playing. Oh! And you can't accuse the person who just accused *you*, obviously."

"You forgot about Jesse again."

"You can accuse Jesse, if you want."

"But everyone knows he didn't do it," Ryan said, exasperated.

"He discovered the body," Joel pointed out. "I admit it's unlikely that he did it, but he certainly could have. So come up with a motive for him, if you can."

When nobody voiced any further objections, Joel held up the bottle of rum, which was nearly empty by now, and said, "Okay. Me first. Ryan—" He pointed the tip of the bottle across the circle. "—I think you killed Stuart because he refused to skip out on the wedding, and you flew into a jealous rage! Everyone knows you want Corrie for yourself, you pervert."

Ryan looked horrified, but Jesse suspected it was less over the murder accusation than dragging his feelings toward his sister into the spotlight. "What the.... *Fuck you, Joel!*"

"Keep your voice down, please."

"Who the fuck do you—"

"Oh, Ryan," Corrie interrupted, rolling her eyes. "Everyone knows."

Ryan stood up, his face looking red even in the dim candlelight, though Jesse wasn't sure if it was from embarrassment or anger. "This is bullshit. I'm going back downstairs."

But as he moved toward the door, Todd jumped to his feet with surprising swiftness and blocked his path. "No, you don't. We all agreed to play. So sit down and answer the fucking question."

"What question?" Ryan looked furious now, but he backed away from Todd's larger bulk. "You're all just making fun of me—"

"Making *fun* of you?" Corrie asked. "More like making you man up instead of hiding behind your doctors all the time."

Ryan whirled on her. "You think I liked being sent to that place? You have no idea what it was like—"

"Don't you fucking dare play the sympathy card with me!" Corrie snapped, her delicate features suddenly contorted in anger. "You're lucky I even *talk* to you after you tried to *rape* me, you fucking freak!"

"Children! Children!" Joel said, laughing in delight. "Don't fight. We have so much more to do."

Ryan made another attempt to move toward the door, but Todd simply shifted to block him again. "Sit down, Ryan. And tell us if Joel's right."

"Of course he's not right," Ryan said quietly. "I didn't kill your brother."

"Sit down."

Ryan looked sullen as he took a seat on the floor again. He refused to look at anybody, staring instead at the burning candle in the center of the circle.

"It isn't enough to just say you didn't kill him," Joel said. "You have to explain why you wouldn't kill him, when we know you had a reason to."

"That doesn't make sense," Ryan said bitterly. "Just because I didn't like him doesn't mean I killed him. Besides, he took the money."

Corrie sat up abruptly. "Money? What money?"

"Dad offered him twenty thousand dollars to bail on the wedding," Ryan said. "I told Stuart on Tuesday that I was going into Concord the next morning to withdraw the cash, but he said if I wanted to give it to him, I could meet him up on the summit that afternoon. I got back from Concord around noon, so I just took the railway up to wait for him."

Corrie's mouth was hanging open in shock. "I can't believe Daddy would do that!"

"It's true."

"Why would Stuart tell you to take it to the summit?" Jesse asked.

Ryan glanced at Todd before looking back at the candle flame. "Because he didn't want his brother to know about it."

The look Todd gave Ryan was ice cold, but he stayed silent. Corrie, on the other hand, glared at her brother and said, "So you took a wad of cash up to the summit to bribe my fiancé into ditching me. And then what happened?"

Ryan shrugged. "He took the money. I came down on the next train."

"Jesus Christ."

"Oh, don't act like you're all upset about it," Ryan snarled back at her. "You didn't love him."

"Fuck you, Ryan."

"Wait! Wait!" Joel interrupted. "That's Ryan's round. And I guess he answered correctly, so now I have to take a drink." He took a swig of rum and gasped. Then he said, "Now Ryan gets to accuse someone else."

"Fine!" Ryan said. He pointed at his sister. "I think Corrie did it!"

A DIFFERENT waiter came around to take Wesley's empty glass and Kyle's empty Corona bottle. By now, Wesley had given up trying to engage Kyle in any kind of conversation and was entertaining himself by playing *Angry Birds* on his iPhone. He glanced up at the waiter and said, "I'll have another soda. My friend needs another Corona."

"No," Kyle interjected. "Nothing for me, thanks."

When the waiter left, Kyle checked his phone for text messages, although he knew it was pointless. He would have noticed if something had come in.

Wesley shook his head. "God, I'd hate to see what you'd be like if you had a teenage daughter out on a date."

"If she was dating a murder suspect?" Kyle snapped.

"You're gonna have to learn to rein that boy in if you wanna keep dating him. He can't be sticking his nose into your cases—*our* cases—all the time, running off to party down with killers every ten minutes. It'll drive you crazy."

Kyle glared at him, but he knew Wesley was right. It was bad enough with Jesse involving himself in just this one situation. The question was, would this become a regular thing with him? That could get Kyle in a lot of trouble—never mind the wear and tear on his nerves. Worse, it could get Jesse killed. Maybe it would be safer for both of them if Kyle ended things after this weekend.

But right now, there were more important things to worry about. "If I don't hear from him in ten minutes, I'm going up there," he said.

"YOU FOUND out Stuart was going to bail on the wedding," Ryan said to Corrie, "so you flipped out on him and killed him."

Corrie gave him a withering look. "You just said I didn't love him. If that's true, why would I give a fuck if he didn't want to marry me?"

"Because you're knocked up," Ryan spat out.

"What?"

"Don't deny it," Joel said. "You told me a few weeks ago."

She tilted her head and flipped him off. "Thanks a lot, Joel. Were you the one who told Ryan?"

"Please! You think I hang out with the perv?"

"I heard all about it when Mom flipped out about the money," Ryan told his sister, ignoring Joel's jab at him. "They had a huge fight. Mom kept going on about how were they going to explain to their friends that you'd just popped out a kid when you weren't married? Dad didn't know anything about it, of course."

"I didn't tell him."

"And now he's hyperventilating about what his golf buddies are going to say behind his back down at the club."

Corrie didn't seem to have a response to that. She shook her head, her mouth closed in a tight line. Then Todd spoke. "You're pregnant?"

"Yes." She reached out for the bottle of vodka and unscrewed the cap.

"Maybe you shouldn't be drinking," Joel said, but he was smiling, mocking her.

Corrie sneered at him and upended the bottle into her mouth. She swallowed deeply, then pulled the bottle away, gasping. After a moment, she said breathlessly, "I wouldn't kill him for ditching me. I'd make his life fucking miserable for a while, but I wouldn't kill him."

"Even if it meant Todd would ditch you too?" Ryan asked.

Apparently, Corrie had had enough of her brother. She swung her fist and connected hard with his upper arm. "Shut the fuck up!"

"Voices down," Joel reminded them.

Ryan clutched his arm and rubbed it, glaring back at his sister. "We all know you were fucking both of them. You probably have no idea whose baby you're carrying."

"That's right," Corrie spat. "I was fucking Stuart and Todd and Joel, and now I'll probably fuck Jesse, just so you can watch and know the only guy on the entire planet I *won't* fuck is *you*!"

Ryan turned beet red at that, but nobody paid much attention to him since Joel suddenly burst out giggling and fell over backward. Jesse sighed and said, "You just told everyone else to be quiet."

"Get up," Todd commanded, grabbing Joel's jacket by the neck and heaving him up to a sitting position again. Joel didn't resist, but it took him a minute to get his giggling under control.

"Okay," he said finally. "I guess there's a valid reason for not killing Stuart in there somewhere—indifference, at the very least. So Ryan has to take a drink."

Ryan didn't need further prompting. He was still holding the tequila bottle, and he took a huge gulp from it. In the brief silence that followed, the candle sputtered, and Todd took the rum bottle away from Joel and downed the rest of its contents.

"I'm next," Corrie announced. She looked at Todd. "Todd… I think you killed your brother, because…." She seemed to be mulling it over, as though she hadn't really given the matter much thought. Jesse suspected this was still just a game to her, albeit a vicious one.

"Don't say because I wanted you for myself," Todd said contemptuously.

At this point, Jesse—and probably everyone else—knew Todd could have had her whether his brother married her or not. Corrie looked wounded, but she made no attempt to defend her honor. She said, a bit petulantly, "Fine. You killed him because he wasn't going to share the money with you."

"I didn't know Ryan had given him any money," Todd pointed out.

"He told you about it," she countered. "He told you he was going to take it so you could both share it. But at the last minute, he decided to keep it for himself."

Todd snorted and took the bottle of vodka away from her. After taking a sip, he wiped his mouth and said, "You're fishing. Stuart was my brother. We shared everything. I could have *anything* he had. I could have had the money, I *did* have you, and I could have had *Joel*, if I'd wanted him." He looked over at Joel, whose mouth was gaping open comically. "Yeah, I knew he was fucking you."

Joel closed his mouth. "He wouldn't have let you," he said, more subdued than he'd been all evening.

"Yeah, he would have." Todd leaned in toward him, his face coming so close that Joel flinched. But he didn't pull away, not even when Todd brushed his lips against his cheek—not a kiss, but pretty damned close. "And you would have liked it."

Joel let out a quivering breath. "Fuck you," he said quietly.

"You know I'm right."

"Fuck you anyway."

Todd sat back and took another swig of vodka. Then he handed it back to Corrie. "I believe I win, and you have to take a drink now."

Defiantly, Corrie snatched the bottle and drank her penalty.

"Now it's my turn," Todd continued. He leaned over toward Joel again, pressing his shoulder into Joel's. Jesse wasn't sure what to make of the gesture. Was Todd getting drunk enough to start hitting on Joel? Or was he doing it to intimidate him? "I think *you* killed my brother because you finally figured out he didn't love you any more than he loved Corrie...."

"Or you," Jesse finished. Everyone turned to look at him, but he was just as startled by the sound of his voice as they were. But now that he'd said it, he knew it was the truth.

Todd raised one eyebrow at him. "Or me?"

"He didn't love you," Jesse went on. "As a brother, I mean. He didn't love anyone. Did he?"

Todd chuckled and rubbed his face against Joel's shoulder for a moment. "No… he couldn't. There was something broken in him. All his life. I think he was born that way."

Joel was looking horrified, as if he'd suddenly realized there was a poisonous snake curled up against him. Or perhaps it was the realization that Stuart might not have been what he thought. "What are you talking about?"

Todd looked at Jesse as if he expected him to take it from there. Jesse realized he was taking a huge risk, revealing what he knew, but he wanted to coax more out of Todd. "I found a news article online about you," he fudged. "About what happened to your parents…."

Todd took a deep breath and let it out slowly. "Why don't you tell us all what happened to them?"

"It looked like your father shot your mother and then shot himself."

"Jesus!" Corrie gasped. Ryan looked a bit wide-eyed too at that revelation. Jesse had thought they might know about the contents of Winchester's report, but now he guessed Mr. Lassiter hadn't shared the details with his children.

"That's what it looked like," Todd agreed.

"But your father was passed out drunk on the living room couch," Jesse said. "It would have been easy to put the gun in his hand and aim it at your mother when she walked in through the front door. Then, as your father jolted up, struggling to wake out of his drunken stupor, the gun could've been turned on him and fired."

"Who would do such a thing to dear Mommy and Daddy?" Todd asked, a sly smile creeping across his face.

"Not you," Jesse replied. "You hated them. And you loved your brother. You would have done anything to protect him…."

"Then why wouldn't I have done it?"

"Because he did it first," Jesse said. It was a guess—an intuition—but the moment he said it, he saw something flicker in Todd's eyes. He'd been right.

Todd's smile faded and he looked away, his eyes clouding as he seemed to be drawn back into a distant memory. "He was capable of anything. I didn't think he would really do it, even though we used to talk about it—fantasize about it. I was upstairs in bed when the shots went off. I ran down, and there he was… all covered in blood, and… grinning… all excited about it."

"So you protected him."

"Why not?" Todd asked defiantly. "I didn't give a fuck about them. I took him upstairs and had him wash off the blood. He wasn't wearing a shirt because he figured it would get spattered. He just put a new one on. We were trying get out the bedroom window and jump down off the porch when the cops got there. If they'd really looked around the upstairs bathroom that night, they might have found something—traces of blood, maybe. We couldn't have got everything. But I don't know if anyone even checked up there. The police knew all about our father's drinking, Mom's whoring around, all the arguments. Stuart and I pretended we'd heard the shots and climbed out on the roof to escape. Nobody looked past the obvious."

Another long silence fell over the circle, until Corrie, her face pale, said, "You're making it up."

"No."

"You're telling me I was about to marry a psychopath?"

"I tried to keep people away from him," Todd said, closing his eyes as if he was about to fall asleep against Joel's shoulder. "I was afraid he'd hurt someone else, if I gave him half a chance. But everyone always thought he was so fucking charming. I was the asshole, but everybody loved Stuart."

Of course, Jesse thought. Sociopaths were often charming. It was all about them. They didn't care about people, but they lived for attention and learned how to manipulate everyone into adoring them.

"Jesus," Ryan said. Knowing he'd been jealous of Stuart, Jesse half-expected him to make some snide remark about not being fooled, but he looked just as shocked as Corrie. Joel looked as if he might throw up. He seemed to be trembling all over.

Finally, when the silence had gone on too long, Jesse asked the question he knew was on everyone's minds. "Why did you kill him, Todd? Was it to protect Corrie?"

Todd's eyes flashed open, and his voice was hard. "Her? He was gonna take the money and run. She would have been safe enough."

Jesse hesitated a moment and then asked, "Joel?"

Todd smiled and put a finger to the tip of his nose.

"Me?" Joel asked, his voice quivering.

Todd said, "Stuart told me he was gonna take Joel to Canada for a bit. Fuck around. Then when he got bored, he'd come back."

"He was going to ditch me?" Joel asked.

"Ditch you? No… I think he was looking forward to doing something more… creative."

Joel stared into space as if everything in his brain had just short-circuited. He slowly slid his trembling hand into his jacket pocket. It was the hand attached to the arm Todd was leaning against, so it wasn't possible to really disguise the movement. Todd reached up and grabbed his forearm. Then he guided the hand out of the pocket.

It was balled into a fist, so Todd turned it over and pressed against the fingers until they unfurled. In Joel's palm were two gelcaps.

"Is this the end of the game?" Todd asked.

"Yes," Joel said quietly.

Jesse looked at the pills in alarm. "What are they, Joel?"

"One's rat poison," Joel said. "The other is cornstarch. One for whoever the killer turned out to be, and the other for me."

"Russian roulette with pills," Ryan said contemptuously.

Corrie looked at the pills, her eyes wide with fear. "Joel… that's pretty sick."

"If the murderer got away with it," Joel said, slowly turning his eyes to focus on her, "I didn't want to be around."

Silently, Todd reached out and took both pills from his hand. Then he popped one of them into his mouth. But when Joel moved to take the second pill from him, Todd balled his hand into a fist and pulled it out of

Joel's reach. Moving with surprising speed, considering how drunk he appeared to be, Todd launched himself across Joel's lap, directly at Jesse.

He struck Jesse full in the chest with his shoulder, and Jesse fell over backward. He hit the wooden floor hard as Todd's fists slammed down on either side of his body. Todd grunted as he lifted his head to look Jesse directly in the eye.

When he spoke, Jesse could smell the vodka and rum on his breath. "I was always afraid he'd go too far, that I'd be forced to stop him before he hurt someone who didn't deserve it. Do you understand me? He was the only thing I loved, but I couldn't let him kill Joel. Joel's an idiot, but he didn't deserve that!"

"I know, Todd."

"And I'm sure as hell not gonna let Joel take that other pill," Todd said. "Not after what his life cost me." He raised his fist and held it up in front of Jesse's face. "But you've been lying to us all along."

"THIS IS RIDICULOUS," Wesley said.

They were standing at the far end of the corridor leading to Todd and Joel's room, but Kyle hadn't dared move close to the door, worried that someone inside might hear him.

So why am I here, then? Am I just going to stand here all night?

"Wait here," he said quietly, "and don't make any noise."

Wesley snorted and gave him a disgusted look, but then he folded his arms across his chest and raised his eyebrows to indicate he'd wait while Kyle made a fool of himself. Kyle didn't want anyone in the hotel to catch him sneaking down the hall, obviously up to something, but he walked softly. He approached the door to the room, stopping a few feet away and close to the wall so he wouldn't be seen through the peephole. Then he had no choice but to look suspicious as he edged closer, mere inches from the wall.

When he was in front of the door, he stopped and listened closely.

Nothing.

He risked leaning his head in and lightly pressing his ear against the door.

Still nothing. Nobody was in the room, unless they'd all decided to take a nap together. Which meant they'd either moved to another room, or they might have even decided to leave the hotel.

Shit.

"TODD!" JOEL shouted, apparently no longer worried about staying quiet. "Leave him alone! The other pill is for *me*, goddamn it!"

Todd was actually stretched out across both of them, his legs in Joel's lap and the top of his body pushing down upon Jesse. Jesse could see Joel trying to shove Todd off his lap, but Todd simply spread his legs and braced his sneakers on the floor. He was big enough that Joel couldn't budge him.

Jesse tried to push Todd off him, but his head was swimming with the alcohol and Todd was like a lead weight across his chest. He swallowed nervously, eyeing the hand Todd had in front of his face with the pill clutched in it. "How did I lie to you?"

"You may not be working for the police," Todd said, "but you're *dating* one of them. Joel saw you mackin' on that Detective Dubois in the parking lot."

Fuck.

"That's no reason to kill him!" Corrie shouted at him, but she made no move to come to Jesse's defense. Neither did Ryan.

Jesse tried again to shove Todd off, but Todd quickly popped the pill into this own mouth, though he held it in his lips, still partly visible. Then he grabbed both of Jesse's wrists and slammed them down on the floor, on either side of Jesse's head. The gelcap protruded from between Todd's lips, and to Jesse's horror, Todd lowered his face as if for a kiss. Jesse tried to turn his head, but Todd clamped it between his forearms and forced him to tilt his face upward. Their lips met, and Jesse felt the gelcap working its way into his mouth. Todd was pushing against the other side of it with his tongue.

Then it was gone. Todd sucked it into his own mouth and swallowed it. He pulled back to give Jesse an evil grin.

"You asshole," Jesse gasped.

Then, as Jesse watched, Todd's smile faded and his brow furrowed. "I think maybe the first pill just broke open." He took several short, shallow gasps and grimaced in obvious pain.

"Jesus Christ!" Jesse shouted. "Somebody call 911!" His cellphone was in his pocket, and he was probably the least drunk person there, but he couldn't move his arms. Todd still had him pinned. "Get off me, you idiot!"

KYLE AND Wesley stepped out of the elevator to find some of the hotel staff clustered around the front desk. They were keeping their voices down, but their demeanor seemed tense. The desk clerk was on the phone, and as they approached, Kyle heard her say, "We're sending someone right up to take a look at it, ma'am."

The manager had been talking quietly with two other men on his staff when he glanced over and saw the two detectives. "Detective Dubois! Are you off duty?"

"Well, sort of," Kyle began, not wanting to get sidetracked into something an on-duty officer could handle—not with Jesse MIA. "Is it an emergency?"

"I hope not, but… the fifth floor is currently closed for renovations, but a guest on the fourth floor just called down to tell us she heard thumping and voices coming from the area over the bedroom in her suite. And she insists someone shouted to call 911. We have called 911, of course, but—"

Kyle didn't need to hear any more. "We'll go up," he interrupted, relying heavily on his years of training to keep his panic at bay. "Can someone show us the way?"

JESSE WAS on the phone with a 911 dispatcher when he heard shouting— Kyle's voice—echoing in the hallways somewhere. He rushed to the doorway and shouted into the semidarkness, "Over here!"

A moment later, Kyle was running toward him, Wesley and two of the hotel staff trailing behind him. When Kyle reached him, Jesse thought for a moment he was going to embrace him—Kyle reached out and grabbed Jesse's shoulder, anxiety and fear etched in his handsome features, and began to lift his other arm. But Wesley said, "You're being watched, children."

Kyle froze and then lowered his arms. "What's going on?"

"Hold on," Jesse told him. He said to the dispatcher, "I have to talk to someone, but I'll keep the line open." Then to Kyle he added, "Todd swallowed rat poison."

"What? Why the hell would he do that?" He and Wesley rushed past Jesse without waiting for an answer. Inside the room, Todd was lying on the floor, doubled up in pain while Joel was rocking back and forth, sobbing and too drunk to be very coherent. Corrie and Ryan were standing over Todd, but they'd been no help either.

"How much did he take?" Kyle asked, kneeling beside Todd.

Jesse started to say, "One gelcap full," but Joel chose to speak up. "Two gelcaps," he slurred, making a gesture with his fingers as if he were trying to estimate how big the gelcaps were.

"You said only one of the pills was poisoned," Jesse said.

"I lied. They were both poison."

The stupid idiot. He'd planned on killing himself either way, Jesse realized. "Fine," he said, disgusted. "Call it a thousand milligrams, then."

"Shit," Wesley muttered. He held out his hand to Jesse. "Let me see the phone." Jesse handed it to him, and Wesley put it to his ear. "This is Detective Wesley Roberts on the scene. We have a man who swallowed approximately a thousand milligrams of rat poison, along with…."

He looked around at the bottles of alcohol and Jesse volunteered, "Rum and vodka. I'm not sure how much…. Right. A lot of rum and vodka. We're waiting for the ambulance, but I need to know what can be done to help him until they arrive."

Jesse knew from the books he'd read on poisons that most off-the-shelf rat poisons used Coumadin or something like it to thin the blood and cause internal bleeding. If they could get him to the hospital quickly, they might be able to give Todd an infusion to restore some of the coagulates to his blood. It was still possible for him to survive.

Kyle stood up and let Wesley take his place beside Todd while he continued to speak with the 911 dispatcher. Kyle looked over the rather sorry collection of drunken young people gathered in the room, and his gaze locked on Joel. "You gave him the pills?"

"Yes."

"Why?"

Joel didn't appear to have an answer. He just started shaking his head, looking as though he were about to start crying again.

"Joel didn't give him the pills," Jesse said. "He had them in his hand, and Todd pried them away from him. Then he took them both pills voluntarily."

"He was trying to kill himself?" Wesley asked.

"I think so."

"Why?"

"Because he'd just confessed to killing Stuart."

Kyle raised his eyebrows and glanced down at Todd in surprise. Then he walked closer to Jesse until he could lean in close and say in a low voice, "You realize a confession to somebody not involved in the case, when he was drunk off his ass, isn't gonna hold much weight in a courtroom."

"I know," Jesse replied, likewise keeping his voice down. "But he did it. Would you like to know why?"

Kyle sighed and looked back at Todd. "Later. After we've saved the idiot's life."

THE EMTs came out of the elevator a few minutes later in a flurry of activity, followed by two police officers from Berlin. Kyle and Wesley filled the officers in on the situations while the EMTs tended to Todd, but since they weren't there in an official capacity—Kyle didn't even have a notebook with him—they stepped back and let the Berlin police take charge of getting statements from all involved.

They were all a bit drunk—except for Joel, who was completely wasted—and that included Jesse, much to Kyle's irritation. He understood there hadn't been any way for Jesse to avoid drinking, not if he didn't want to be kicked out of the "party." But it had been incredibly dangerous for him to go along with it. From what the Lassiter kids were telling the police, and what fragments Kyle overheard from Joel's incoherent statement, Jesse had come damned close to being on that stretcher himself. It took all Kyle's self-control to keep from breaking out in a cold sweat as they relayed the scene with Todd trying to force a pill into Jesse's mouth. They all thought Jesse had swallowed it until he managed to get out from under Todd and call 911.

"You were damned lucky," one of the officers told Jesse. "Are you sure you didn't swallow any of those pills?"

"Of course I'm sure," Jesse replied, frowning. "I'm not dumb enough to swallow one and then not tell anyone."

The officer's expression indicated he wasn't convinced of Jesse's intelligence, and at the moment, neither was Kyle. But they moved on to Jesse's statement. Unfortunately, hearing Jesse's much more detailed and coherent account did little to assuage Kyle's fears. If anything, it made it worse.

At some point during the statements, the EMTs carried Todd out on the stretcher, heading for Androscoggin Valley Hospital in Berlin, just north of Gorham. Todd was still conscious, but only barely, and he wasn't in good shape.

The Lassiter kids were told to go back to their parents' suite, but Joel was escorted down to his room by the police. There, as Kyle understood it, they planned to confiscate the rat poison he'd used, and possibly the vitamin pills he'd taken the gelcaps from. Most likely, he'd spend the night at the station in Berlin. Kyle wasn't sure if they'd file charges against him, since he hadn't actually tried to make anyone take the pills, but that wasn't certain. His actions had definitely endangered Todd and the others.

At any rate, having someone watch over the kid for next twenty-four hours was probably a good idea. He was falling apart. He'd barely stopped sobbing long enough to say anything the officers could write down.

As for Jesse, he was more or less free to go. Except he was drunk, and nobody was going to let him drive back to the Lodge, even if it was just across the road.

"I'll give him a ride," Kyle told the officers. He'd been downplaying his relationship with Jesse during the whole mess, but he wasn't going to just abandon him. And a ride probably wouldn't look like anything more than him doing his job, anyway.

The Berlin officers were fine with that, so Kyle, Wesley, and Jesse left together. Jesse seemed to be as irritated with him as he was with Jesse—maybe because he hadn't immediately lavished praise on Jesse for solving the murder—so the ride across Route 302 was coldly silent, except for Wesley making irritable remarks about how much trouble this was going to cause them back in Concord.

Back at the Lodge, Kyle resisted the urge to drag Jesse up the outer stairs by the arm like a child. But once they were inside the room with the door closed behind them, he grabbed him by both shoulders and snarled, "He could have killed you."

"I know, but he wasn't actually—"

Jesse wasn't allowed to finish his sentence because Kyle mashed their mouths together in an angry, possessive kiss. Jesse resisted him for a moment, but eventually he melted into Kyle's arms.

When Kyle finally allowed them to breathe, he said, "You scared the shit out of me, kid."

The sound of Wesley clearing his throat caused them both to turn. He was standing in the doorway, arms crossed and eyebrows raised. "Nobody better be getting any ideas about makeup sex, 'cause I need to hit the sack."

TODD DIDN'T make it through the night.

Jesse woke up the next morning to Kyle talking quietly on his cell phone. He was sitting at the desk in his tighty-whities, laptop open while he talked. Wesley was still asleep in the other bed, snoring softly.

Jesse couldn't hear what Kyle was saying, but after the detective closed the phone, he looked over and saw Jesse watching him. He came over to the bed and climbed back under the covers. "That was Officer Stanley from Berlin," he said softly. "Todd Warren went into cardiac arrest early this morning. They couldn't save him."

Jesse wasn't sure how he felt about the news. Todd had never been anything but a sexist pig in the few days Jesse had known him. Still, he'd killed Stuart—sacrificed him, in a way—because he thought it would save Joel. And he hadn't killed Jesse. Not that choosing not to kill someone ranked high up there on a scale of good deeds, but Jesse was grateful nonetheless. And really, in the final analysis, everything Todd had done, from covering up the murder of his parents to killing Stuart to save Joel to swallowing both pills so Joel wouldn't take one, had been motivated by compassion.

Jesse did feel bad that he was dead. But Todd hadn't wanted to go to prison. He'd taken the pills to avoid that—or perhaps more to the point, to avoid living his life without Stuart, the only person he'd ever cared about. So he'd gotten what he wanted.

"Does that mean Joel's in more trouble now?" he asked.

"Yes," Kyle replied. "Depending on what they want to charge him with—they have to decide that soon, if they want to keep holding him—he might find himself facing manslaughter or negligent homicide. He did have intent, though he didn't really go through with it. Frankly, even if they do charge him, I doubt much will come of it."

He shifted so they were front to front, their legs intertwining and their crotches pressed together. Jesse could feel Kyle's erection pressing against his, but there were two layers of cotton between them, and with Wesley sleeping less than ten feet away, that wasn't likely to change soon. Jesse brushed his hands across Kyle's naked chest and belly under the blankets, feeling the heat of him, breathing in the musky scent of sweat and Old Spice. Even though he knew Kyle was probably still a little irritated with him for putting himself at risk the night before—and truthfully, he was a little irritated that Kyle hadn't acknowledged he'd found the solution, even if his method had been risky—he couldn't think of anywhere else in the world he'd rather be right now than snuggled up against Kyle.

"We're pretty much done here," Kyle continued. "We'll need to run around a bit, talk to the Lassiters, talk to the hospital, the Berlin police…."

Jesse got a sinking feeling in his stomach as he realized what Kyle was saying. "You're telling me I need to go home."

Kyle leaned forward and kissed him. Then, sliding his lips across Jesse's cheek to nuzzle gently at his earlobe, he said, "Yeah, I guess I am. There isn't anything for you to do here except hang around the hotel. I'll be too busy to see you. And we'll be checking out tonight."

"Fine," Jesse said, "but what happens when I get back to Dover and you get back to Concord?"

Kyle glanced over at Wesley, perhaps verifying the man was still asleep before he rolled on top of Jesse. In this position, with Jesse opening his legs for him, they were about as close to having sex as they'd be able to get. Kyle's swollen cock rubbed against Jesse's as he slowly and subtly began to grind their crotches together. Jesse couldn't help but let out a small gasp of pleasure.

"What do you want to happen?"

"I don't know…." He was lying. Jesse knew what he wanted. He was just afraid to say it in case Kyle came up with a reason to say no. But there was little point dancing around it. "How do you feel about being my boyfriend?"

Kyle looked into his eyes for a long time before answering, "I think I'd feel pretty good about that."

He lowered his face for another kiss, but Wesley's sleepy voice interrupted them. "Jesus.... Are you guys *fucking*? I thought we had an understanding!"

Epilogue

IT WAS Friday night, and Kyle still hadn't called Jesse. At the beginning of the week, there had been too much chaos, too much wrapping up to do. Kyle had come home every night and pretty much tumbled into bed. He hadn't wanted to call when he was half-asleep.

But then, later in the week, he'd started getting nervous, and all the doubts he'd had before about being too old for the kid, and Jesse's fascination with Kyle's line of work maybe not being all that good for him—especially after what happened Saturday night—started creeping in. He kept thinking about calling, but then he chickened out.

How the fuck is this going to work?

At least Wesley had been cool. He hadn't pressured Kyle either way about ending the relationship or calling Jesse. He'd left it completely up to Kyle. That was the great thing about Wes. He had your back if you needed him to, but otherwise, he left you the hell alone.

But here it was, nine o'clock on Friday night, a gorgeous young man possibly wanting to have sex with him, and Kyle was making himself a cup of coffee and thinking about watching a movie—alone.

God, I'm pathetic.

When he heard his cell buzzing in his jacket pocket, he nearly tripped over one of the kitchen table chairs to get to it. His heart soared to see Jesse's name on the touch screen, but almost as quickly, he remembered he'd been a total shit all week, putting off calling. Jesse probably thought he'd been dumped.

Nervously, Kyle swiped the phone on and put it to his ear. "Hey, bud!" he said with forced cheerfulness. "How's it going?"

"Jesus, Kyle! I'm so glad you picked up! There's a dead body here, and I didn't know who else to call!"

"A dead body?" *Christ.* How the hell had Jesse gotten himself wrapped up in *another* murder? "Where is it? Do you know who it is?"

"I'm not sure who he is," Jesse replied. "I just stumbled across him in the kitchen. I think he's been shot!"

"Why didn't you call 911?" Kyle growled. "You know better than this. It'll take me an hour to get over there."

"They'd be useless! I needed somebody who could solve this before the killer gets away."

What the hell had gotten into him? He wasn't thinking rationally. "Jesse, where are you?"

"My house."

Kyle had his address, but even as he was reaching for his jacket, he hesitated. "Somebody was shot in *your* kitchen?"

"Well," Jesse said thoughtfully, "he might have been bludgeoned. And it might have been in the library."

"You have a library?"

"Doesn't everybody?"

"And you don't know what room the body's in?"

"Not yet."

Kyle sighed. "Jesse... are you playing *Clue?*"

"Of course not," Jesse replied. "It takes two people to play *Clue*, and I'm all alone here. Naked."

"You asshole."

"Did I mention I have popcorn? And hot chocolate. And... oh yeah. I'm naked."

Kyle laughed and took his jacket off the hook. "I'll be right there, kid."

JAMIE FESSENDEN set out to be a writer in junior high school. He published a couple short pieces in his high school's literary magazine and had another story place in the top 100 in a national contest, but it wasn't until he met his partner, Erich, almost twenty years later, that he began writing again in earnest. With Erich alternately inspiring and goading him, Jamie wrote several screenplays and directed a few of them as micro-budget independent films. He then began writing novels and published his first novella in 2010.

After nine years together, Jamie and Erich have married and purchased a house together in the wilds of Raymond, New Hampshire, where there are no street lights, turkeys and deer wander through their yard, and coyotes serenade them on a nightly basis. Jamie recently left his "day job" as a tech support analyst to be a full-time writer.

Visit Jamie: http://jamiefessenden.wordpress.com/
Facebook: https://www.facebook.com/pages/Jamie-Fessenden-Author/102004836534286
Twitter: https://twitter.com/JamieFessenden1

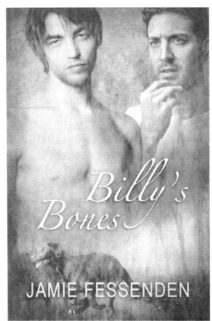
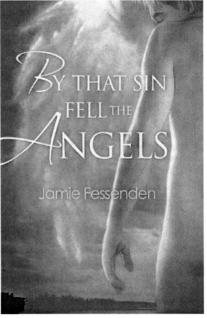

Also from DREAMSPINNER PRESS

http://www.dreamspinnerpress.com

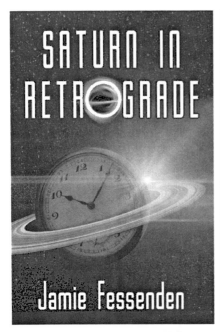

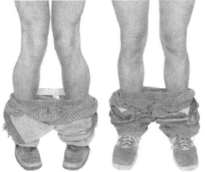

Also from DREAMSPINNER PRESS

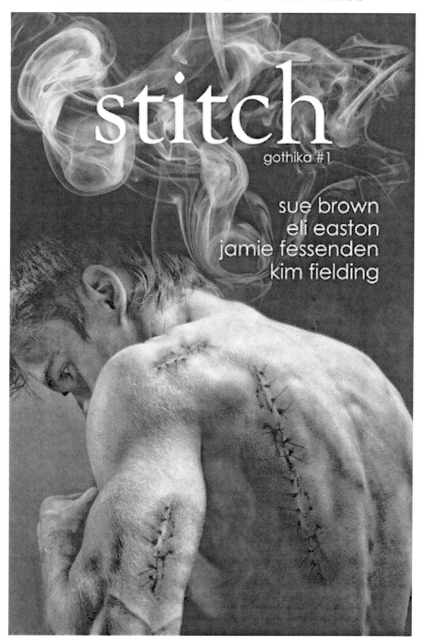

stitch

gothika #1

sue brown
eli easton
jamie fessenden
kim fielding

http://www.dreamspinnerpress.com

CPSIA information can be obtained
at www.ICGtesting.com
Printed in the USA
LVOW10s1114071117
555290LV00009B/99/P

9 781632 162021